FRONTIER

FRONTIER

GRACE CURTIS

SOLARIS

This edition published 2024 by Solaris

First published in hardback 2023 by Solaris,
an imprint of Rebellion Publishing Ltd
Riverside House, Osney Mead,
Oxford, OX2 0ES, UK

www.solarisbooks.com

ISBN: 978-1-78618-882-3

10 9 8 7 6 5 4 3 2 1

A CIP catalogue record for this book is available from the
British Library.

Designed & typeset by Rebellion Publishing

Printed in Denmark

MIX
Paper | Supporting
responsible forestry
FSC® C104608

Contents

For Katie

THE HUNT FOR THE FALLEN STAR

IT WAS A night like any other on Earth. Silence on the land, stillness in the sky. Stars glittered like sunken jewels, and from the ground below human eyes regarded them as one might a benign tumour.

Something trembled. A shard of silver detached itself from the great black canopy and hurtled down in an arc, ember-hot, vomiting smoke. It landed in a shock of sand and debris that rose high into the air before settling back down with a sigh.

Many miles away, in a ramshackle nest at the peak of a column of criss-crossing metal beams, Bolton Strid snapped his telescope shut.

'Crawley,' he hissed, not daring to look away. 'Crawley, wake up!'

Behind him, a bundle of sacking groaned and slumped onto one side. 'S'not my turn yet.'

'Wake up, you old bastard!' He aimed a kick with his heel. It glanced off Crawley's shoulder, and the older man sat up, blinking. 'God's tits, *what?*'

7

'Grab your things,' Bolton replied, stuffing the telescope into the lining of his jacket. 'We're rich.'

MARIE MARAKOVA, DRIVER, fixer, and sometime-mechanic, leant against the struts of the front porch with her broad forearms crossed, watching narrow-eyed while the scavenger Bolton examined her van. He came to the rear doors, stuffed one hand in each pocket, and sniffed.

'Bit small.'

Marakova raised an eyebrow. 'You got a better offer?'

'Ms Marakova, please disregard the words of my good friend Mr Bolton here,' Crawley said, clasping his hands together. 'I can assure you it will be sufficient. However, about the matter of *you* driving—'

'I stay with the truck.' She shifted her bulk, casting a shadow over Crawley. 'Or no deal.'

'Of course.' Crawley nodded quickly. 'Quite fair. Quite fair indeed.'

'You know where it fell?' she asked Bolton.

He shrugged. 'Roughly.'

'And you really think…' Marakova paused. Despite his slack posture, there was a dull excitement in Bolton's eyes. Ever since they arrived, Crawley, the smaller one with an actor's voice, had been darting from place to place like a hoverfly, dampening an old rag on his forehead and spouting a continual stream of nervous nonsense. But Bolton stayed still. He watched the horizon.

Optimism was a disease of which Marakova had long since cured herself. She fastened the money with a bulldog clip and pushed it into her back pocket.

'Let's go,' she said.

Buckette was a scrap trader's town, tucked away in

safe obscurity at the edge of civilisation. Most of the shopfronts they drove past lay empty. The few that were in use displayed cardboard boxes stacked high with quasi-legal valuables: lithium batteries, tinned food, cans of gas. Armed guards stalked the base of the water tower, through which passed a sad trickle of people lugging jerrycans. A similar trickle slid in and out of the chapel, thumbing their beads, loosening their collars, muttering apologies for sins committed against the sacred Earth. The border to the wasteland was marked by a circular mound of decaying grass and a weathered marble plinth. There'd been a statue on top of the plinth once, evidenced by the two slender legs of a rearing horse that were still welded there. Someone had taken the rest down with a buzzsaw.

At Bolton's direction Marakova drove out for many miles, until Buckette receded to a line of bleached stubble in the rear-view mirror. Crawley unpeeled himself from his seat, revealing a moist stain the length of his spine.

'Pardon me, Ms Marakova,' he said. 'Would you mind turning on the air conditioning, if such a service is available?'

She cranked the driver's-side window open half an inch, belching hot air and dust into Crawley's face.

'Keep your eyes open,' said Bolton. He was sat with his boots up on the dashboard, sucking at the nub of a cigarette that had long since burned out, fanning himself slowly with the brim of an old ranger's hat. His eyes were bloodshot and unblinking. 'We're close.'

'Hope so.' Marakova glanced down at the fuel gauge.

They came at last to a sort of crest, a crease in the land that ran down to a dried-up riverbed. Bolton raised a hand, and the van stopped. 'There.'

'Where?' Crawley asked, leaning forward eagerly.

Across the valley a thinning pillar of smoke rose faintly into the sky. Something glimmered at the base. Marakova's lips peeled back, showing a pair of sharpened silver incisors.

'Well I'll be damned,' she declared. 'You were right.'

There was a trail of gutted soil and black grass some quarter of a mile long scarring the ground where the star had slid on landing. Bolton rolled the window down and stuck his head out as they drove along, peering down at the charcoaled earth. 'It's big,' he said.

'That good?' asked Marakova.

'Oh, yes, ma'am.' Crawley'd shuffled forward so that his whole head and shoulders were wedged between the front seats. 'When it comes to the scrap trade, volume is everything. Our very bread and butter.'

Marakova ignored him. 'What is it?' she asked, watching the thing getting closer.

'Probably an old satellite,' said Bolton. 'Hedonists used to use them to power their, uh' – he made a gesture with his hand that was equal parts vague and derogatory – '*devices.*'

Marakova nodded. Everything from the old world was stained by sin. But sin, fortunately for her, had no bearing on market value.

She edged the pedal down a little further.

It was about the size of a car. That was the only thing Marakova could think to compare the fallen object to, though the resemblance quickly fell short. It was huge and pill-shaped, chrome body scored with bright red paint, small thrusters built into one side still dribbling smoke. There was lettering scored on the base: **LIFEBOAT – 01.**

No solar panels, no radio dish. No fragile gold casing.

And no signs of wear, either – it wasn't brand new, but it certainly wasn't centuries old.

It dawned on her slowly. This was no satellite. It was part of a ship.

With some effort, Marakova kept her composure. 'Say,' she called to Bolton. 'What's the bounty on space tech these days?'

'Can't recall,' he replied mildly. 'Quite high, if I'm not mistaken.'

'It's a gift from Gaia!' Crawley howled. 'Thank you, O Mother beneath me! Thank you!' He lowered himself onto his knees and started kissing the ground.

'What're you thanking God for?' asked Bolton. 'It came from the sky.'

Crawley stood up, scowling, ashy dust darkening the creases of his face. 'Always one for the details, aren't you, Bolton?'

They stared at each other.

'I found a door!' Marakova shouted. Hatch would have been a more accurate term. It was oval-shaped, curved to sink into the rest of the structure. She grabbed the handle and yanked with all of her considerable might, bracing one foot on the side. 'Stuck,' she grunted, waggling her hand. 'Shit.'

'There's a window over here,' Crawley said, kneeling at the far end. In front of him was a thick circle of hardened plastic, smeared with dust. 'Can't see inside. Maybe we can break it—' He started to cast around for a rock.

'Stop,' said Bolton. 'The pair of you. *Stop.*'

They stopped, watching Bolton amble towards the pod. He studied it much as he'd studied Marakova's van; as an indifferent and slightly sceptical customer, deciding if the purchase would be worth his time. From his front pocket he drew out a matchstick, which he struck on the plated hull and used to light another cigarette.

'Here's what's gonna happen,' he drawled. 'Crawley, you take the van and go find a Sheriff. Tell him what we've got, where we are. When you're done come straight back here and don't speak to anyone else.'

'Of course n—'

Bolton hooked a finger in Crawley's collar and drew their faces together. '*Anyone.*'

'Whatever do you take me for,' he muttered, not meeting Bolton's eye.

Bolton released him. 'Me and her will stay here and guard the loot. That okay with you?'

The last sentence was directed at Marakova. She pondered for a moment, chewing her cheek. It seemed wrong to separate from the van, but the cost of that old tanker was a pittance compared to what they had here. Against her better judgement, there was a fantasy blooming in Marakova's mind: a fantasy of an auto shop with a whole fleet of trucks, dozens of overalled underlings at her beck and call. Some place in the South, maybe with an office in New Destiny itself. To even see the city was a dream. But living there?

The thought alone made her mouth water.

She nodded. 'Alright. Call it collateral.'

'That we will.'

They spat and shook. Crawley rubbed them both on the back, the grin returning to his face. 'Oh, my friends,' he chuckled. 'Just think what we'll get. Even with a three-way split. Oh, this is tremendous. God keep you both, my friends. May she hold you down.'

He climbed in the van and, after a few stutters and false starts, trundled off in the direction of the town.

12

Bolton and Marakova watched him go. Neither spoke.

Bolton circled the pod again, pausing to squint down into the window. Marakova attempted to work some of the red paint off with her thumbnail. It wouldn't loosen.

Both were thinking the same thing, but neither of them could incriminate themselves by speaking the idea out loud. They had to dance towards it.

'You known that guy long?' she asked at last, picking a scab at the base of her chin.

'Longer than I'd care to.'

She crossed to the hatch, pulling idly at the handle. 'It weren't him that spotted the wreck, were it?'

'No.' Bolton nodded slowly. 'That honour does go to me.'

'So he ain't really done anything, has he?'

'Not really.'

'Yet he spoke of a three-way split.'

'Yeah. Funny that.'

'Funny.'

Another pause.

'I never been a big one for close-up stuff,' said Marakova.

'I've known him longest.'

And just like that, the matter was settled.

Earth days were long. Crawley was gone for several hours, but when he returned the sun was still high in the sky, bearing down on the diseased planet with resentful passion. He found Bolton and Marakova sitting a few yards apart from one another, staring out at nothing. They both stood as he approached. There was a strange atmosphere around Crawley as he climbed down from the van – his chin drooping, his back hunched.

'Well?' said Bolton, stepping forward, all anxious aggression.

'I found a Sheriff,' Crawley began, reordering a mound of dirt with his toe. 'I was obliged to drive all the way to Springwell, but I found him.'

'And?'

'I told him what we have: the weight, the shape of it. He was rather sceptical, but I talked him around. He was able to give me an estimate as to what we could expect in compensation.'

Marakova's hands were on her hips. '*And?*'

Crawley motioned for them to come closer. They did. In a low voice, he told them the figure.

Marakova took a deep breath. She leant forward, one hand on her knee, and stared at the ground. Then she raised up in a great wave of noise –

'*WHOOOO!*' She slammed one hand between Crawley's shoulders. 'Are you *kidding me?*'

A winded smile cracked across his face. 'No, Ms Marakova, I am not.'

Bolton was shaking his head, skipping like a record, slapping his hat against his knee: 'Well I'll be damned. Well, shit. Wow. God forgive me. I'll be damned.'

Marakova ran her tongue back and forth along her teeth, tasting the metal that had stained her breath for almost a decade. Those silver teeth were her backup in the case things ever went bad. She wondered if platinum would taste any different.

'A convoy should arrive in a few hours to hoist it away,' Crawley said. 'I gave them our coordinates. I hope you don't mind, Bolton.'

'Of course not. You did good, Crawley.'

Crawley tried to look modest, but the muscles in his

face kept pulling into a smile. 'I thought…' He bustled back to the van and pulled a clinking paper bag from the seat. 'I thought that celebrations were in order.'

'I'll say so!' Marakova yanked the offered bottle from Crawley's hand and popped the cork free with a slick move of the thumb. She raised it to her lips and downed a third. 'Gaia!' She belched. 'Tastes like spicy petrol.'

'Waste of good petrol,' said Bolton, taking a lengthy sip.

'You may complain, friends,' said Crawley, 'but to me, it tastes like freedom.'

'To freedom, then.'

They clinked nozzles. For a fleeting moment, caught in the crossfires of booze, hope, and minor heatstroke, the three of them were taken in by a genuine sense of joy. Then Marakova caught Bolton's eye.

'Hey, Crawley.' He turned to his friend, who was downing the drink like he was afraid someone would take it from him. 'Guess what? While you were out, Marakova figured out how to open the hatch.'

Crawley threw his bottle to the ground. It bounced and rolled. '*Did* she now, my fine old friend?'

Marakova crossed her arms. 'Uh-huh. We thought we ought to wait for you to come back. In fact…' She trailed off, looking back at Bolton.

'…in fact,' he picked up. 'We were thinking you ought to do the honours.'

Crawley looked between them, his eyes glazed. 'You two – you two think I'm not aware of your little game?'

Bolton's posture stiffened. 'Uh…'

'Like you'd ever let me have any sort of *honours*.' Crawley spat. 'You don't want to get hit by anything that might spring out, do you? You mangy old *dog?*' He smacked Bolton on the arm hard enough to make his teeth rattle.

'Aha—' Bolton chuckled, shrugging helplessly.

'You sussed us,' said Marakova, grinning silver.

'You're glass to me, friend.' Crawley tapped his temple. 'Glass. Well, to space with it—' He marched over to the hatch and wrapped both hands around the handle. 'Let's see what the heathens have been so kind as to send us, eh?'

Crawley yanked. The hatch didn't budge. He yanked again, face reddening. He turned and was startled to find Bolton standing close behind him. The scavenger stepped away, swiftly hiding a hand behind his back. 'You, uh – you need to twist it.'

'Oh, do I?' Crawley went to try again.

It was a wet noise – or rather, a hardness that turned into a wetness. Crawley fell like a cut puppet, first to the knees, then to the face. Totally silent. His fingers trailed down the hatch and fell limply to the ground.

Marakova squatted down and checked his eyes. A pair of marbles. The man was gone. She nodded to herself.

'There'll be trouble if the Sheriff sees. We ought to hide him before—' She realised she was being ignored. 'Hey.'

Bolton's body was contorted, one hand braced on the star's chrome shell, the hat pulled low to cover his eyes. He was still clutching the rock.

'You alright there?' Marakova put a hand on his shoulder. He brushed it off.

'I don't feel too good.'

'Look, we *both* said—'

'Sweet Mother Earth, would you just give me a damn *minute?*' His voice cracked on the last word.

A surge of white-hot irritation passed over Marakova's

face. She mouthed a few unpleasant words at the back of Bolton's head, and then said, in an affectedly sweet tone, 'Take as long as you like, darlin'. I'm gonna drag the body down into that scrub, okay? Then we can start talking numbers.'

Bolton nodded.

Marakova grabbed Crawley's corpse around each of the ankles and pulled him easily towards a patch of high, yellowing grass, coming to a halt a dozen yards in.

'Hey!' she called. 'This far enough?' The scavenger didn't respond. She squinted. 'What're you…?'

He was standing with his legs apart, pointing at her.

Not pointing – aiming.

The first shot caught her in the shoulder; the second in the centre of the chest. Marie Marakova fell backwards and vanished into the grass.

BOLTON STUFFED THE handgun back into his jeans. His face glowed with sweat. But he was alone now, finally, just him and his treasure. He ran his fingertips along the surface, feeling the otherworldly metal under his palm – smooth and well formed, still cool under the sun's heat, still unmarked despite the incredible distance it had fallen. All his life, Bolton had made do with what was old and rotted and cobbled together. Clothes that didn't fit. Tools that didn't work. Someone else's hat. Leftovers. That was all he knew, all that Earth had given him: the scraps and the cast-offs from the people they called sinners, just because they'd had the good sense to leave. But now he had something of theirs. Something new. Something of his own. Something, God's disapproval be damned, that would set him up for *life*.

17

He peered through the window. Dark shapes lay unmoving within. Then he took out his telescope and turned it southwards.

A small sound came from the back of Bolton's throat. A whine, dissolving into a gurgle as the muscles contracted one by one. The sensation was that of a throttling fist. He dropped the telescope and seized his neck with both hands, clawing, grasping, tendons leaping forward like taut ropes against the skin. He tried to stumble towards the trio of bottles that lay empty in the dirt, but his legs seized up before he could arrive, and he had to reach out and pull them towards himself. On the corner of the label someone had etched a small cross. The other, also a cross. The third – the one Crawley had drunk from – was marked with a circle.

The bitter taste. He should have known.

'Crawl—' He couldn't even get the name out to curse it. 'Crawl—'

He convulsed another moment, and then lay still.

After a while a breeze picked up. The collar of Bolton's shirt flapped feebly against his jaw, and his hat, broad-brimmed, lifted and fell a few times before coming altogether clear of his head and settling face up on the ground beside him. Half an hour passed.

The star shuddered. It was just a tremble, followed by a faint sound from within. Then it shook again, harder this time. Once more, and finally the hatch door flew open, slamming against the outer shell and bouncing forward again to dangle delicately on its hinges.

Sticking out of the star's interior, into the arid atmosphere of Earth, was a single boot.

It is the general principle of any Empire to leave no swathe of land untouched, unless that land is so barren and hostile as to be not worth touching in the first place. So it was with the Central Galactic Empire (also called the Centralian Empire and the Empire of the Never-Setting Sun) in regards to Earth. Abandoned for over three centuries... [the] planet was officially evacuated less than a few decades after the Empire's founding. Only a scattered few chose to remain, almost all of whom were members of a group officially known as the 'Latter Day Church of Gaia', a fringe religion dating back to the late 20th century... [now] revived in a more radical form. Central to the Church's dogma was the deification of Earth.

Though their presence on the planet was technically illegal, the Church's doctrine forbade the use of contemporary technology, rejecting anything associated with the so-called 'sin' of space travel. They considered climate change a form of divine punishment to be meekly accepted, rather than a natural disaster to be escaped at all costs. Considering this, and the state of the planet's atmosphere, Imperial experts predicted that the remaining population would not last more than a handful of generations... To put it bluntly, they were not worth nuking.

– A Potted History of the Periphery, Vol 1

A FISTFUL OF NOVELS

HERE IS A fact that does not change: the best place to go for information is a library. Even if you're countless miles from home, dirty and worried, even if your mouth has a copperish tang where you bit your tongue on landing, and you want to scream or pummel your fists into the dirt, or tear down a wall, or kick something, all out of pure fear and frustration. Even if you don't like to read.

Head to the library. They'll set you straight.

A Stranger walked into town – and then she walked right out again. To call the looks she got 'dirty' would be an insult to dirt. Locals watched her pass with open venom, so she kept moving without so much as a nod, fearing that any slight gesture would be taken as an invitation to fight. It was a fight she'd probably win, but that wasn't the point. She needed help.

Specifically, she needed to send a message.

A message to someone who might be dead.

She didn't know. There was a lot she didn't know.

So she went to the library.

It was a trailer hunched low on rusted axles, parked a half-mile from the centre of town. A cart nailed to the rear bumper carried a brightly coloured sign: *Good books for rent! Generous prices!* The door was propped open with a brick.

After taking a moment to count her options – they numbered in the low zeroes – the Stranger ducked inside, praying for a friendly face.

The interior was close, dusky, low enough that her ranger's hat nearly brushed the ceiling. Cracked paperbacks covered every inch of the wall space and most of the floor. At the back of the library, over a makeshift counter, two people were ruining what should have been a cosy atmosphere by having a blazing row.

The librarian was short, maybe 5'2" on a good day, made slightly taller by a bouquet of dreadlocks she kept tied up over her head with a bright orange rag. Around her waist she wore a sort of belt, which had attached, among other things, five pens, a small knife, a spool of semi-translucent tape, an inhaler, a pocketbook, and a hand-cranked machine that dispensed receipts. Her right leg was held stiff by a brace. She was arguing with one of her customers, almost nose to nose with the man. His tones were silky, but the Stranger could see bloodless spots on the tip of each knuckle where he gripped the counter's edge.

'Ms Keeper,' he was saying. 'Don't be foolish. I cannot give back what I have already bought.'

'You didn't buy *shit*, Sheriff,' snapped the librarian. 'It was a rental. I only do rentals.'

'I don't think that's true.'

'Oh yeah? I have your signature right here.'

She slammed something down on the counter – a

plastic ringbinder, thick as her arm, with yellowing sheets. 'You're in the ledger.' She swivelled it towards him, indicating a page. 'Right there. See?'

The man leant over, tugging thoughtfully at a tuft of white hair on his lower lip. 'Right here?' he asked, pointing.

'Uh-huh.'

With the same considerate energy, he reached across and ripped the page clean out of the binder. She squawked with outrage, snatching the ledger away. But the damage was done.

'I'll repeat,' he said, mashing the page in his hands. 'Don't be foolish. You know what I want.'

'You…' The librarian breathed deep, and then spoke in a torrent: 'You can keep your heathen fuckin' money and every penny of your heathen fuckin' change. I'd sooner throw my entire collection down a mineshaft and let *God Herself* find out who Mr Darcy marries than sell a single page to you. *EAT SHIT!*'

The customer clenched his fists harder, white spots spreading into a bloodless fist, and the Stranger was certain he was about to hit her – so much so that she flinched forward, ready to catch his elbow. But he relented with a chuckle and the words, 'You'll regret this.'

'Like space I will,' she snarled. 'Get outta here.'

The customer left, pausing to bob his head at the Stranger, who was trying lamely to conceal herself behind a bookshelf. 'Ma'am.' Then he kicked the brick that was propping open the door, sealing them in with an angry slam.

The librarian started muttering, picking paper scraps out of the metal clasps and flicking them at the wall. It seemed like a bad time to approach, so instead the

Stranger moved around the trailer, scrutinising her collection. Though the books were worn, they showed signs of tender repair: neat threading, well-placed glue.

'I'm sorry you had to see that, friend,' said the librarian, closing the ledger with a sigh. 'The name's Amber. Now what can I— God's tits! What is *that?*'

The Stranger jumped, then followed the direction of the librarian's pointing finger to the thing on her hip. It was a sleek, aquiline contraption of chrome and black glass, no magazine or scope, clean metal surface peeking out of a faded leather holster.

'Where are you from?' demanded Amber. 'Are you with the Sheriff?'

'No—'

'Did you *kill* a Sheriff? Where in God's good name did you get that?'

'I-I-' She stuttered, grasping for an answer. 'I-I found it.'

'Oh.' The librarian calmed. 'Scavenger, eh? Space junk?'

She nodded.

'Guess it's your first time this far north?'

'Yeah.'

Amber shook her head. 'Always the same.' Then, sharply: 'Listen up, friend. You're not down south anymore. This is a God-fearing land, and our Holy Mother beneath does *not* sanction that sort of unnatural machinery. You got that?'

'I'm sorry,' she said, adding in full honesty: 'I didn't know.'

'Well, now you do.'

There was an uncomfortable lull – at least, uncomfortable for the Stranger – broken when the librarian asked: 'What happened to your hair?'

'I shaved it off.'

'And your face?'

'That's just how I look.'

'You look like you've seen a couple fights.'

'Yeah.' She reached compulsively for her nose, feeling the spot where the bone went awry. 'A couple.'

'Hmm. And what sort of book are you after?'

'No books. I need a communicator.'

Amber cocked her head. 'A what now?'

The Stranger winced, searching for the right words. 'Uh – a radio.'

'A radio? I already told you, we don't keep shit like that around these parts.'

'Oh.' The Stranger sagged lower. 'Right. Yeah.'

Amber watched her another moment, expression softening. 'Look, what's your problem? Are you lost?'

'Yeah,' she admitted. 'Very lost.'

The librarian planted her elbows on the desk, and said, with the affect of a friendly bartender: 'You wanna talk about it?'

'I shouldn't, uh…' The Stranger tugged her hat down over her eyes, clearing her throat. 'No, it's okay.'

'Come on now, it's all therapy. And anyhow,' she gestured around at the paperbacks, 'I like a good story.'

'It's not a big deal.' A throb of pain formed in the Stranger's forehead, and she winced again. 'I'm looking for someone. Someone missing. Or I'm the one who's missing. Anyway, it's urgent.'

'Sounds rough. They must be someone special.'

'Yeah, well.' She felt herself blush. 'Yeah.'

They both mulled for a moment. Then Amber smacked her fist into the palm of her hand. 'Tell you who's got something like that. That weasel who just left. The Sheriff.'

The Stranger brightened. 'Really?'

'Uh-huh. I've seen him using it. Bold as anything.' The librarian grew gloomy. 'But you'll have to be careful. He's a slimy, cockroachy, boot-licking, dust-sucking little toenail of a man. Thinks because he owns the well, he owns the whole town.' She made a motion with her hands as if to strangle the air. 'He still has my only copy of *The Count of Monte Cristo.* Keeps trying to send me money for it. As if that's something money can buy. Pleh!' Her eyes jerked upwards. 'What's that face for?'

'Nothing.' The Stranger shook her head, smiling faintly.

'It ain't funny. You don't know how hard it is to find a good book. Or any book.'

'Tell you what,' she said. 'I'll get your book back for you.'

'Oh, come on now.' Amber flapped a hand dismissively. 'There's no need to – I mean, I couldn't hardly ask—'

'I'd like to. You're the first friendly person I've met, since – since I got lost.' They looked each other full in the face, the Stranger bending a little at the hip to make their gaze level. 'I should pay you back.'

'Well.' Now it was Amber's turn to blush. 'Aren't you sweet.'

'So, this Sheriff. What's his name?'

'He calls himself Emollient.' The librarian grimaced with second-hand embarrassment. *'Emollient Du Cream.'*

THE DU CREAM MANSION had been fake old at the time of its construction, but enough decades had passed since to grant it the status of genuinely ancient. It stood apart from the low tin roofs and whitewashed church spire of Springwell, upon a hill tall enough that most townsfolk were a little red in the face by the time they arrived. It was multistoreyed, with long windows and a tapered slate roof. A handsome porch with four white pillars faced out towards the horizon.

The Stranger took this all in from the top of the cracked driveway, pushing her hat up with one finger. *Please,* she thought. *Please let this work.*

If you put fear, confusion, heartbreak, a dash of lime and a half-cup of crushed ice into a shaker and gave it a good swirl about, what poured out the end might look something like the inside of the Stranger's mind at that moment. She was fighting every moment to stay calm – or at least, stay looking calm. Her emotions were a law unto themselves.

As she climbed the porch steps, a man came into view. He was leant up against the mansion door, a rifle cradled comfortably in the crook of his elbow. Dark circles of sweat stretched down from both armpits.

'Hey,' she said, nodding.

The man did not return the greeting. Instead he sniffed, a long draught of air rattling through two bulbous nostrils, and asked, 'Fuck're you supposed to be?'

'I'm here to see the Sheriff.'

He didn't respond, except with a stare.

'…Is he in?'

The doorman grunted.

'Yes?'

Another grunt.

Calm, the Stranger reminded herself, *calm.* 'This is urgent,' she said. 'Can I go in or not?'

'It's a free planet,' he muttered, stepping out of the way.

She pushed inside. He twisted round and watched her from the doorway, bouncing the rifle up and down on his forearm. 'Careful how you go now.'

The entrance hall was wide and stately, with a strict colour palette of pale pink and lime green. Windows, fringed with frilly curtains, stretched down to the floor, giving her a view over the rows of dahlias and geraniums that lined up across the garden – and, in the distance, another patrolling guard. A grandfather clock ticked morosely on the far wall.

'Hello?'

No answer.

There was a door ajar at the far end, and she stepped through, calling out, 'Hello? I'm coming in…'

It was a huge, vaulted room, a full two storeys tall, ribbed from floor to ceiling with dozens of bookshelves – at least five times the number in Amber's trailer. And where hers were all carefully mended and re-mended over years of use, Du Cream's collection was as pristine as a tomb. The spines were leather, the titles embossed in gold. A pair of plush candy-coloured armchairs lay in front of a marble fireplace. At the centre of the room was a desk, meticulously set out: papers neatly stacked, a pen set at a perfect right angle beneath, and more books, stacked up in castellated piles, their pages marked with bits of ribbon. A pair of sliding glass doors led out to the garden.

But nothing that looked like a radio. Nothing with so much as a battery. All analogue, primitive. The Stranger's teeth set with frustration. She was on the verge of rifling through his drawers when a voice called out from the entrance: 'Did it hurt?'

Startled, her hand twitched towards her holster. She forced it down. '…hurt?'

'...When you fell from heaven?'

The Stranger choked. 'Wh—'

'Mercy, there's no need to blush.' Du Cream chuckled, placing his hat on a waiting stand. He was a soft-spoken, smooth-skinned, besuited Swiss roll of a man, with a white goatee and an indulgent twinkle in his eye. 'I use that line on everyone. Never get too far with it – angels are out of vogue, you know,' he added with a wink.

'Right,' she croaked.

'Take a seat.' He indicated one of the hideous couches. 'Rodrick told me I had a lady caller.'

'The doorman?'

'The very same.'

Remembering the revulsion in Rodrick's eyes, the Stranger doubted that *'lady caller'* was the phrase he'd used. Du Cream ambled towards a claw-footed table, where a glass chalice lay, filled with amber liquid. 'Will you take a tipple?'

'No. I'm here to borrow—'

'I know, I know, it's so early in the day. But I must steady my nerves.' The Sheriff threw down a measure and wiped his lips on his sleeve. 'I just returned from the most *awful* scene.'

He paused significantly.

'...scene?' she asked.

'Yes, of a crime, you know. Dreadful thing.' He shuddered, filled another measure and lowered himself down on the opposite couch. 'And so strange. Three bodies, scattered out in the middle of nowhere. All dead by different means. Bludgeoning. Poison. Gunshot. One man stripped of his hat and shirt, *post-mortem*. Who'd do such a thing?'

The Stranger paled, twisting a cuff button in her fingers.

'Yeah,' she said. 'Awful.'

'All low lifes, of course, scavengers and such. Normally I'd write it off. But my superior in the south – the good Deputy Seawall…' There was a portentous pause, as if the name was supposed to evoke something. The Stranger arranged her face into an awed shape. Pleased, he carried on: 'He's taken an interest for some reason. Apparently there's more to the case. We've been told to look for anyone carrying a lot of *heathen kit*.' His eyes flicked demurely down to the Stranger's pistol. 'Personally, I'd put it down to a scrap between ne'er-do-wells. But what Seawall wants, Seawall is bound to have…'

Du Cream sighed, leaning back against the overstuffed cushions. 'Tell you the truth, I don't have the stomach for these murderous things. I'm a scholar at heart, as you can see from the shelves around you. From a young age—'

'Do you have a radio?' the Stranger asked, cutting him off. She was sat on the edge of the couch, poised to spring up and run. 'It's urgent.'

Du Cream blinked. 'A what?'

'Your communicator. I was told that you have one.'

'Oh, that thing?' He recovered quickly and chuckled again. 'Why, I do.' He patted his pocket. 'Right here. But who told you?'

'The librarian did. Out on the edge of town. She'd like her book back, by the way.'

Du Cream raised an eyebrow. '*Her* book?'

'Yes.' In a flash of panic, the Stranger realised she'd forgotten the book's title. 'The Counted Minty – uh…'

'*The Count of Monte Cristo*.'

'Yeah.'

'I see.' He pressed his hands against his knees and stood up with a sigh. 'Very well. I'm sure it's around here somewhere.' With a rueful smile, he added: 'I'm afraid she doesn't care for me much.'

'I know.' *Calm,* thought the Stranger. *Calm, calm, calm.* 'She said.'

'It's because I'm trying to *buy* her collection.' He inspected the shelves as he spoke, hands clasped behind him like a pair of nestling white voles. 'I dislike this rigmarole of withdrawing and returning, withdrawing and returning. We are not living in the age of barbarism and bartering anymore. I can afford these items as a businessman, and I deserve them as a hardworking keeper of the law...' He glanced at her. 'You understand I offered her a reasonable price.'

'Sure.'

'But she wouldn't sell.' He beamed at her, eyes twinkling. 'And now she's leaving, and all I have to comfort me is one trite volume of Dumas. Very irksome.'

The Stranger nodded vaguely. She was looking past the Sheriff, through the windowed doors, at the trim garden and the ocean of wasteland beyond. There was a black scratch in the sky – a buzzard – and her imagination followed it, over the smooth hills and on to parts unknown, and she realised that the forty-thousand-kilometre radius of this one planet troubled her far more than the unmeasurable reaches of space.

'Ah, here it is!' From the bottom of a stack on his desk Du Cream lifted free a book that was roughly the size of two bricks. He grabbed the cover by one corner and the rest of it fell, spine snapping with an audible crack. 'One moment...' He fumbled in his breast pocket and pulled out a cigarette lighter.

Pulled from her daydream, the Stranger got to her feet. 'Wait—'

But it was too late. Flame ate over the surface in a matter of seconds. Du Cream laughed and lit it from the other corner, his face awash with orange. Words melted, the cover warped and receded into nothing. When at last the fire petered out, he beat the book against his leg to smother the embers.

'There.' He dropped the book into the Stranger's hands. Nothing remained but a few curling blackened pages bound by the scrap of a spine. 'Do we understand each other now?'

'No.'

'I don't want one book. I want *all* of them. Bring them to me, and I'll help you contact whoever you want.'

She balked. 'Are you serious?'

'Deadly.'

'What about—'

'The asthmatic? With the lame leg? Your heathen pistol should take care of that.' Du Cream turned back to the shelves, running his fingers delicately over the spines, as if to make them shiver. 'The scriptures say, *when the fires burn, bathe in ashes*. Besides, we do have that dreadful case to worry about. If I am left idle for long enough I may be forced to start making arrests…'

THERE WAS A bone-rattling jolt as the library rolled over yet another chunk of desert rock. Du Cream's mansion wound into view, and the Stranger jerked the gearstick up, revving the complaining engine against the steepness of the driveway. At last, with a sigh of relief, she wobbled the trailer over the hill's crest.

Staring up at the house, in that threadbare seat surrounded by the librarian's things, the Stranger felt something unfamiliar touch the edge of her heart. She wondered what sort of person she was becoming.

'*Oi!*'

Something sharp tapped against the window. The Stranger obligingly wound it down, only to have the long nose of a rifle thrust its way inside.

'Hey now.' She lowered the barrel with two fingers. 'It's only me.'

The gun retreated, replaced with the heat of Rodrick's glare. 'He's round the back.'

'Thanks.'

Winding the window back up, she crawled the trailer around the side of the mansion and reversed it so that the rear entrance was a mere step away from the library doors. She cranked the handbrake and hopped outside. Du Cream was clapping.

'Marvellous, my friend!' he called. 'Simply marvellous!'

The Stranger smiled, slamming the door shut. Du Cream was rubbing his hands together. 'Let's see what we have, shall we?'

He wrenched open the back door and climbed inside, giggling as he went. The Stranger crossed her arms and waited. There was a thud. The trailer bounced as something heavy hit the floor. Amber poked her head out, looked swiftly left and right, and stepped out. 'This is crazy,' she said.

'Did you get it?' the Stranger asked. 'The communicator?'

Amber nodded. 'Let's make this quick.'

The Stranger watched the door while Amber, half cautious, half giddy, walked the length of Du Cream's collection, pulling books off the shelves.

'Crap,' she declared, dropping a book flat on the floor

after reading the first few lines. 'Crap.' She dropped another. 'Dull.' Thud. 'No good.' Thud. 'Space, doesn't the man have anything *readable?*'

'Amber…'

'Yeah, yeah, sorry.' Amber moved faster, coming to a discarded shelf right at the back and pulled something out. '*The Three Musketeers*. Haven't read this one yet.' She tucked it approvingly under one arm, then stuck her hand down the back of the row and pulled out another five, hoisting them up to her chin. 'This shelf's all fiction. Help me carry 'em and we can get outta here.'

The Stranger scanned the garden one more time, then hurried over to the shelf, stooping down.

A gunshot. Amber screamed.

Somebody yelled, '*I fuckin' knew it!*'

The Stranger turned, a book in each hand. Rodrick was walking swiftly towards her, raising his rifle, but before he could pull the trigger *Jane Eyre* spun across the room and hit him across the knuckles.

'Fuck—'

Wuthering Heights smacked into the soft meat of his nose.

'*FUCK!*'

Rodrick stumbled back, arms pinwheeling, blood and paper rippling away in a fine arc, as the Stranger scooped up the two fallen books and slammed them neatly into either side of his head. He fell.

'Hey. Hey!' She sprinted across to where Amber lay on the floor. 'Hey. Still here?'

A long, agonising groan drew from Amber's lips. 'Fuck,' she spluttered. 'Little – rat.' She propped herself up on one elbow and lifted *The Three Musketeers* from the pile scattered around her. She gave it a vigorous shake. A long bullet clattered to the floor and rolled away. Rodrick's violent intent had made it as far as the epilogue.

'Fucking ruined,' she spat. 'Son of a bitch.' She flung the book to one side and staggered unevenly to her feet, holding the Stranger's arm for balance. 'Grab the rest, c'mon.'

With the books gathered, the Stranger climbed into the library front and threw the stolen merchandise over the headrest, while Amber tumbled, wheezing, into the passenger seat. 'Go,' she ordered, slapping the dashboard. '*Go!*'

The Stranger hit the gas and made a perilously tight turn back onto the driveway. Behind them the books swayed right, then left, as she spun the wheel to make a nosedive back down the hill.

There was a click.

An antique silver pistol trembled in Du Cream's hand.

'Turn around,' he said.

'Shit,' said Amber, to no one in particular.

Du Cream ignored her. 'I know where you're from, friend. So does the Deputy. You're finished.'

The Stranger revved the engine.

'I said *turn around*,' he repeated.

'I will.' The pedal was on the floor, but they still gathered speed. The Stranger could feel her stomach rise with the momentum.

Du Cream's voice was shaking. 'I-I'm going to count to three!'

'One—'

'Two—'

'Th—'

As the trailer hit the base of the hill, the Stranger

locked the wheel to the left and yanked the handbrake as far as it would go.

There was a moment of weightlessness. The right wheels lifted, one foot, two feet. The Stranger held onto the roof handle, her expression serene, while Amber's cheek smacked against the passenger window. But it was Du Cream who fared worst of all: from Amber's overstuffed shelves the books slid loose all at once, hitting him dead on as a solid wall of paper. He didn't have time to scream.

The library wavered balletically for a moment. Then it crashed back onto its haunches, still intact, but with one less conscious being inside.

There was a long intermission of silence – broken, eventually, by Amber's question: 'What did he mean by that?'

'Mean by what?'

'"*I know where you're from*"?'

The Stranger rested her forehead on the wheel.

'Nothing,' she said. 'Don't worry about it.'

Later – when the evening winds had cooled the surface of the cracked earth, and the stars had begun to pierce the upper reaches of the frazzled atmosphere – once Du Cream's unconscious body had been dumped unceremoniously by the side of the road, and the trailer had driven many miles to what was deemed a safe distance – Amber, still basking in triumph, took out the communicator and laid it on the desk between them. 'Here she is,' she announced. 'As promised!'

The Stranger looked at it. 'Shit,' she said.

It was a chipped plastic rectangle with a greenish screen and a set of buttons, hardly the size of her hand.

A phone. An ancient mobile phone.

'I can't use this.'

'*What?*'

Amber was insulted, truly, in her bones; not just for the effort they'd gone through, but because she really thought they'd acquired something dangerous. 'Why not?'

The Stranger opened her mouth to explain, then closed it tight, and took a slow breath. 'I need something that can send a signal out. Not just to a specific device. A *planet*-wide signal. Something that'd get picked up by the scanners. This won't work.'

'Scanners? What are you jabbering about?'

'On my ship!' she burst out. 'The scanners on my *ship!* Understand? To let them know I'm alive, so I can *find* her and—'

Amber gripped the shotgun. The barrel was trembling, and so was she.

'Get out,' she said. 'Before I damn myself just for talking to you.'

The Stranger's expression did not change. 'Please don't do this.'

'You get out now, and I'll do you the favour of forgetting we met.'

'But—'

She cocked the gun. '*Out!*'

But the Stranger didn't move. 'At least tell me where to go.'

Amber's eyes darted down to the Stranger's pistol. 'New Destiny,' she said, with a delicate curl of the lip. 'The High Sheriff can help you. Anything heathen, he takes it for himself.'

'Okay.' With a nod, the Stranger backed up to the

entrance. She nudged the iron door open with her toe, spilling a square of moonlight into the cramped interior of the library. She turned to go. Then she stopped.

'Can I just—'

Amber pulled the trigger.

There was a second, or maybe one half of a second, where Amber lost track. The first thing she noticed when her awareness returned was that her ears were ringing. Beneath the ring she could hear the sound of something inorganic, an electronic pulse whining from a high pitch to a long low note, and then to nothing. She saw that the Stranger had her pistol drawn. Then came the pain, worse for having been delayed, stemming like so many petals from the spot where the shotgun stock had recoiled into her shoulder. She and the Stranger were aiming at one another. Nobody appeared to have been shot.

The Stranger touched her hat, offering a thin smile. 'Apologies. Thanks for aiming over my head.'

With those words she ducked back outside. Amber said nothing. There were no marks, either on the wall or the ceiling, which suggested that the shotgun had gone off. Slowly, she brought the muzzle to eye level, and saw that it had melted into a glowing, mangled stub.

FIRST INTERLUDE

THE PHONE LOOKED like roadkill: a pancake of glistening metal in the centre of the road, buttons warped, cover split by a net of fissures. Even the most desperate scavenger wouldn't have bothered to prise the thing free from the tarmac.

It lay facing the moon.

Light appeared, a square of cheap thrumming green. And music, too, some 8-bit loop of a classical melody, bright and shrill in the desert night.

Flashing in the centre of the screen, beneath a symbol of a bell, was a single name etched out in blocky black text:

SEAWALL

GARRATY

'How're you doing, Garraty?'

Garraty said nothing. But the Courier (for that was her role, at least for that day) had expected this: she'd been travelling with Garraty for several hours, and he was yet to say a word. So she pressed on: 'I'm feeling good. I've seen better days. But it could be worse.'

The old highway stretched far into the distance, an unbroken ribbon of weedy tarmac melted and shimmering in the midday sun. She beat it down with long, even, rubber-soled steps, her ranger's hat pulled low to shade her eyes. 'I'm moving,' she said. 'And I'm alive. Which is good. Better than not moving. And, uh. Being dead.'

Garraty grunted, squatted low, head dipped serenely towards the ground, and, with a look of martyred perseverance, relieved himself directly onto the floor of his cardboard hutch.

'You know,' she said, 'sometimes I get the feeling you're not listening to me.'

Garraty made no moves to defend himself. She turned her attention to the unblemished horizon. 'Do you really think we're gonna die on this road?'

Garraty sighed. The Courier nodded. 'Me neither. I think we're going to be *just fine.*'

Onwards, onwards, onwards. Two weeks since Springwell. The Courier had been walking for half a month. Constantly kicked out into the night, constantly stiff in the struts of her neck, constantly asking for directions – which way to the city? How far from here? Also: can I have some food? Answers were invariably, 'south', 'very', and 'yes, but it is ground pulses and grilled lizard, for that is all we have to spare, may God keep you and hold you down'. Using pain like coal shoved on an engine, using that thought that repeated so often, as often as a heartbeat, drilled into every footstep:

I miss her. I miss her. I miss her.

Over time she'd learned a little better how to blend in on Earth. She kept her pistol out of sight, avoided talking too much in quiet rooms. Didn't speak at all if she could help it. But when she'd expressed an interest in taking the twenty-mile highway down from Rat Junction to Moneta, the other travellers at the junction pump house became chatty, almost *animated*. It turned out there was nothing Earth people loved more than a good depressing story.

The attendant spoke first, growling out from under a heavy moustache: 'Oh no, I wouldn't go down there, no ma'am. Bad idea. Real bad idea.'

Rumbles of agreement from every side, a slow blur of nodding heads. She was wary of so much attention, but couldn't resist asking: 'Why not?'

'Cursed road. Folks fir.' Like it was a matter of fact.

A trucker piped up: 'My husband's cousins, they took the pickup down there last week. Never got to Moneta. Gone like they'd been plucked from the air.'

'I heard a whole caravan went missing,' came another. 'Three cars total. It's no good.'

'No ma'am. You want to take the East road out to Churny, then come down longways.'

'To space with *that*.' At the corner pump, a wild-bearded man was filling the tank of a rusty moped. He'd been listening with a gradually blooming scowl. 'Problem with cursed roads is people always travel in groups,' he said, gripping the handles. 'If you go on your own, move fast, you'll be just fine. I've gone down Moneta that way a dozen times. You folk don't have the stones for it, that's all.'

The attendant sucked his lips. 'I wouldn't be so sure, son.'

'How far is it to Churny?' asked the Courier.

He shrugged. 'About a week.' With a meaningful glance at her boots, which had long since lost their shine, he added, 'Longer on foot.'

'A *week*? For the love of—' The Courier clamped a hand over her mouth to keep herself from swearing on the wrong God. Two deep breaths, and then, as steadily as she could: 'I don't *have* a week.'

'Me neither,' said moped man. 'Thank you for the advice, but I'll take my chances. And respectfully, friend' – he nodded at the Courier – 'you ought to invest in a vehicle as soon as providence allows.'

The Courier looked at the man's moped – mud-caked, springs rusted together, exposed wiring slung low beneath the corroded engine – with burning envy. 'Wish I could,' she said.

There was a whistle from the crowd. A man, squatting in the open container of a beat-up semi; scrawny, fingers drumming on the bumper, a valley of chest hair between elastic suspenders. 'You're going to Moneta, son? Do you need some work?'

'Heck no, Jordan.' The moped man turned and spat in the dirt. 'D'you think I'm stupid? I know what you trade.'

'I just need one package moved,' he said. 'It's urgent.'

'It's *always* urgent with you.'

'Come on.' Jordan's voice was keening. 'I've got a little money – some food…'

The Courier perked up. 'Food?'

'Sure.' He noticed her. 'What, are *you* gonna take it? On *foot?*'

She shrugged. 'I'm going that way.'

'Space, if you're volunteering…'

'It's not heavy, is it?'

'Not *heavy,* no…'

'I've heard enough.' The moped man straddled the bike and pushed himself over on his toes, close enough to put a hand on the Courier's shoulder. 'Just keep moving, friend,' he advised. 'Keep moving, and keep God in your heart.' He nudged up the kickstand, and urged the bike on south with a bronchial splutter and a wheeze of smoke.

The attendant sniffed. 'Stupid bastard.'

As soon as the moped was out of sight, Jordan started shoving things into her hands: a cardboard box, a brown paper bag. 'This box needs to get to Moneta tonight,' he was saying. '*Tonight.* Don't hang around. Don't chat to nobody. I'd go myself, but I can't risk it. You swear you'll get it there on time?'

'Sure.'

'This is a matter of life and death, friend. Promise me you will.'

'I told you I'd do it,' she said, exasperated.

'Promise!'

From the front of the semi came the sound of doors slamming. The engine stuttered into action, and a voice called, 'We're away! Jordan, come on!'

'Okay,' she sighed, thinking: *whatever.* 'I promise.'

The man glanced over his shoulders, then carried on rapidly: 'Take it to Rochelle. Okay? Rochelle. In Moneta. The house with the red door. If she asks, tell her you've got Garraty.'

'Got what?'

'Garraty!' With a groan of powered gravel, the truck pulled away. 'And keep the lid on! *He bites!'*

The Courier looked into the bag and sighed. Bread and raisins. She'd been hoping for a sandwich. And so, with the package in tow, the Courier set off for the town of Moneta – down the cursed road.

Walking was nothing new to the Courier. She'd spent most of her youth on foot, wedged shoulder to shoulder in a long concrete hangar, sterile air souring with vaporised sweat. They called it primary training. You'd march in circles all day, then find out there was another five hours' marching still left to do, and you and your buddies would groan and bitch and maybe kick something over. Then you'd carry on, five hours, ten, twenty, till you could circle the moon three times over without checking the time, singing some filthy tune to the rhythm of your own feet.

No singing here. No voices at all. Rat Junction was far behind, and the quiet smothered her ears like cloth. And flat, so flat you could stand on a chair and see over the rim of the world.

She tried to recall how the planet had looked from orbit. Burnt, she remembered. Overgrilled. Oddly lumpy, like a dry sponge. Any oceans? It was hard to recall. She'd had other things on her mind at the time.

A contaminated memory. She set it aside.

Her free arm was still wrapped around the cardboard box. She hadn't opened it, but an hour of lugging the thing around had soured her feelings towards the package. It was irritating, really, to have something like that thrust into her hands. *First sign of trouble and I'll chuck it in the scrub,* she thought. *I'm sure 'Garraty' can take care of himself.*

Curious now, she began to study the box's exterior. It was a foot long, rectangular in shape, unmarked and unsealed. This struck her as odd. If Garraty was something precious, why not transport it securely? The lid wasn't even taped down.

She held the package higher and gave it a tentative shake. Something stirred inside.

She jerked her head back, thinking, *surely not...?* Bringing the box closer, she placed one hand on the base and shook it again.

Definite movement. It seemed she'd woken him up.

The Courier was unsettled. Of course, it was none of her business what she was being paid to transport. But what if there were some kind of monster waiting in there? Her mind filled with myriad images from museum-screens: some bastard oversight of nature, skittering sideways on too many legs, gnarled black body twisting unnaturally upwards into a swollen, glistening stinger. *It bites.*

The box's weight shifted as the thing inside moved over to the opposite corner. She placed it down on the ground and took a step back. There was nothing for it. Drawing her pistol, she stretched one leg out and nudged the lid off with her toe.

Nothing emerged. She waited another moment. Still nothing. Keeping her gun trained on the opening, she inched forward until she could peer inside.

The Courier let her gun drop. She squeezed her eyes shut and tilted her head up to the sky, letting out a sigh, which turned into a sort of relieved, self-effacing laugh. Then she squatted down and lifted her cargo free of his cardboard prison.

Garraty regarded her mutely, ink-drop eyes peering out of a walnut head.

'Hey, now,' she said. 'Not so scary, are you?'

He groaned, his horned legs swimming sluggishly through the air. It seemed strange that such a weird, harmless little creature needed to be moved so urgently, that his presence anywhere would be a 'matter of life and death'. She peered at him from all angles, noting the scowling curve of his mouth, the mottled hexagonal pattern on the back of his shell. No clues.

The Courier could name a handful of Earth's extinct lifeforms: rhinos, bears, owls, panthers. All of them gone, reduced to a strand of DNA in a lab somewhere. But she couldn't recall the name for the grumpy green hunchbacks.

'Ah, well.' She set him back inside his box. 'You're fine, whatever you are.'

She resumed her journey with the lid of the box slightly ajar, pausing every now and then to peer approvingly down at Garraty. It felt good to have a companion.

Time passed. The last of the winds dropped away. In the far distance the silver arc of a warp tunnel glistened, hauntingly huge, half buried in sand. The Courier squinted at it, wondering how long it had been since a ship had passed through that gate – three centuries? Four?

There was a faint ringing in her ears.

Garraty started pooping not long afterwards, which she found funny at first, but it became distasteful after the smell began to waft upwards. This coincided with the first roadside attraction they'd passed in several hours of travel: rotting plastic cubicles, luminous blue for no reason that she could discern, arranged like turrets guarding an empty lot. Scattered around was the detritus of some failed project – a section of collapsed fencing, oil drums, bleached rubble. The ground glittered with broken glass.

'Stay right there.' She placed Garraty down on the ground. With a piece of slate she scraped his box clean as best she could, tipping the droppings, which had already started to harden, out onto the earth.

'Okay. Great.'

Great. The words hung in the air for a moment.

She sat down on the oil drum, cradling her head.

'Keep it together, Captain,' she muttered. 'Keep it together.'

A disturbance in the distance caught her eye, and she looked up. Somewhere ahead of them, on the boundaries of human vision, a scarf of dust trailed upwards into the pure blue sky.

There was a truck coming.

'Huh.'

The Courier watched with interest for a minute as the

speck of an outline formed and drew closer. When she glanced down again at her feet, Garraty was gone.

'Shit.' She crouched down. He was nowhere to be seen. 'Oh, you little *bastard*.'

But there was no anger behind the words – in fact, the Courier had to repress a sense of panic as she scanned the empty road. When this proved unsuccessful, she dropped to her hands and knees, picking through the rubble.

'I'm going to leave you here,' she threatened. 'I'm going to pack up and go. Serves you right.' But she kept looking.

She found him in the sliver of shade behind the plastic shacks, tucked contentedly into himself. 'Look what you've reduced me to,' she said, picking him up. 'A decorated war veteran, babysitting a goddamn – a goddamn – what are you called again?'

She paused, distracted by the sound of an engine. It rumbled to a slow halt, and a woman's voice emerged from within: 'For the last time, stop fucking calling. It's under control.'

At the end of the row, one of the blue shacks shuddered with a sudden impact. Then the next along, then the next. Though the driver was out of view, the Courier could imagine her working down the line, flinging open doors and slamming them shut again in hasty disgust, one hand fixed to the device at her ear. 'Because I thought I saw someone, alright?' A pause. 'Well, someone's gotta be carrying the fucking tortoise around. It's not gonna come up by itself.'

The Courier felt a shock of recognition, and fixed Garraty with a cool, accusatory stare.

Tortoise.

A bark of laughter from the driver as another cubicle

shook to its foundations. 'Of course it's fucking worth it. With this stuff, you just need to name your price. They'll do anything. *Anything*, Mother God.' One final slam. The Courier hunched down as far as she could go, submerged in the weeds and the broken glass.

'Never mind. False alarm. They must be further north.' A pause. She laughed again. 'Are you kidding? I'm the best shot on two legs. This'll be like pissing in a barrel.'

The Courier waited until the sound of the engine had long faded away, and then commando-crawled to the end of the lot, one hand clenched around Garraty's midriff. She looked at her ward, and he at her, blinking innocently.

'What the hell have you gotten us into?'

The tortoise's mouth cracked open, and for a brief, surreal moment she thought he was going to say something in response. Instead he yawned. The Courier stood, beating herself up and down with the brim of her hat. Thick clouds of rubble-dust came free and dissipated into the windless air. She retrieved the box, placed Garraty back inside, and resumed her walk southwards, craning her head regularly in the direction the truck had gone.

'Do you think she'll be back?' she asked. 'Your friend?'

She glanced at Garraty, who was turning in slow, ponderous circles, probing the edges of his habitat. 'Why's she chasing you, anyhow? Do you taste really good? Maybe she'll grind you up into something. Your shell could be some rare... aphrodisiac, maybe.'

A contemptuous glare from Garraty.

'Whatever it is, she must want it really badly to go through all this trouble. Not that I'm worried, I mean. I can look after myself. Did you hear what she said? *Best shot on two legs.*' The Courier snorted. 'As if.'

Silence settled down again, much as the dust from the truck's tyres settled back into the shiftless earth. When the Courier spoke again, she chose her words with caution: 'I used to do a lot of that kind of talk. When I was younger. I liked to brag.'

A deep sigh.

'But not anymore. I made a promise to myself. No more violence. Because people can do that, you know?' She jostled the box, and said brightly: '*Change!* I changed, didn't I? I'm better now, aren't I?'

Garraty spun on.

There was no way to track the time except the painfully slow rotation of the planet's bulk. The sun was three quarters of the way across the sky, sinking towards the uneven hills that hugged the horizon, when the Courier noticed she was nearing something. A shack. Little remained of the original building – just a few lengths of white tin and a faded sign that read, in chunky, cheerful letters, **Muddy Gap Cafe**. The rest was a patchwork of plywood and canvas. The whole structure looked more than a little precarious, but the thought of shade was too tempting to pass by. The Courier walked to the entranceway, lifted a wall of hanging tarp, and called out, 'Hello?'

Nobody answered. She stepped through.

It was dim inside, but mercifully cool. Plastic furniture littered the room, pushed up against one side of the wall to make space for a singed patch of floor that had presumably housed a campfire. A door frame at the back led through to the kitchen.

The Courier stepped around, noting each little detail with a tourist's curiosity. There was a bent teaspoon, a discarded sock worn down to nothing at the heel, some scribbles of graffiti REPENT! and below in a different hand, *why?*, and an empty, upturned tin. The latter made her stomach rumble. She wiped a mummified fly off one of the chairs and sat down, unclipping a canteen from her belt and pulling the lumpy bag of food out her back pocket.

To the Courier, who'd spent years of her life surviving mostly on purification tablets and tubes of flavoured paste, the food on Earth seemed comparatively fresh. Not *good* fresh, but 'fresh' in the same way you might talk about droppings. The bread was seasoned and not too bad, but the raisins were awful – chewy and dry, with not a hint of sweetness. She brought one up to eye level and saw that it had legs.

The Courier's jaw froze mid-chew. Bile rose rapidly up her throat. There was nothing for it. She shut her eyes, inhaled deeply, and shoved the rest into her mouth all at once, gagging violently as half a dozen bug bodies lodged in the back of her throat. Stuffing in some bread only made things worse, so she fumbled the canteen lid loose and took a desperate gulp, spilling a measure of precious water down her shirt in the process.

Garraty watched from his box. She lowered the canteen and glared at him. 'What're *you* looking at?'

Then the Courier's head pricked up.

Another engine. A surreptitious peek out the doorway revealed the same truck from before driving the opposite way, close enough now that she could see the thick, glistening hubcaps.

The Courier swore. She could run for it – there might be a back exit in the kitchen – but, then again, maybe not. Her panic subsided as she realised the upside. The driver would have to come in on foot, which would give the Courier the upper hand. Positioning herself against the wall, she rested her hand against her holster and waited.

Wind stirred outside, tarp moving lazily inwards. The truck rumbled ever closer. The Courier shifted from foot to foot, waiting for the squeal of brakes, the slam of a door. It didn't come. Still the sound grew louder.

She whispered to Garraty: 'Do you think she'll drive past?'

And louder.

'Oh,' she said.

And louder.

'*Shi*—'

The wall burst open. There was an explosion of plastic and splinters, and the tin roof of the shack lurched nauseatingly downwards where the plywood struts had been knocked away. It held, but only just. The truck idled, half in, half out.

But the cafe was empty.

Under the bumper, the Courier waited. It had missed her by half an inch as it came through the wall, and she'd managed to wriggle in between the wheels before the dust settled. But now she was stuck. The metal underbelly pressed down on her from above, radiating heat and the stench of fried oil. She had two options: either crawl backwards and escape from the rear, or stay still and risk getting squished as the truck backed up. Neither felt all that preferable.

A pair of boots materialised on the floor, the truck springing a little as it came free from the driver's weight. The Courier watched, chin to the ground, as the boots circled around to the front and vanished into the kitchen.

Down in the darkness, the Courier smiled. One shot from her could slice right through the driver's heel. No more cursed road. She'd take the truck, and the driver could limp back to Moneta. Serve her right.

She reached for her holster, suppressing a yelp of pain when her elbow jostled up against a chunk of hot engine metal. She dug her teeth into her bottom lip and tried again, slower this time, pulling the gun by the handle across the floor and up level with her face. Only when her finger was on the trigger did she let herself exhale.

Floorboards creaked up ahead. Another object crossed into the Courier's frame of vision, something humpbacked and low to the ground, moving with surprising speed.

It was Garraty. The little animal was marching towards his doom with a look of intense, bloody-minded purpose.

'*Psst!*' the Courier beckoned desperately, but Garraty didn't so much as turn his head. 'Stupid little…'

She peered forward. The kitchen door was just out of sight. The driver would see the tortoise as soon as they turned around. That would put her on alert, and then they'd be finished. After another half a second of hesitation, the Courier crawled forwards, reaching out to grab Garraty by his rear leg. He let out a mewl of protest, trying to retract into his shell, but she was too fast. With one rough yank the two of them vanished back beneath the bumper.

Garraty kept growling. The Courier wiggled back, pulling him up against her chest. Rapid footsteps from the kitchen. She fumbled, desperately pulling the pistol up, but the driver was in a hurry, and their boots stomped past and vanished in a second.

The engine thrummed into gear, bathing the back of the Courier's neck in fetid heat. She had no choice but to press her face to the ground as the truck slid backwards over her head, then scramble back behind the sagging wall with Garraty in one hand and her gun in the other.

She listened. Thick tyres ground the soil to pulp as they turned, and then rolled away, continuing their journey south. The Courier sighed.

Holstering her gun, she lifted Garraty to eye level. He'd retracted himself in protest at all the rough treatment. 'What's your problem, starshine?' she asked.

Garraty glared resentfully out of the gloom of his shell.

'Don't be like that,' she coaxed. 'Come on, it's safe to come out now.'

Still he refused to emerge. She turned him upside down and shook hard. 'Give it up! Ungrateful—'

She stopped. On Garraty's shell, in the pattern of thin rivets and interlocking shapes, there was a line that seemed to go deeper than the others. The Courier reached in, running her fingers around the edge. It was definitely raised.

Cautiously – Garraty stayed motionless – she stuck her thumbnail in. The centre of the shell lifted away with a click. From under the lid a shower of small pale things came free, scattering over her lap. She swore, wiggling backwards, but nothing attacked or bit or swarmed. She picked one of the things up, holding it between her thumb and forefinger. It was a pill.

'Son of a bitch,' she said.

With this stuff, you just need to name your price. They'll do anything.

'So you're a drug mule.' A pause. 'Or a drug tortoise, I guess.'

The revelation left her feeling strangely deflated. Somehow she'd imagined that the holy people of Earth were above such mundane vices. But they weren't, of course they weren't. She pressed Garraty's shell against her forehead. 'Gods above. What am I—'

Sensing an opportunity for revenge, Garraty poked out of his shell and clamped his jaw across the bridge of her nose. The Courier swore, yanking him off, but his pointed lip managed to tear free a sizable strip of skin. 'That's *it!*'

She jerked her arm back, fully ready to throw him against the wall. But something stopped her. Well – someone.

Someone who wasn't there.

Thinking of that person now, the Courier sat back, sighing and slumping like a slit tyre.

'Sorry.' She set Garraty down at her side, idly rubbing her thumb back and forth over his grizzled head. 'I guess I can't just leave you here, can I? She wouldn't like that.'

Extending his limbs out as far as they would go, Garraty pushed out of her hand, digging his curled paws into the fabric of her trousers to haul himself up and over into her lap. He twisted round a few times looking for just the right spot, then crouched down, head lolling to one side, and promptly fell asleep. His nostrils expanded, letting out a warbling, contented whistle.

'Trying to be cute, are we?' she asked. 'I'm not that gullible.'

She placed a hand on his shell, feeling the warmth beneath.

Half an hour later the Courier was walking again, this time on high alert. Two near misses – they might not survive a third. Worse still, the water was nearly gone, and she had a headache like a sharp-cornered brick nestled in the centre of her skull. Garraty slept obliviously in his box, the white pills scooped up and secured back into the compartment in his shell. She'd shut the lid, worried that he'd shrivel up in the heat. Well – shrivel up more.

Another object pushed into her line of view, and she startled, reaching for the pistol, relenting when she realised her mistake. It was motionless, broken and sagging, weeping rust. Railing around the flat side helped her identify the thing for what it was: the corpse of a watership, banked helplessly on one side. Bone-pale brambles crowded over the bridge. The prow was sharp as an open tin.

Good cover, she thought. *Maybe I could camp out...*

Then, a sound. A puncturing of the air. At least a mile south, but it echoed like thunder across the open plains, and the Courier knew the sound at once. A gunshot. Then another.

The Courier passed the ship. She was moving faster now, trying to outpace the growing sense of dread.

At first she thought he was a bag of rubbish, sprawled and formless in the far distance. Then she saw the curl of his limp fingers resting on the roadside. She broke into a sprint, dropping to her knees as she reached the man's side. But there was nothing she could do. Nothing any of us can do for the dead.

He was lying in a small mound of what had once been his own face. His arms, already stiffening up, were splayed at either side in a gesture of mild surprise, wild beard clotted with blood. Beside him lay the moped, weeping oil from a wound in the front tank.

The Courier leant back, swallowing. For a second she sat like that, eyes shut, lips pressed tight. Then she got up and looked around.

A few yards ahead lay a leather knapsack. Someone had turned it inside out, so that the crumpled thing looked like a body in and of itself. Possessions were scattered around: a couple of shirts, a cracked hand mirror, a folded photograph.

In her mind she could visualise the last moments of the man's life. Hearing, or perhaps seeing, a car on the approach behind him, he'd steered to the side of the road to let it pass. The driver had then leant out of the window and shot him once in the back of the head, and another shot in the face. Thorough, accurate. *Best shot on two legs.* Pulling up – the Courier could see tracks curving the dirt – the driver had hopped out and rifled through his things, turning out his pockets, emptying his knapsack.

Then she'd climbed back in their truck and driven on, leaving his body to bake and rot.

She looked again at the corpse.

'Where were you headed?' she asked. 'Back home, like me?'

He didn't respond.

Walking on, she placed a fist softly in the palm of her hand and popped the knuckles one by one.

AT THE EDGE of town, the truck did a U-turn. There was no warning beforehand. It crawled up to the slanting roadside shacks at the same modest pace it had been driving all day. Then, as if repelled by a forcefield, it spun a tight semicircle and shot back the way it had come, leaving a smear of black markings on the highway. A casual observer might say that the driver was showing signs of violent frustration. But who could say for sure?

The truck powered back down the road, the engine

groaning under its own weight. It wasn't long before she came into view: a traveller, walking south, languid as anything. The truck snarled into a higher gear. Hearing this, the traveller's head pricked up, and they moved over to one side to let them pass. There was no sign of fear on the woman's face, only a kind of dozy curiosity. Yard by yard the truck closed the distance between them, slowing a little on the approach. Range was reached. With a mechanical purr, the driver's-side window started to lower.

That was the signal. The Courier moved. In two bursts, the leftmost of the truck's tyres exploded, swinging the whole vehicle violently to one side. The driver did not brake. Instead she accelerated, urging the runaway vehicle towards the Courier, who realised too late the miscalculation she'd made.

They collided. Caught as she was trying to leap away, the Courier's legs clipped the headlight and she was thrust diagonally over the bonnet, landing with a thud back on the ground. The handbrake shrieked. Metal wheels scored the tarmac as the truck swung around to face the fallen Courier.

But she was already up.

The Courier's reflection shone dark and distorted in the tinted glass. She could plant six rounds through the truck's windscreen in the time it took most people to take off their safety.

But she wouldn't. Or maybe couldn't. Same difference.

The engine cut off. Neither the window nor the door stirred. She knew the driver was armed, but where would she shoot from? The driver's seat? The passenger's? Had she moved to the back? What angle did she hold the weapon at? Was it a—

No time to duck. The Courier jerked her head to one side. The bullet licked her cheek, leaving a faint red line. There was a white hole, cracked all abouts like a spiderweb, right into the centre of the windscreen. Into that hole the Courier aimed, lifting her pistol to replicate the angle exactly.

The driver screamed like the air was being ripped from their body by force.

She wouldn't die. The Courier was certain of that. An upside to her pistol's design was that wounds it made were instantly cauterised, so there was no danger of blood loss. The driver would be fine, eventually.

Eventually. But not for a while. If the Courier had aimed right – and she always aimed right – her shot had split her forearm lengthwise, knuckle to elbow.

And so the driver screamed. The Courier walked south, towards the town where scattered lights clustered under a blackening sky.

The silence between Garraty and the Courier, the silence that had been there since they met, grew awkward as the streets of Moneta rolled out around them. It was late, and dark, and as quiet as a held breath. The Courier cleared her throat.

'I'm sorry you had to see that,' she said. 'I thought, you know, if I got her shooting hand she would stop...'

Excuses trailed away.

'Look, you can bite me if you want.' She stuck her hand in the box, waggling a finger beside his jaw. 'Go on.'

But Garraty turned his head.

'You know, we could make a run for it,' she mused. 'Sell those pills, buy a car, drive south. Find a communicator. Find her. Go home. What do you think, eh? You and me?'

But you promised you'd do it.

'Yeah, but…'

You promised.

'Damn it.' There was a buckled can lying in the street; she kicked it against a cinder-block wall, watched it bounce. 'Damn it, damn it, damn it. It could all be so simple. You make everything harder, you know that? You make everything so damn *hard*.'

Garraty didn't respond. Perhaps, somewhere in his wizened mind, he knew she wasn't really talking to him.

The red door swung open after a single knock. There was nobody there.

A voice called: 'Who're you?'

She looked down. A girl of maybe eight stood before her, hair mussed, squinting upwards.

'Oh,' said the Courier. She cleared her throat. 'Hello.'

The girl's eyes adjusted, and she gasped. *'Garraty!'*

'Yeah. Um, here.'

She passed him down, legs swimming, and the girl nuzzled the tortoise to her forehead. Garraty cooed in return. 'You're late!' scolded the girl. 'Bad Garraty!' Then, in an unnervingly well-practised motion, she popped open his shell, took out a pill, and popped it in her mouth.

The Courier moved forward – and then watched, fingers slack in empty space, as she swallowed it whole. *Oh crap,* she thought.

'Hello? Who's—' An adult presence appeared in the doorway, half-faceless in the yellow backlight. 'Oh, Mother God,' he said. 'Garraty.'

'He's back!' the girl cried.

'That's great, honey. That's really great.' He took hold

of her shoulder, squeezed it tight, looked at the Courier and said with a voice that would cut ice: 'You cut that fine.'

'I'm sorry,' she said, still in shock. 'I'm sorry. She just – I mean she just took...' There is no easy way to explain to someone that their child needs to be compelled to vomit in short order. *'She took a pill.'*

'What, just now?' He looked down. 'I know you've been waiting, but next time with water, okay?'

'Okay.' She sealed Garraty's hatch and placed him on top of her head. 'Back home!'

Home, indeed: he nestled happily into her hair, legs lolling out. The whole scene hurt the Courier almost physically, and it took no small amount of resolve not to grab him back and sprint away into the night, never to be parted again. Instead she asked: 'What did she take just now? Is it safe?'

'Safe?' The man snorted. 'Gaia, don't you even know what you were carrying? It's insulin.'

'Insulin,' she repeated. 'Shi—' She remembered the child. 'I see.'

'I'm sorry they didn't tell you.'

Garraty turned circles in her hair, dark curls whirling around.

'You can buy them down in the city, but up here... it's harder. Less oversight.'

'Of-of course.'

He gave the girl a little pat on the back. 'The lady is going now, Rochelle. Say thank you to the lady.'

'Thank you!' She waved frantically. *'Bye!'*

'So long,' he said. 'Safe home.'

'But—'

It was no use. She was talking to a closed door.

A list of longings as long as an arm was piling up in the Courier's mind, not the least of which was a need for some word of comfort, some sugary lie to sip on, some flavour of *It'll be okay.* But of all the words tossed around that day, there were only three that really mattered: *Keep moving, friend.*

And so the sore-footed Courier walked into the night – dreaming of mopeds, and other things besides.

…Examining the case of Radovid 5, it is clear that the technology exists to pull back even the most devastated planet from the brink of uninhabitability – provided the aforementioned planet is of strategic importance to the Empire. The decision to abandon Earth should therefore be recontextualised as more political than humanitarian. While they are outdated, readings from the southeastern continent indicate…

– 'Abandoned planets: A socio-climatical reexamination', Dr Noelle Daley. (2805, unpublished)

Incoherent partisan gibberish. Has she lost her mind?

– Peer review notes

SECOND INTERLUDE

Du Cream and Seawall had been talking for about half an hour, give or take, judging by the shifts in the midday shadows. Rodrick stood guard as always. He was even more nervous than usual – not for fear of attackers, but because he'd spent the morning trying to make himself look presentable, combing his hair into a pair of well-greased curtains and tucking his best shirt into his best jeans. Even the rifle had a fresh coat of polish.

This was the Deputy, after all. Everything mattered.

They'd been summoned to Churny, a mean little town with an oppressive stink of burnt garbage and motor oil, to meet with the High Sheriff's right-hand man on the latest leg of his manhunt. Du Cream had pulled rank to get them access to the town's grandest building, an unlovable cube of orange brick with concrete steps and a slabbed floor. Rodrick stood watch by the naked flagpole at the entranceway and glared at passers-by. The boss had warned him they might be a while.

'What's done cannot be undone,' Du Cream admitted,

straightening his tie before the mirror. 'I shall have to accept a scolding.' Even Rodrick, who didn't pay much attention to anything, noticed the tremor in the Sheriff's fingers as he undid and rethreaded the tie once, twice, three times. At last he pulled the whole thing loose and threw it on the floor. 'Open collar,' he said, feigning a smile. 'Better to look relaxed, hmm?'

Du Cream seemed to be shrinking by the day. His cheek still bore traces of his run-in with the fugitive, that grim morning two weeks ago when he'd staggered up the front driveway with a face like a basket of plums. 'Of course, he's sure to catch her soon,' he muttered. 'Then all will be forgiven. It was a silly mistake, that's all. He'll catch her in no time.'

The Sheriff's nerves were a mystery to Rodrick, and he didn't understand why there was such a fuss over one outlaw. But Rodrick was also an incurious man and didn't waste energy on things outside his interest.

At least this shit's nearly over and done with, he thought, shifting his rifle from one shoulder to the other. A mule pounded past, hooves dragging, a sealed wooden barrel strapped to either flank. *Maybe I can grab a glass of something before we go.*

'Anything to report?'

The tone was soft and friendly, but it took Rodrick by such surprise that he almost levelled his rifle. Deputy Seawall was standing beside him with his arms crossed, chewing on a toothpick. He'd arrived without so much as a whisper.

'That a no?' asked the Deputy, giving him a wry look.

'N-no sir!'

'Okie dokie.'

Seawall was a slight man, smaller than Rodrick by a

good few inches, rough-shaven with a permanent half-smile. He plucked out the toothpick and inhaled. 'I bet you fancy a nice stiff drink right about now,' he mused to Rodrick.

'Sure do.'

'That makes two of us.'

'I'll bet.'

Rodrick was already feeling warm towards the Deputy. For a leader of men, he spoke plainly – much plainer than Du Cream, who could hardly lead a single town.

'Yeah,' the Deputy went on, 'I'd love a nice drink and a good long sleep. But now I've got a big mess to clear up instead. They always leave us to clean up when they make a mess, don't they, son?'

'Yes, sir.' Rodrick nodded emphatically. 'Every time.'

'Darn irritating, huh?'

'You said it.'

The Deputy gave him a friendly whack on the back. 'I'd better make tracks then. So long now.' He ambled away, whistling through his teeth.

Rodrick stayed still, waiting for Du Cream to call him in. The Springwell Sheriff was very particular about his rituals: nobody was to see him unless summoned.

A quarter of an hour passed. Two quarters. Rodrick peeked through the entrance. He called out, 'Sheriff, sir? You in there?'

No response. Another quarter. Rodrick was parched. He could feel his shins starting to cramp up. He tried again. 'Hello? Sheriff?'

Feeling impatient now, he advanced further in, finding the office door ajar. After a swift knock, he nudged it open. 'Hey, Sheriff? Are we going or what?'

There were no windows in the office, just a small

portrait of a snowy forest – snow, Rodrick knew, was a sweet edible cream that once fell from the sky, one of the many gifts God had revoked on account of humanity's sins. Du Cream seemed enthralled by it. He'd turned his armchair to face the wall and sat there, staring.

'Sir? Are you sleeping?' He clapped a few times. 'Hello?'

A little spark of hysteria was forming inside Rodrick. He knew his boss was not asleep. There were stains on the floor. Stains on the armchair. But he couldn't turn around; something compelled him closer, to where he could see the man's face.

'Let's go now,' he said softly, coming to the Sheriff's side.

Rodrick looked at what was left of Emollient Du Cream. Then he walked outside and vomited on the concrete steps.

SAINT'S CRADLE

THREE DAYS' TREK from the town where a drug-smuggling tortoise dozed in a little girl's hair, in a natural basin scooped and lined like the palm of a giant hand and surrounded on all sides by low balding hills, there was a town called Saint's Cradle, where there lived a boy by the name of Jovah. Jovah had always lived in Saint's Cradle, though he knew that Saint's Cradle had not always been the town's name. It had an old name that nobody was allowed to speak, because it brought back memories of dark days that followed the Departure, the starving-time, before the town was reborn in the lap of Gaia's glory.

Jovah knew about these things because his father was a Preacher. That would have been a mark of honour anywhere, but Saint's Cradle was more than an ordinary wasteland parish. It was the holiest town for miles around, where currency came in blessings and the whisper of heresy could do to a human life what fire does to a bundle of dried hay. A Preacher's son was naturally assumed to be more learned than other children, more mature than other children, more obedient than other children. He was revered and therefore desperately lonely. You couldn't steal fruit with the Preacher's son, because what if he told his father? And what if his father told God?

That wouldn't do. For God was the Earth they lived on, and her wrath was mighty.

So Jovah played alone.

Four days out of seven, when the children came to the chapel for school, it was Jovah's job to hand out the notebooks and pens. They'd thank him with a blank smile and return to their conversations, and he'd stand at the back of the class and listen to the steady murmur of lapping voices until the crowd became a voice all of its own.

Jovah asked his father once if Earth was ever lonely.

'She's the only one of herself, isn't she?' he asked. 'The only world-god.'

His father looked a little surprised, as Jovah was a quiet boy and not prone to asking questions. But then he smiled, and drew a napkin along his mouth. 'That's correct, Jovah,' he said. 'She is alone in a vast expanse of dead rocks, which look to her like corpses that were never alive.'

Jovah nodded solemnly. 'Planets.'

'But Gaia is not alone. She has us. And we are always with her, see?' His father dropped the napkin, and it fell to the table. '*This is the mark of her love.* She's pulling us closer, even now.'

'But doesn't she hate us?' Jovah pressed. 'Because of all the sinning?'

The Preacher chuckled and shook his head. 'No, Jovah. She does not hate us. She punishes us out of love, in order to make us holy again. When the waters run dry...'

'...*drink dust,*' Jovah intoned. A psalm. No matter what they spoke about, it always seemed to end in a psalm. His father nodded approvingly.

'That's right. Now be a good boy and clear the table.'

When he was little and did not understand how his father's words worked, Jovah had tried to 'drink' some of the thinning soil that coated the backyard of the chapel. It tasted – not unpleasant. Just of nothing, except for a salty tang underneath the musk. Afterwards he got terribly thirsty.

That memory embarrassed him these days.

Jovah was a model child, and he had a problem that most model children do: he was invisible to adults. Once they understood that he would do what he was told the first time, they ceased to think of him. He did nothing to gain their attention, performed no tricks, told no stories. He vanished into obedience. When he wasn't helping his father in the chapel or running errands in town, Jovah would walk through the foothills outside his house where the yellow grass grew waist-high and the air buzzed with hidden crickets. There he'd crouch down and watch ants march back and forth over tiny fault lines in the Earth's crust. That was his only pastime as far as anyone knew.

But Jovah had a secret.

To understand Jovah's secret, one must understand Saint's Cradle itself, how it was built and why it existed. It had never been large, but the passing centuries had shrunk it further still, so that the skeletal ruins of abandoned homes surrounded it on every side. The town's main features were a chapel, a general store, an auto mechanics, and an inn called The Motel with a few dozen rooms stacked atop each other in a grid. All these features could be seen by a traveller in quick succession, spread out as they were along either side of the highway that cut down through the town centre. There had been farms there not too long ago, but the gradual stiffening of the soil underfoot had forced the farmers south, to the other half of the continent, into the High Sheriff's verdant inner territories.

Like a con artist, the town had always been running some scheme or other to keep itself alive – blowing glass, brewing spirits, fixing cars. But it could never compete with the larger settlements nearby. The strain of living on exports gradually took its toll. Year after year the town bled dry, until the only people remaining were those who could not afford to leave. Flies buzzed over rubbish bins, keys turned in locks, and stray dogs ran caterwauling in the street, lips bubbling, ribs pressed white against the skin. Passers-by stopped staying overnight. There was a stench of death about the place that curdled a man's stomach.

But Saint's Cradle was loved by Gaia, and she did not want it to die.

In the middle of the town, split off a hair from the highway, a pitted road led down to a crater filled with old-world rubbish. Before Jovah was born it had been little more than a backcountry trail to a forgotten scrapheap. Now the entrance was marked by a magnificent archway, wrought out of various items found in the crater itself – a twisted old table leg, a bent kettle, a rotten robotic toy – and shot through with electric lights. The path down had been widened and decorated in a similar fashion.

At the end of that path was the Saint. He sat there as he always had, at the bottom of a sharp slope, shadowed in the remains of an overturned lorry, garlanded on every side by weeds and stiff bracken. Not sleeping. Not moving. Not even *eating*. But still – somehow – wonder of wonders! – alive.

It was one of Jovah's favourite bedtime stories.

'I'll never forget the day I found him,' his father liked to begin. 'I was just a boy back then, not much older than you, and I was scared – *he* scared me. Just sitting there like a corpse. So I threw a rock to try and make him move. It hit his head, and all this blood flecked out' – he made a spray with his hands, whooshing over Jovah's face until he giggled – 'but he didn't even flinch, Jovah. I sensed Her then. Sensed the touch of God. Right here.' He tapped his chest. 'Reaching up from the ground.'

'*What did you do?*' Jovah whispered.

'I fetched my father, of course, and showed him what I found. I thought he would laugh at me, but he understood right away. Your grandfather was a very holy man. He sent word out to all the other Preachers in the land, and they all came to see, though I don't think most of them believed. Those were hungry days, Jovah, and it seemed unbelievable that a man could subsist on God's energy alone. But they were curious. So they came.'

'One by one they went down into the crater. One by one they sat with him, watched him, listened to him breathe. And one by one they were converted. The last to arrive was Ursula Ramirez.'

Ursula Ramirez of New Destiny. Ursula Ramirez who supposedly lived on leaf tea and lima beans and could feel the shifts in God's body beneath her uncovered toes. Ursula Ramirez, who'd united the disparate desert parishes into a single community, One Church Over God, so that one struggling town might send help to another, and important news might spread, and that each Preacher might not feel so alone. Ursula Ramirez, who most folk called the High Preacher. She insisted she was nobody's leader and not to be revered – and for that, they revered her all the harder.

'She went down to the crater. We waited and waited. Almost for an hour. When she came back, she walked past all the other Preachers, and came straight to me. She took my hand, just like this.' The Preacher took his son's hand. 'And she said, *well done.*'

Jovah exhaled. Those final words always made him shiver.

After the High Preacher gave the nod, faithful folk started arriving in swathes. The inn filled up. The shop ran out of stock. Everything was coveted, even the rubbish in the crater; a wealthy home was incomplete without a piece of sacred garbage on the mantelpiece. And they didn't just come once – the impression left the first time was strong enough that many made it an annual pilgrimage, returning the next year with families in tow.

Jovah had seen the Saint's power at work again and again. Old men climbed out of the crater with shining eyes, wiping their cheeks with crisp white cuffs. Couples would leave hand in hand and whisper new affirmations to one another in the light of the sun. Even squalling babies fell silent in the weight of God's presence.

And so the town became Saint's Cradle, and fed itself on nothing but faith alone.

JOVAH AWOKE AS he always did, half an hour before dawn. His first conscious thought was: *Today is the day.*

Ten years old. Jovah had been waiting to turn ten for a long time.

Light was a precious commodity in most places this far north, but Saint's Cradle was rich, so that before he even opened his eyes he could grasp around his bed and find the compact metal torch. He flicked on the beam and cast it over the familiar shapes of his room – Jovah knew he was far too old to have nightmares about heathen spacemen coming to drag him up to their endless void. But it didn't hurt to check. The room was clear, so he tiptoed into the hall, pausing outside the master bedroom. He could feel his father's presence on the other side of the door: lying down, eyes closed. Not sleeping.

They never acknowledged Jovah's secret work, even when they were alone. But Jovah's father always listened for his footsteps.

He pulled his shoes on and padded downstairs.

The dawn sun cast a grey curtain over the parish yard. Buzzards circled one another in the sky, calling out across empty space. *Pitiable creatures*, Jovah thought. They lived so far from God, from the Earth. Perhaps that was why they were so ugly.

He bent over the cellar door and hauled it open, stepping down with the torchlight stretched out before him. The air was cool and dry and a little stale. He walked through to the back, towards a wooden chest much older and larger than he was, and hauled up the lid. From deep within he took out a single string-bound parcel.

Slowly – as he always did – Jovah lifted the parcel to his face and inhaled.

Flour. Warmth.

He released the lid, and the jaws of the chest clamped shut.

Saint's Cradle was all dawn and silence. The lights that marked the path down to the crater had been switched off, and the old truck was little more than a smudge in the gloom. As he got closer, Jovah flicked on his torch again. At the crest of the slope was a painted wooden signpost, which read:

Touch Not the Saint.

Speak Softly Near the Saint.

Tempt not the Saint with material things.

Stay No Longer than an Hour with the Saint.

In Gaia's Name.

Jovah took out the package and walked down the slope. With each new step his heart quickened a little more. There was a sense of something heavy weighing on his lungs as he descended, as if the very air was thickening with holiness.

And there sat the Saint, inevitable as death. His bare shoulders did not twinge at the touch of torchlight, and only a slight fluttering of the eyelids acknowledged the boy's arrival. Age had made a sunken caricature out of his face: scooped cheeks, sagging eyes, drooping, withered lips. Veins stood out like worms through the delicate skin.

Jovah hardly dared to breathe. He bowed once and placed the package within arm's reach of the Saint's body. He stepped back and bowed again. Then he turned and left.

By the time the first visitors arrived, the package would be gone, paper and all.

*   *   *

A FEW YEARS earlier, when they were packing up after a class, Jovah had confronted his father about something that had been troubling him for a long time. It built and built, until he blurted it out so loud his words echoed back to him from the arched ceiling of the chapel.

'*We're giving him food, aren't we?*'

There was no need to ask who '*he*' was. It was still early, and they were on the pulpit, getting ready for the morning's sermon. Jovah's father levelled a handful of books on the floor and pressed them into place on the shelf. 'That is correct,' he said quietly. 'He is a mortal man. He needs food like you and I.'

'But people think he does not eat.'

Jovah looked steadily at his father, searching for something – a glint of fallibility, some instinctive response to this shattering contradiction. There was none. 'It is true,' he admitted. 'People think that.'

'Why don't they know? And why must I do it in secret? And where—'

'Jovah—' His father held up a hand. 'I'll explain when you're older.'

'*When?*' Jovah was a meticulous boy; he liked things to be set by parameters. 'When will I understand?'

His father paused. 'When you are ten.'

Jovah counted on his fingers – two years to go. A lifetime. But he could wait. 'Thank you, Father.'

He'd been counting down the days ever since.

Jovah's tenth birthday landed on Saturday, the day for sermons. Sermons were a weekly ritual in Saint's Cradle, and attendance was mandatory, even for travellers. For the duration of the service the town reverted to the ghostly state of the long past, all darkened windows and the occasional whine of a stray mutt. Only the chapel buzzed with life. Most days the benches overflowed and the walls were lined with faithful folk, and sometimes they even had to open the doors just to make more room. Before the sermon began there was always a tempestuous rustle of whispering and shuffling feet.

When the Preacher started to speak, silence fell like an axe. Faces, even children's faces, turned as one to the podium, to see the man who stood there.

'Once…'

Jovah's father always started with a story. Smaller matters – births and deaths, local news – could wait until after. His voice was low and powerful, sounding out from a neck garlanded with holy beads. Nobody ever strained to hear.

'Once, during the time of the Great Departure, there were two brothers. They ran a farm together on the eastern continent. The time was coming to board the ships that would take them away to a colony in the sky. The elder brother, whose name was Steel, said to the younger brother, whose name was Wood, *"Brother Wood. Our land grows dry and arid. Our weather grows stormy and unsafe. Our seas rise salty and vengeful, and our fresh rivers run dry. Come, let us ascend with the others to the heaven that man has built in the stars."*

'And Wood said to him: *"Brother Steel, the land grows arid because we have separated ourselves from it with gross machines. The clouds are angry because we have attempted to touch them with our buildings. The sea is rising because we have littered it with ships. Let us stay here, and atone for what we and our ancestors have done, so that one day our Mother who is Earth might know peace.'"*

Jovah listened keenly. They hadn't yet discussed the Saint – his father hadn't the time, he assumed – but it seemed there might be some explanation hidden in this *particular* story. His father spoke on:

'The brothers argued and argued, but they could not agree. So Steel left with the rest of the people, and Wood stayed behind alone, and worked the land with his coarse tools, built by his own hands. He worked and worked, but still the soil would yield no life. At last he threw down his tools and pressed his forehead to the ground. *"Mother!"* he called. *"Why have you forsaken me, the most loyal of your sons?"* And on that spot he died.

'Wood's body fertilised the lifeless soil that he had appealed to. And so there grew on that spot the silhouette of a man, drawn in green grass and flower buds. It stands there to this day. So the story goes.'

Jovah's father clasped his hands together as if he were closing a book. But there was no text to read from. There wasn't a story in the world the Preacher didn't know by heart.

'Amen.'

The spell of silence was lifted, and the congregation rumbled back: 'Amen.'

After bidding goodbye to the final guest, Jovah hightailed it to the back of the chapel, following the warm scent of flatcake all the way to the kitchen. He found his father working over the stove, white apron tied neatly over his robes, dropping two dollops of batter into the pan. He moulded them with deft, one-handed movements, tucking in and pressing down, until each was a solid disc. Both flatcakes went on a plate, which his father set down on the table in front of Jovah. 'Eat up, now,' he said, wiping his hands.

Jovah nodded, murmured a prayer of thanks, and took a bite. A crisp outer shell crumbled into a soft sweetness inside. His father's flatcakes tasted the way that clouds looked.

'I'm hitching a lift to Whistler today,' said the Preacher, hanging the skillet on a hook over the hob. 'The Sheriff there has just had a son. She wants him baptised right away.'

Jovah swallowed. 'That's wonderful news, Father.' He didn't dare show it, but Jovah was becoming worried. He had been ten for several hours and the topic of the Saint was yet to arise.

'It is.' The Preacher folded the apron, laying it over the back of a chair. 'She sets a good example. I wish all lawmen kept the faith so closely.'

'As do I.'

'Make sure the floors are swept. I'll be home by noon – with a surprise.'

Jovah lit up: 'A surprise?'

'Of course. Do you think I'd forget?'

Jovah beamed. 'No, Father. Thank you, Father.'

He stooped to plant a kiss on the crown of Jovah's head. 'Good boy. God hold you down.'

Noon came and went, and Jovah's father did not return.

It was a quiet day in Saint's Cradle, but that still meant visitors – wealthy men who drove in wearing starch-stiff collars, gaggles of pilgrims moving on foot and in packs, families bickering in respectfully lowered voices. Many of them wanted to see what the chapel of such a holy town looked like. They found a steepled tin shack, sparsely furnished with long oak benches and a threadbare rug on the floor, and a grave, grey-eyed little boy who stood before the pulpit and answered their questions. He was neither friendly nor unfriendly, but acted more as an extension of the furnishings. Parents asked cautiously where his parents were, and he would bow his head and say he did not know.

But Jovah's stomach was starting to groan.

The flatcakes had been many hours ago now. He had checked the kitchen and found nothing to eat. There was no money to go to the general store with – no friends he could call on – and the thought of asking a stranger made him burn with shame. Preachers' sons did not beg. So he bowed and nodded at the guests and tried to ignore the rabid little animal clawing at his stomach. Sometimes he muttered psalms to keep himself distracted.

> *When the waters run dry, drink dust.*
> *When the floods rise, breathe water.*
> *When the fires burn, bathe in ashes.*

More than one curious traveller was driven away by this straight-backed boy whispering to himself before the pew.

Night fell, and the world was smothered. The moon was a white marble dropped on a sheet of silk. Jovah's hands shook as he locked the chapel doors. At no point did he feel any concern for his father. It didn't occur to him that something bad could have happened – only that he'd found something more important to do then come home and feed his son. Such things were to be expected.

A Preacher's duties were manifold; no doubt it was something worthy keeping him away.

Still, the hunger gripped him hard.

There was *one* place where he could get food. But that would be the height of heresy, the very peak of sin. It would be wrong, dreadfully wrong. Like stealing from Gaia's very mouth.

He paced. He chanted. Nothing worked.

Jovah found himself standing before the cellar doors. He opened them, peering into the darkness. It was like a mouth itself: a watering mouth, hungry to be fed. The torch trembled in Jovah's hand. His mind mixed excuses: *I shall admit all to Father and beg forgiveness. I shall replace it secretly out of my own labour. I shall recite psalms for an hour, a day, a week...*

Nothing stuck. He was too hungry to think. He stepped down, clicking his torch on, pointing it at the old chest.

A pair of eyes stared back.

Jovah gasped, and the figure leapt up. 'Don't scream!' it said.

Jovah screamed.

'Stop screaming!'

Jovah continued to scream.

'I'm just a person!' It slapped its chest with both hands. 'See? I'm not gonna hurt you!'

Jovah stopped screaming.

She blew air out her nose, a kind of laugh. 'Finally.'

'What are you doing in my basement?' he asked.

'Stealing food. Sorry. I was hungry.'

'I'm hungry too.' He dropped his hand, scattering torchlight along the floor. Brown paper was scattered around her feet. 'That's the—' He nearly said *Saint's food*. 'That's ours.'

'I know, I know.' She wiped some crumbs from her mouth. 'I said I'm sorry, alright?'

He brought the light back up to her face, making her squint. She was tall, with a broken kind of nose and a broad-brimmed hat. Her face was grimy in the creases.

'You're a tramp,' said Jovah.

She laughed through her nose again. Jovah felt odd. He'd never been laughed at before; it made him sort of angry. But he was a man of ten now, so he kept his temper.

'I'm not a tramp,' said the Tramp.

'Okay. Where do you live?'

'Uh…' The Tramp scratched at her neck. 'Nowhere, right now.'

Jovah tilted his head, frowning. 'Tramps are people who don't have homes.'

'I've got a home. I'm just a bit lost, that's all.'

Jovah pondered this.

'You live upstairs, right?' she asked.

He nodded, and spoke with a voice edged in pride: 'Yes. I live in the town chapel with my father. He is the Preacher of this town.' For no particular reason, he added: 'I am ten years old today.'

'Oh.' The Tramp cleared her throat. 'Happy birthday.'

'Thank you.'

It struck Jovah that nobody had said those words to him yet. This realisation brought on a new emotion: a foreboding whisper of future adolescent misery, like the time-honoured shiver of footsteps trod on an undug grave. He shook it off.

'Please stay here and do not eat any more food. I'm going to go and get some help.'

She paled. 'What-what sort of help?'

'My father. He will know what to do.' Jovah back paced a few steps. 'Please do not tell any other tramps about what you have seen here today,' he added.

Another laugh. 'Yeah, sure.'

Jovah nodded again. Then he turned and hurried out, shutting the cellar door behind him. In the darkness he suddenly felt a lot less certain. The Tramp had snuck into the cellar without his permission. That made her a thief, surely. Thieves were dangerous, because they were a type of bandit, and he knew stories about bandits from the old days – those weren't the sort of stories people told in church.

Something else, too. She'd had something on her hip. A funny kind of gun. Jovah realised that he was sweating.

Light spilled out from the parish window, and Jovah crumbled with relief. His father was back. He was already speaking as he burst through the door. 'Father, there's—'

Two faces stared back at him. The familiar, that of his father; and the unfamiliar, a rough-stubbled man whose eyes glinted like twin shards of glass.

There was an interim of silence. Then Jovah's father cleared his throat.

'Jovah. This is Deputy Seawall. He's come all the way from New Destiny.'

Jovah looked between them, suddenly lost. There was something strange in his father's face. Why wasn't he drawing himself up as he always did? And why did his voice sound so weak?

The Preacher cleared his throat again. 'Say good evening, Jovah.'

Automatically, Jovah straightened up and clasped his hands behind his back. 'Good evening, sir.'

Deputy Seawall squatted down, bringing with him a warm smell of cigarettes and boiled meat. 'Hey there,' he said. His voice sounded like there were burn holes in his throat. 'How's it going?'

'It's going well, sir.'

'You been here all by yourself today?'

'Yes, sir.'

'Been bored?'

'No sir.'

He scratched a yellow fingernail along the base of his jaw. 'Formal little feller, aren't ya?'

Jovah didn't know how to respond. Deputy Seawall stood up with a sigh, slapping his thighs. 'You got anything to drink here?'

'I'll have to do some searching.' The Preacher looked down at his son, staring through him. 'Jovah, why don't you go play in your room?'

'Yeah.' The Deputy grinned. 'Me and your da need to have a talk.'

Jovah knew about New Destiny; everybody did, even little babies. A distant dreamland, hidden in a cloud of rumour, to which human souls were drawn as inexorably as a ball on an uneven table is drawn to the edge. It was the place where the law came from, a place where the citizens were supposed to live like decadent kings – running water, cooled air, everything. Supposedly it was built out of a ship, though Jovah could not understand that. It had been centuries since people had travelled across water.

Sometimes the young and zealous parishioners spoke out against the city, calling it a tumour, or a nest of sin. They said the High Sheriff had heathen sympathies and kept the High Preacher like a dog on a leash. But Jovah's father always came to their defence: 'If you were old enough to remember what life was like before the High Sheriff, you would not be so quick to speak against him,' he would say. 'As for Preacher Ramirez, she has given her whole life to God, every minute of every day. How many of you can say the same?'

Shameful silences: Jovah's father was good at making those. Almost as good as he was at making flatcakes.

Normally Jovah would never have done it. The horror of punishment was planted too strongly within him: even if his father never found out, God would know, and Her retribution would come up on him from beneath. But this visitor from New Destiny had pushed him over the edge. All day long he'd waited to hear the truth about the Saint, but he'd had nothing but strangeness upon strangeness. The Tramp – Seawall – perpetual hunger – and that look on his father's face that, if it were any other adult, he would have called fear.

So Jovah lingered on the stairwell. They spoke low, but he could hear it all clearly. There was a clink of glass, the sound of liquid pouring.

Then Seawall spoke: 'That's a funny lad you've raised, Preacher.'

'He's a good boy,' came the reply.

'Where's his mother?'

'She left us.'

'I'm sorry to hear that.'

'Thank you.'

Jovah couldn't hear a trace of gratitude in his father's voice.

'If you ask me, it's kind of fucked-up that you've made him a part of this.'

Jovah's pulse throbbed in his temples. He waited for his father to leap in, to defend them – or at least tell the man off for cursing. He only heard silence.

The Deputy went on: 'I kinda feel sorry for the little guy. Maybe I oughta take him under my wing. Show him how the real world works. Perhaps if he learned how to—'

'Jovah will be a Preacher,' said his father softly. 'Unless Gaia chooses another path for him.'

'See, you say Gaia, but I've got a feeling you mean *yourself*.' The Deputy smacked his lips. 'Damn. You Preachers are all the same.'

Again Jovah's father did not respond. Jovah squeezed his hands under his armpits to keep them from trembling.

'What do you want?' his father asked at last.

'Nothing. For now. High Sheriff says I'm not to move against you, so I won't. But you can't keep this scam up forever, Preacher. If people knew you'd been feeding that hobo there'd be riots in the streets.'

Tell him he's wrong, Jovah thought. *There must be a reason. Tell him he's wrong.*

Nothing.

'Don't misunderstand me,' said the Deputy. 'I'm a God-fearing man. More than you, I'd wager.'

'I'm not sure that's true.'

The Deputy chuckled softly. 'No?' A pause, from the sounds of it so that the Deputy could take a draught. 'I grew up on a homestead out in the eastern valleys,' he said. 'My folks were pious. They led a hardscrabble life, just like the scriptures say. We grew our own food. Dug water from a well. All that shit. We were isolated, Preacher, out on that farm. Vulnerable to the whims of God.'

Like Jovah's father, the Deputy had a talent for stories; a way of sucking you in, even against your own will. Jovah was hunched up on the third step of the staircase. The elevated position gave him a view of the space above the lampshade where, between brittle paper and the bare ceiling, a cylinder of cobwebs hung, dense and matted as a pile of hair. The Deputy went on: 'One day God in Her wisdom decided to dry up our well. I'm sure you can imagine what kind of days followed. My folks thought it was a test, see. A test from God. So they kept working that crusty soil, and hiking mile after mile to the river, and praying. And for their faith our sweet Mother Earth rewarded them with a very slow and very unhappy death. So I gotta wonder – why does God love your Saint more than She loved my old ma and da? What did they do wrong? Can you tell me that?'

Silence. Shameful silence.

'Thought not.'

A chair scraped backwards over the floor tiles.

'When the old man dies, his office *will* pass to me. And as the new High Sheriff I will see to it that you're investigated for promoting conspiratorial fantasies and unlawful subversions of the truth. Investigated, convicted, and punished to the full extent of the law.'

Suddenly his father's voice grew loud. 'You wouldn't just punish me, Seawall. You'd destroy this whole town. Understand?'

'I get you, Preacher. It's just business, ain't it?'

Footsteps. The creaking of the door. The Deputy again:

'By the way – I know everyone and their mule passes through this town. You seen any strange folk mixed in with the travellers recently?'

His father's voice was strained. 'Strange how?'

86

'Oh, y'know. Tall, scruffy. Funny accent. Funny gun. There's this woman we've been looking for... a pain in the ass, much like yourself.'

Jovah's heart seized.

'No. I've not seen anyone like that.'

'Okie dokie. Well, g'night then.'

The door slammed shut, and the man was gone.

In the white static of Jovah's mind, a memory formed. The memory of a question from long ago. She was a pilgrim from the far edges of the wastes, who'd cut through the flowing crowd to speak to Jovah's father after a long-ago sermon.

'Preacher, sir,' she'd said. 'Respectfully. That stuff you said about the heathens. I don't get it.'

He frowned slightly. 'What's wrong, sister?'

'All those people who chose to leave.' She looked down as she spoke, picking at a loose thread on her cuff. 'So many folk, a whole planetful, all born of this soil. Must have been all kinds of people who left. Were they really all evil? Every last one?'

'Oh, sister.' It was rare to hear Jovah's father laugh: it boomed, loud enough that people turned their heads. 'Of *course* they were.'

'But—'

'Listen to me.' He put a hand on the woman's shoulder. 'We all carry sin. All of us, by our nature. But some folk are sin incarnate. You cut them open and the void of space bleeds out like tar. And you know the worst part?'

With the slightest motion, the woman shook her head. The Preacher finished in a whisper: '*Some of them walk among us still.*'

Jovah waited for an hour, until the sounds of his father's

pacing feet had long ceased. Then he slipped out, torch in hand, and made his way to the cellar. The Tramp was still there. She was dozing, one head against the side of the trunk. He stuck the torch in her face, and she blinked and spluttered.

'Hey now—'

'You have a gun, don't you?' he asked.

'Uh…' She pushed herself up higher. 'I mean – yeah, I do…'

'Good.' Jovah's mind was a roaring blur. All he had was an image: the hateful Deputy on his back, tar oozing from an open wound. 'There's someone you must kill.'

Jovah seemed to have left himself behind.

He knew that he was hot, and also that he was shivering. This seemed wrong, but he couldn't understand why. He couldn't understand anything. Someone was speaking to him from very far away.

'Hey! Can you hear me? C'mon now…'

Jovah found himself being shaken vigorously by the shoulders. It was the Tramp. She looked younger up close, he thought. Her eyes were darting all over his face.

'It's okay,' she was saying. 'You, uh, I think you fainted.'

'He's coming for you.'

'Who?'

'The Deputy. He's coming for all of us.'

She tried to laugh, but the sound came out forced. 'That's just a mix-up—'

'He is staying in town.' Jovah sat up eagerly, remembering his plan. 'You have to go kill him. You have to!'

She let him go and stepped back quickly as if she had burned herself. 'No,' she said. 'Don't joke about that. About… killing people.'

'I'm not joking. And *he's* not a person. He's all void inside. I know it.'

'*Sweet heavenly*—' The Tramp wiped her eyes. 'Look. This gun I carry?' She lifted it free of the holster. It looked like water made solid, and Jovah was torn between wanting to touch it and wanting to run away. She knelt down, showing it to him. 'It's a special gun, okay?'

Jovah was dubious. '...why?'

'Because it's never killed anyone.'

'Then it's a broken gun!' he retorted furiously.

'Maybe.' She smiled, holstering it. 'Either way, I can't help you.'

'You have to! Or-or...' Jovah was horrified to find his throat pulling tighter, his face turning hot and prickly. The Tramp's expression softened, and she reached out for his shoulder.

'Do you, uh... Listen, do you need help?'

Jovah shook her off. 'You'll be sorry,' he hissed. 'You'll be sorry when he gets you.'

He expected her to shout or cry, but she said nothing, only looked at him with an expression that he could not understand.

Jovah turned and ran.

It was dark, but Jovah knew the way. He ran down and down, with the sleeping town on one side and the wasteland on the other, until the jagged shapes of the old scrapyard came into view. He scrambled past the signs and down into the shadowed hollow.

The Saint was a silhouette. His hooked body sat silent and magnificent as ever. Jovah took to his knees and pressed his forehead hard against the ground.

'Please help my father,' he whispered. 'Please help my

father, oh Saint. Please make that Deputy die. Don't let him take me away. Please please please.'

Something rustled. Jovah looked up. Particles of dust trickled down from his forehead into his eyes, and he wiped them away, blinking.

The Saint was looking at him.

He'd hardly done anything except open his eyes and tilt his chin down a fraction, but to Jovah it was as miraculous as seeing a statue move. He'd done it.

The Saint's cracked lips parted by a hair's width, and he breathed a word:

'Come…'

Jovah's stomach tightened to a ball of pure excitement. He stepped forward.

'Come…'

Another step. They were less than a foot from each other now. The Saint's right arm twitched. He raised it, reaching out his withered fingers. Jovah stayed still. The Saint hadn't told him to move. He wrapped his fingers around Jovah's arm and started to move it gently upwards. The Saint's mouth opened, slightly at first, but then wide, wider than Jovah thought a human mouth could open. The smell was astonishing. It was a living decomposition, the scent of something that grows only to feed its own rot. He tried to wiggle away, but the Saint's fingers burrowed deeper into his arm, pulling him in. His teeth were brown and sharp and fused together, a string of drool clinging to one out-turned lip, low enough to wet the dirt. Jovah felt damp breath on the back of his hand, and his body went limp with fear.

Another hand grabbed him, jerking him backwards. Just in time – the Saint's mottled incisors clasped around the tip of Jovah's sleeve, tugged so hard against the hand that it tore cloth like skin from a roasted animal. The jaw opened again, this time aiming for flesh. Then: a flash like a grin of white teeth. It went whistling over the Saint's head.

'Let him go,' said the Tramp. '*Now.*'

The Saint's grip slackened just long enough for her to wrench Jovah free, and he collided headfirst with her legs.

'He-He...' Jovah didn't know what to tell her. It wouldn't come out.

'Yeah.' The Tramp's hand was on his back. 'I know.'

Jovah turned and looked back through his tears. The Saint was sat just like always; eyes closed, perfectly still, like the end of a nightmare where everything suddenly reverts to normal. But he could still feel the fingers where they'd gripped his arm.

'It's a lie,' Jovah sobbed, burying his face against her jacket. 'That's not a saint. It's a lie.'

The pistol caught a shard of moonlight as the Tramp slipped it back into the holster. 'Come on,' she said. 'Time to go home.'

Jovah's father was sitting alone, his posture alert, his fingers outstretched and drumming on the table. The sound of the door brought him immediately to his feet.

'Jovah! Where in space have you been?'

He stepped towards his son, and then stopped when he saw the look on his face. He looked up and saw the Tramp. She lingered behind Jovah, one hand clasped lightly on his shoulder. 'Who are you?' he demanded.

'It's okay.' Jovah spoke to a spot just below his father's chin. 'She saved me.'

His father's face drew tight. 'Who did this?'

Jovah looked down. There were no words inside of him.

'Was it Seawall?'

Jovah could only shake his head.

'Jovah. Look at me when you talk to me.'

'It was the man in the junkyard,' said the Tramp. 'He nearly bit his hand off.'

The Preacher froze.

'I went to pray for help,' Jovah said miserably.

Jovah's father took a step back and fell into his chair. His eyes stared at nothing. Seeing this doubled the hopelessness already brewing in Jovah, and he felt his face growing hot as the tears rose back up to the surface. 'I'm s-I'm sorry…'

'No, Jovah. I'm sorry. Come here.' Jovah stumbled closer and his father pressed him tightly into his chest. He stroked his head, whispering, 'I'm sorry, I'm sorry.'

The Tramp coughed. 'Right then.'

'Wait,' his father said sharply. 'The Deputy—'

'I know. I've got to keep moving.'

Jovah's father swallowed, looking down. 'It's too quiet in these parts. You need crowds to hide. Take the rail.'

'Rail? You mean there's a—'

Something volcanic shifted in the depths of Jovah's stomach, rumbling loud enough to cut her words off. Jovah's father put a hand to his forehead. 'Gaia. The food. I forgot.'

Jovah straightened up. 'It's alright.'

'No, it's not alright. It's not alright at all…'

He started to rummage around in the folds of his coat, pulling out something misshapen wrapped in grease paper. 'I'm sorry it's cold. This was supposed to be your birthday present, but that damned Deputy…'

Jovah realised what was in the package and started to shake. It was a pie. A real pie. Even in the wealthy Saint's Cradle, children whispered about such things.

They watched him as he ate, ravenously, in small quick bites. When the pie was gone he licked the wrapping free of crumbs, and then his lips. It was the best thing he'd ever tasted.

Then the shyness returned. He balled both hands on top of his knees.

'Jovah,' his father began. 'I've been treating you like a child, and expecting you to act like a man. I'm sorry.'

Jovah said nothing.

'Ask me whatever you want. I'll tell the truth.'

Jovah spoke quietly. 'He's a monster, isn't he?'

There was a lengthy silence.

'Yes,' his father said at last. 'To himself, maybe. Maybe even to you, or to me. But not to the travellers. Not to the people who live here. But then, he's a piece of God.'

Jovah banged the table. 'But he's *not!*'

His father sighed. 'Listen, Jovah…' He leant forward, placing a hand to his temples, the place where the hair turned silver-grey. 'You can choose your own – your own way of feeling about it. But I'll tell you what I think. I think that God is a being that you *make* real. You make Her real by deciding She exists. That's what we're doing, Jovah. We're keeping God alive. As long as we keep Her in our hearts, She'll be alive.'

Jovah chewed his lip. Then he nodded. His father embraced him, apologising again, and this time Jovah said it was alright.

He saw the Tramp over his father's shoulder. She'd turned her face away.

There were no bedtime stories that evening, and Jovah lay awake a long time – not because he was scared, but because he was thinking. It seemed so strange to him that God, the being who brought so much wrath and suffering in the old stories, could turn out to be so fragile. In the stillness of his bedroom he lifted his blanket up and let go. It fell in a heap on top of him. Feeling gravity's presence – feeling the touch of God – he whispered the psalm:

'This is a mark of Her love.'

JOVAH'S LIFE AS a ten-year-old went on as normal; if normal is the right word for any life. Lonely school days came and went, travellers flooded through, and the weeks were punctuated by sermons, by fire and brimstone, wood and steel.

And Jovah still kept the secret.

The truth that was not true.

Every morning, before the sun rose, he and his father went down to the scrapyard and built a God out of brown paper bags.

THE HUMANITARIAN SOCIETY has quietly announced the launch of a new single-ship aid mission departing from the Centralian system sometime next week. Their destination? Earth. Yes, THAT Earth.

This marks the first voyage to the homeworld in almost three centuries. It seems that giving free handouts to the living is no longer enough to satisfy the pearl-clutching members of the HS, and they have been forced to start coddling skeletons.

Readers concerned about Imperial finances being wasted on such a spurious endeavour need not worry. Funding for the mission is reported to be entirely private. Team lead Dr Noelle 'Crackpot' Daley (whose God-awful book The Extinction Myth was given a thorough trashing in this publication last year) managed to wheedle the money from her long-suffering father, Duke Daley V of Radovid.

But the question remains – why all the cloak and dagger? Perhaps it has something to do with the security force accompanying the aid mission, which, according to rumour, is set to be led by veteran of the Bretonian war, the famed Captain…

– Article in the *Scrutinizer*, Central edition, 2812.

MURDER ON THE GLOW HILLS RIDER

CLOTH, CLOTH, CLOTH. Hattie Warbler wished that the world was woven out of cloth. She loved the touch of it – thick denim, gleaming buttons, fresh linen. Soapy leather, smooth one way, rough the other. Even silk, once, an ancient necktie that shone like something born beneath the ground. She loved the way a well-cut collar hugged the collarbones, how a clean seam could trace the natural symmetry of a thigh. Clothes were a wonder to Hattie.

It was people wearing them that were the problem.

She remembered as a young apprentice how she'd been lectured – *we took you on for your talent, Harriet, but if you can't learn to be civil with the customers then we may be forced to find a replacement*. Ha! As if Hattie could be replaced. She was well past her apprentice years now, and had her own shop that she could run how she pleased, in a town far enough to the south that *disposable income* meant more than toilet paper traded for a pack of matches. People came all the way up from New Destiny to get measured – and if they had a problem with her service they could damn well go all the way back down again.

She'd had a blazing row with the last assistant – or maybe the assistant before last? – and before he slammed the door, he'd said something to the effect of, *you see the clothes, Hattie, but not the people inside of them.*

A childish distinction. Clothes told her everything she needed to know.

Take the young woman at the back of the carriage, for example. The suit she wore was no hand-me-down: it hung well on her slight frame, and was so stiffly starched it probably could have stood up under its own power. The only sign of wear was a minor softening around the cuffs and elbows, as if she habitually rolled her sleeves up. A pair of spectacles, balanced low on the end of her nose, was secured around her neck with a chain fine as a spiderweb. In her lapel a brass badge glinted, etched with some kind of crest, and she was reading a book emblazoned with a scalpel. A surgeon then. Trained in the city. Intelligent. Talented. Rather neurotic. Likely dull in conversation.

Hattie ticked the designations off in her mind, quite satisfied, and turned to the other passenger. This one was a gentleman of contrasts. His jeans were clearly ancient, layered with an architect's delight of stains and moulded to his legs through thorough weather and wear. But the shirt he wore was brand new, a brightly coloured button-up that struggled to contain him. Windswept hair, expanding belly, the ruddy complexion of an uncooked steak – he was a farmer, and a wealthy one at that. Growing food had once been a bitter battle for survival, a contest of ever-failing returns. Now, under the High Sheriff, it was an increasingly good way to get rich, provided you were willing to play the rules. Hattie didn't understand it, and to be frank, she didn't care to. Leave politics to the privileged few who controlled it and the underprivileged many who suffered by its whims. Neither party was paying *her* bills.

Hattie looked down, saving herself for last. Her outfit, which naturally she had made by hand, was by far the most tasteful in the carriage – a high-collared dress, ruffled in layers of paling grey like the feathers of a pigeon. Comfortable, breathable, classical but with a nod to the contemporary. It wasn't hard to look good, Hattie reflected. You just needed to know what *good* looked like.

With the people-watching possibilities all exhausted, she drew a book out of her handbag (a trashy paperback – Hattie's books were the most tasteless thing about her) and cracked open the well-thumbed pages. She read one line, and then the world went black.

The carriage constricted like a throat, close and hot, and the floor shuddered to the rhythm of the engine, *du-dum, du-dum, du-dum,* a relentless coal-fed pulse.

Hattie's thumbs pressed against the paper. She shut her eyes, counting the seconds.

One
Two
Three
Four
Five

A *whoosh* like an intake of breath, and sunlight flooded back into the train. Hattie exhaled. She hated going through tunnels.

* * *

THERE WERE PLACES on Earth that had been touched by death in such a way that even the hardiest of planet-folk could not make a living there. One such place – perhaps the worst of such places, at least on the western continent – was called, with a little humour, the Glow Hills. It was a wasteland within a wasteland: a rock-and-rubble desert irradiated beyond hope of repair by man or nature. There were putrid lakes that stung to the touch; strange, malformed creatures that had survived at a terrible cost. And everywhere, in the air, on every surface, the little seeds of death, which could plant themselves in your cells in less than an hour and blossom into multitudes within a month. A journey on foot would be a death sentence, and the drive around it cost a fortune in fuel.

So came the *Glow Hills Rider*.

Twice a day it crossed those poisoned lands, from Whistler to Riggsby, connecting the sandy archipelago of settlements in the North to the further reaches of the South. A shining artery of life, so technologically convenient that it spawned mutterings of heresy among the faithful folk. But even Preachers were forced to use it from time to time – muttering, eyes shady, counting their beads.

Hattie hadn't ridden the *Glow Hills Rider* in almost a decade, and after this journey she did not intend to ride it again. She had nothing left tying her to the barren, barbaric North. Besides, it was a morbid way to travel; dangerous even. Hattie was not much one for shows of faith – it seemed narcissistic to assume God took time out of Her busy day to care about one person's individual habits – but you didn't have to be a zealot to see the potential problems in a high-speed metal tube flinging itself across a poisoned desert. That was why she always sat at the back of the rear carriage; it seemed obvious that this would be the safest place, in the event of a crash.

At the far end of the aisle a shape appeared in the porthole window, a blurred silhouette made distinct by the peak of a pointed cap. There was some indistinct rattling, the scrape of a lock. The door opened, and in marched the Conductor, suited up in white and blue. Immediately Hattie sensed something strange. His expression betrayed a hint of nerves, despite the rigid posture. He locked the door behind him, pocketed the keys, then turned back towards the passengers with an important air, pushing up the hat to the top of his forehead.

'Ladies 'n' gents,' he announced. 'May I have your attention, please?'

The Surgeon shut her book irritably. The Farmer, roused from a doze by the sound of the door, sat up a little, rubbing his eyes.

'You will have noticed that I have locked the door that does connect our two carriages here,' the Conductor went on. 'That is on account of the fact that we have apparently got ourselves a, uh… little…' He stumbled over the words. '…*ahem*… a criminal on board.'

A ripple passed over the benches. The Conductor pressed on: 'The Sheriff of Riggsby, who is remaining behind to ensure the safety of the driver, has asked me to conduct a thorough search of the carriage, as well as the usual examination of the tickets and such.'

So we're all to be treated as criminals, then? Hattie thought. She could tell from her expression that the Surgeon was none too delighted either. The Farmer, who was still waking up, sat forward, rubbing his broad forehead. 'Eh? Who's a criminal?'

'We don't know,' said the Surgeon quietly.

'Rest assured, sir.' The Conductor patted an oblong lump in his jacket pocket. 'I'm armed and I have got authority to act.'

Hattie suppressed a groan. This was why she didn't like leaving her shop. It was always like this – lawmen and bandits without a brain cell between them, playing hit the bottle with their piddling little peashooters, while normal, *sane* people like her could only keep their heads down and pray not to get caught by a stray. The Conductor meandered over to the young Surgeon, who handed over her ticket without a word. He held it up, nodded, stamped it through, and handed it back.

'Travelling alone today, miss?'

'Yes.' The Surgeon did not make eye contact as she spoke.

'Know where you're headed?'

'Yes.'

The Conductor waited for her to elaborate, but she did not.

'...and where might it be?'

'I'm a travelling Surgeon. I go where I'm needed.'

A vindicated smirk pricked the end of Hattie's lips.

'And have you seen anything funny around here, so to speak?' the Conductor asked.

The Surgeon shifted to look out the window. 'No.'

'Suspicious persons, and so on?'

'No.'

He pulled open the overhead compartment, peered inside, and shut it again. 'Very good.'

Crossing the aisle, the Conductor repeated the process with the Farmer's compartment, this time finding a huge duffle bag, the weight of which nearly toppled him over as he tried to pull it free.

'Careful there, son!' the Farmer protested. 'That's real cow's hide, you know!'

'Under-understood,' the Conductor panted. He undid the clasps and peered inside. 'Lots of things here, sir. You been travelling long?'

'No.' The Farmer looked affronted. 'I just like to be prepared is all. I'm a man of means.'

'What's this?' He pulled out a black object that looked like a gun handle.

'Oh, now, see, that's one of the new bits of gear I've been shopping round.' The Farmer took the device, holding it up in his palm like a salesman. 'Latest pro-tee-type, see?'

'Mm-hmm.' The Conductor redid the clasps and returned the bag, with difficulty, while the Farmer sat and fiddled with the device. He closed the compartment, still puffing. 'Your tickets, please, sir?'

'Oh, right, yes, right.' He rifled his hands through each of his jeans pockets in turn, finally pulling free a crumpled paper stack. 'It's a real situation with this criminal, eh?' he said, handing it over.

'Certainly is, sir, quite the situation, as they say.'

'I'd be sweating *bullets* if I were you!' the Farmer added cheerfully.

The Conductor clipped and returned the ticket. 'And what's the purpose of your journey today, sir?'

'Coming back from a business trip.' He leant in, and spoke in his idea of sotto voce: 'I'm no stranger to the odd scrap myself, you know, son. You can call on me if you need a hand.'

The Conductor pressed his lips into a smile. 'I hope that won't be needed.'

He turned towards Hattie. Her handbag was beside

her, and the Conductor picked it up, running his hand along the base. 'Begging your pardon, ma'am.'

'So I'm a ma'am, am I?' asked Hattie. 'Not a miss?'

The Conductor blinked, midway through undoing the zip. 'Uh-that's to… and, have you seen anything suspicious at all?' He glanced inside.

'I saw a stranger in uniform going through my things.'

An ugly pause. He dropped the bag back on the bench, took her ticket, and scrutinised it for what Hattie felt was an unreasonable length of time before clipping the corner and handing it back. 'And why are you travelling today?' he asked.

'I had a funeral to attend.'

He bowed his head. 'I'm sorry to hear that.'

'I'm sure you are,' she said, pulling her handbag closer.

He sighed, reaching up to snap open her compartment drawer. 'You know, ma'am, this is a highly dangerous situation. We're just trying to keep everyone safe and sound, as they say.'

'If you say so.' Hattie lifted her chin up. '*I've* got nothing to hide.'

An entire human being fell out of Hattie's overhead compartment.

Hattie gasped; the Farmer swore; the Surgeon shut her book again with an even more irritated expression. The unfortunate Conductor was pinned to the ground in a mess of apologising and confused limbs. There were some words of muffled protest, a couple of pathetic kicks, and then the two people extracted themselves from each other. The Conductor was the first to his feet, trembling and pale, but with a look of triumph.

'Looks like the jig is up, as they say!' he exclaimed, adjusting his cap, which kept sliding down over his head.

Sloppy milliner, Hattie thought. 'Why don't you come quietly, my frie—'

The Conductor lost track of his words as the Stowaway stood up. *Unfolded* might be a more accurate term. She seemed to brush the roof, towering over him with a face that was almost comically criminal: a jutting broken nose, and eyes so hollow they looked like they'd been scooped out with spoons. But that wasn't the most unsettling part for Hattie. It was the *boots.* Something about them riled up against Hattie's spirit. She couldn't have specified what was unfamiliar. It was everything and nothing. Not out of fashion. *Outside* of fashion. Pre-retro. Hattie was about to ask who her supplier was, when the Conductor pulled out his gun and pointed it at the Stowaway's chest.

Hattie winced. It was one of those horrid *heated* guns that you could buy in the city, the ones that shot light instead of lead. The Stowaway was unperturbed, smiling genially down at the Conductor.

'Hey now,' she said. 'I don't want trouble.'

'If you've got something to say, say it to the Sheriff.' He gestured towards the door. The Stowaway moved, and the Conductor followed, prodding her with the barrel.

'Look,' her hands were up, placating, 'I can pay you, just not now.'

'You're in bigger trouble than a couple unpaid tickets.' *Jab.* 'They got you down for murder, assault of a Sheriff, breaking and entering, and armed robbery.' *Jab.* 'So you just come quiet, and there won't be any need for any kind of violence, pardon the expression.'

'What?' Just as they reached the end of the carriage, the Stowaway stopped. Then she moved, circling around the Conductor with unnerving speed. He tried to step back and collided with the door, knocking the hat back over his eyes.

'I...' He raised the pistol. 'I'm warning you now...'

In the corner of her eye, Hattie saw the Farmer and the Surgeon both rising to their feet. She herself was ready to dive under a bench. This was turning into a terrible afternoon.

'I will,' said the Stowaway, her smile widening like a crack in a pane of glass, 'but you need to tell me what's really going on. Before anybody decides to get *violent*.'

Whoosh.

Blind blackness surged in through the windows.

Hattie heard shuffling, a thump. An intake of breath – female? Then, up ahead, some sort of flash, a flint-spark through the darkness. All in a couple of seconds. Then light flooded back in.

In the aisle, two people had collapsed. The Conductor was slumped over, propped up against the door. The Stowaway was down on her behind, blinking. The pistol lay between them.

The Conductor was dead.

The Surgeon's small voice was the first to break the silence.

'What did you do?'

It was directed at the Stowaway, who took a second to gather it all together. Then she started up wildly, away from the corpse. 'Not that!'

The Surgeon took a step closer, and Hattie saw something metallic slip out between the lines of her pale fingers. 'Do you take me for a fool?'

'*No, I—*'

The scalpel leapt forward through the air, jolting to

a halt a centimetre shy of the Stowaway's throat. The Stowaway had clamped her fingers tight around the Surgeon's wrist.

'Listen—'

The Surgeon grunted, thrusting with the other hand, only to have the blow neatly batted down. She went in for another slice and was countered by the Stowaway with an appalling *thump* of a knee to the stomach and a one-handed shove that sent her sprawling.

'I'm sorry,' the Stowaway said, shaking out one hand. 'I'm telling you, it's not what it—'

There was a crackling sound. The Stowaway's body tightened like a wound coil. Then she dropped. Behind her the Farmer stood, his face shiny with sweat, black *pro-tee-type* held out triumphantly.

He grinned, slapping one thigh. 'Well I'll be sky-high. It works on people too!'

'SWEET MOTHER EARTH!' Hattie found this too much, and shrieked at the Farmer before she could contain herself. 'Well done, you DOLT! Now we've got *two* corpses!'

The Farmer's face fell. 'She ain't dead,' he said petulantly. 'It's just a buzzer stick.'

'It might have killed her if she had a weak heart,' the Surgeon remarked. She tugged up the pleats of her trousers and moved to scrutinise the unconscious face. 'Not that it matters. She'll get defenestrated for this.' Using a pocket handkerchief, she picked up the Conductor's gun and placed it on the bench behind her, next to the suitcase.

'Oh, that's alright then,' declared the Farmer, sitting down.

Hattie stuttered. 'You don't mean...'

'Oh, yes she does.' He made a grotesque chucking motion with his hands. 'Right off the train, *into* that oh-so-lovely radiation! Never thought I'd see the day.'

'I'll tell the Sheriff everything that happened,' said the Surgeon, shifting her gaze to the Conductor's corpse.

'*Thrown off?*' Hattie demanded, advancing towards them. 'Isn't that a bit *much?*'

'Oh, yeah.' The Farmer chuckled. 'Used to happen all the time, back when there were proper bandits about. Conductor would just chuck 'em over, out into the funny air.'

Outside, across the thrumming open space, was the sound of urgent knocking in the next carriage along.

'Drat.' The Surgeon stood, yanking off her spectacles. 'The door's still locked. Has anyone seen the key?'

'Oh, uh…' The Farmer glanced between his feet while the Surgeon checked the Conductor's pockets, frowning. Hattie felt like she was drowning.

'Pardon me,' she said. 'But are you both insane?'

'You've had a shock.' The Farmer patted the bench next to him. 'Why don't you come have a little sit-down—'

'Don't condescend to me, you great *beetroot*. And you' – she pointed now to the Surgeon – 'Forget that key! We're not leaving here until we sort out what's really happened!'

The engine beat steadily under the long silence that followed.

'What's that supposed to mean?' asked the Farmer. 'You're saying the criminal didn't do it?'

'Of course she didn't,' snapped Hattie. 'You saw it, didn't you? In the tunnel?'

Somewhere in the back of Hattie's mind, her rational side was erupting in protest. *You're sticking your neck out, Harriet!* it wailed. *Yank it back in, before it's too late!*

But it *was* too late. Hattie had slipped into the mode she used when a linen delivery came later than promised, or a customer tried to underpay her for a suit. Her elegant heels were stuck firmly in the ground and they would not be released until the wrong was righted.

And she was right about this murder. Wasn't she?

The Farmer's arms were crossed. 'What am I supposed to have seen?'

'The spark!' Hattie insisted. 'It was after the thump!'

'So?'

'So she was knocked down *before* the gun was fired.'

There was something else, too, though Hattie wouldn't say it out loud for fear of looking foolish. She'd sized up the Stowaway well and good in their brief encounter, and though she'd noticed some interesting things, she'd seen nothing that suggested a capacity for murder – at least, not murder in cold blood.

'Must've shot him from the ground then.' The Farmer shook his head. 'Poor bastard. If only he'd asked me for help.'

Now it was the Surgeon's turn to look troubled. She turned her back on them both, bending over the Conductor's corpse. She beckoned them with a narrow finger. 'Come here, both of you.'

Hattie and the Farmer looked at each other. They stepped over the Stowaway to the Surgeon's side, each taking a shoulder to peer over.

'The entry wound is right in the centre of his forehead, see?' In a gesture that Hattie found quite disrespectful, she tilted the Conductor's head up by the chin, bringing his wound into the light. The Farmer took a sharp breath. Looking at the murdered man, Hattie couldn't help but remember her mother's emaciated corpse – dwarfed by the coffin and paler than the shroud it was wrapped in. Such a contrast with this body, which was intact save for a narrow tunnel through the centre of the head.

'Shouldn't there be more…' Hattie paused to swallow. 'More blood?'

'The wound is already cauterised,' explained the Surgeon. 'This is not the work of an ordinary pistol. There's no exit wound, see? The flesh on the back is equally—'

The Farmer cut her off. 'Yes, miss, we see it.'

The puncture was neat, open, still faintly smoking. Hattie had the nauseating idea that if she wanted to she could have peeped through the man's head as if it were a keyhole.

'My point is that you were right,' said the Surgeon. Perhaps it was natural reverence for the recently deceased, or just the fact that their heads were so close together, but she spoke in a half-whisper. 'And look here.' She straightened, and the other two followed. There was a smooth hole in the frosted glass, level with where the Conductor's head had been. 'He was shot clean through, from standing.'

Hattie could make out the blurry shape of something moving in the window of the next carriage along. 'I think they're waving to us,' she said, half to herself.

'So what's this mean then?' asked the Farmer. 'The criminal is innocent?'

'*Yes,*' said Hattie. 'Obviously!'

'You realise what that implies, don't you?' The Surgeon's voice had a sliver of ice in it.

'Of course I—' Hattie stopped. All of a sudden she felt acutely aware of her physical proximity to these two perfect strangers.

The Farmer looked from one serious face to the other.

'… He shot himself?'

'She's saying it must have been one of us,' said Hattie bitterly.

'Wha…' He gawped a moment. Then his brow knotted. 'Now you listen to me here. I am a man of means. D'you hear me? A businessman. Everything I have, I worked hard for. So don't start accusing on me just because—'

Hattie groaned. 'Nobody is accusing *anyone*.'

'On the contrary, that's exactly what you're doing,' the Surgeon said. 'To one, or both of us. You've even implicated yourself.'

'Don't pin this on me!' she exclaimed.

'I'd pin it on the *pair* of you,' added the Farmer.

'Let's think through this rationally.' The Surgeon gestured to the Farmer. 'You were standing by the benches to the immediate left of the victim at the time of the shooting. And I was to the immediate right. Now the hole in the window suggests the killer was facing the victim head-on. Meaning that the assailant must have leapt into the aisle, grabbed the Conductor's gun, taken the shot, and returned to their place before we emerged from the tunnel.'

Hattie raised her eyebrows. 'Quite complicated.'

She sniffed. 'I'm only following your line of reasoning.'

The Farmer looked puzzled. 'How was the criminal woman knocked down anyway?'

'I've no idea,' said Hattie. 'Shame we can't *ask* her.'

'It would have been possible to take the shot from the rear benches.' The Surgeon consulted the floor as she spoke. 'Easier, perhaps.'

'Wha-' Hattie stuttered. 'But the *gun* was over *here*. I was miles away!'

'You might have your own,' offered the Farmer.

Hattie spun on him. 'Why in Gaia's name would I be carrying a *heat* pistol?'

'You might if you were a criminal.'

Hattie was so furious she was almost at a loss for words. 'Are – are you joking?'

'You were rather stand-offish during your interview,' said the Surgeon mildly.

'Oh, *I* was stand-offish, was I?'

'Did you say you were at a funeral?' asked the Farmer.

The Surgeon nodded curtly. 'She did. Whose was it?'

He grinned. 'Not a victim of yours, I hope?'

'God beneath me!' Hattie exclaimed. 'It was my *mother's* funeral!'

'That doesn't prove anything,' said the Surgeon.

'Exactly,' Hattie retorted. 'It doesn't prove anything at all!'

'But it's still *suspicious*, though,' pressed the Farmer.

'*NO IT ISN'T!*' Hattie exploded. 'No more than *you* carrying a scalpel in your sleeve, or *you* constantly bragging about how you're a "man of means", whatever *that* means. As a matter of fact, you both seem exceptionally keen to pin this murder on someone else – first that woman, and now me – why? I don't know! But I think *suspicious* is a good word for it!'

Hattie stopped to catch her breath. The Farmer looked at her solemnly.

'Did you and your mother have a good relationship?' he asked.

'Shut up about my mother! A man is dead!'

The banging from the next carriage had resumed, louder and more urgent than ever.

'God's tits,' Hattie exclaimed. 'Where is that *damned key*?'

'I've got it.'

Under better circumstances it would have been funny. The three of them turned as one to see the Stowaway standing, brass key dangling between two fingers.

'And I'm not giving it back,' she added.

On the bench between them lay the Conductor's pistol. The Surgeon started towards it, and then leapt back with a shrill scream as it exploded in a crackling flash. In the Stowaway's hand – Hattie swore aloud, it was unbecoming, but she couldn't help it – was a *second* pistol, sleeker and cleaner and newer-looking than the first. Too good for a criminal, too good even for an ordinary Sheriff, unless that Sheriff enjoyed an obscene level of private wealth.

The three of them huddled together, the Farmer shifting his shoulder an inch to place himself between Hattie and the gun. A fruitless and positively condescending gesture; she appreciated it nonetheless.

'Here's what we're doing,' said the Stowaway. The smile was back on her face, which Hattie found irritating. *Learn new expressions!* she thought. 'We're going to wait out this journey together. Quietly. No chats. And when we arrive, I'll go out the rear door and none of you will ever see me again.' She reached down slowly, taking her hat by the rim and fixing it comfortably back onto her head. 'I wish I could stay and explain myself. But I can't. There's no time.'

'I knew it,' muttered the Surgeon.

The Farmer was stuttering helplessly. 'But-but the thump—'

'She knocked him down first. Shot him through the head. Then put a second shot through the window.' The Surgeon looked icy. 'Quick thinking, I must say.'

'Why don't you three sit down?' The Stowaway gestured to the benches. 'This'll be a long enough ride as it is.'

The Farmer grumbled something about how he didn't need to stand for this, and the Surgeon glowered and slipped a hand into her pocket, feeling for something sharp. Hattie wasn't paying attention. She was staring at the Stowaway's hat. Staring hard, scrutinising every detail like it was the face of a liar.

But clothes never lied. She knew that for a fact. So what was the Stowaway's hat trying to say? It was too snug, that was the thing. Or rather, just snug enough. Which was perfectly normal – after all, who in their right mind would wear a hat that didn't fit?

And then she knew.

'You've got it all backwards,' Hattie said, quietly. Then louder, 'Stop! You've got it all *backwards*!'

The other passengers stared at her – quizzical, angry, frightened.

'Listen to me,' she said, turning eagerly to the Stowaway. 'You need to give me that key. I'll fix everything.'

She gripped the key harder. 'Why?'

'Just—' Hattie shut her eyes. She forced herself to be rational. In her mind she was still stitching it together, thread by disparate thread. 'Look there, on the far wall.' She pointed down the aisle to the back of the carriage. 'Then come back here and tell me what you think.'

The Stowaway looked back. She struggled a moment, visibly torn between sense and curiosity. Then she jabbed the pistol at the other passengers. 'None of you move, okay?'

Nobody moved. The Stowaway hurried over to the far wall. The Farmer leant down and whispered to Hattie, 'D'you want me to jump her?'

She shook her head.

'Are you sure? Worked last time…'

'Just *wait,* you blithering idiot.'

The Stowaway scrutinised the far wall. Hattie's world was drained of everything except the tension, the quiet, the double-thud of the tracks.

Then the Stowaway turned, walked back, and dropped the key into Hattie's palm. 'You're pretty smart, huh.' The smile, for once, looked genuine.

Hattie felt her cheeks flush. 'Well, it was obvious, wasn't it?' she said, preening. 'None of us wanted him dead. So none of us murdered him. Simple as that.'

Throughout this whole exchange the Surgeon looked ready to explode. 'What's back there?' she demanded. 'What did you see?'

The Stowaway wiggled her pistol knowingly. 'Just stay there. You'll see soon enough.'

Hattie turned towards the door and remembered the Conductor's body was still in the way. She looked to the Farmer with an apologetic grimace. 'I'm sorry. Would you mind?'

'Course not.' The Farmer stepped past her. 'Pardon me, brother,' he murmured, lifting the corpse by the armpits and laying it easily down across a bench.

Hattie slotted the key in and opened the door. Rank air whooshed in.

'Wait,' said the Surgeon. 'You're not going to go *out there,* are you?'

'Stop whining,' she snapped. 'I'll only be a moment.'

There was a two-foot gap between their carriage and the next. Pale earth surged beneath the gangway, rail spikes like gnashing teeth. Hattie glanced back at the three faces that watched her, and sent thanks down to God that she was wearing her sensible shoes.

She jumped across. The key rattled in the door. On the

other side, in an otherwise empty carriage, stood a man with a face like hot cheese.

'It's about damn time,' he said.

'Come quickly, please.'

'Anybody hurt?' he asked, passing her.

'No.'

The cheese-faced man stepped over the gap, and Hattie hopped after, slamming the cabin door behind them. The other three waited inside. He waited till he had everyone's attention before speaking with a tone you might use on a group of squabbling children:

'Right. Can y'all see this badge?' He pointed to his chest. 'That makes me a Sheriff. *She-riff*. Meaning I'm representative of the authority of the *High* Sheriff. Meaning I am in charge here. So someone had better tell me what's going on, before I arrest the pack of you.'

Everyone started talking at once:

'Mr Sheriff, sir—'

'It's been nothing but—'

'I'll have you—'

'This *criminal*—'

He held up a hand. Silence fell.

'Now I can see that you're all worked up,' he said. He stuck a hand into either side of his vest and rocked back on his heels. 'But I can say one thing for sure – you don't need to worry about any criminal. I shot the bastard.' He looked down at the Conductor's corpse with naked contempt. 'And just in time, too.'

The Farmer was quickly enlisted to help the Sheriff remove the corpse, and to provide a more thorough explanation of everything that had occurred for the purposes of official record. He obliged quite happily,

saying: 'Of course, I saw through it all right sharply...'
Hattie suppressed a roll of the eyes. Before he departed,
he winked at her, making a slight two-fingered salute.
'Safe travels, ladies.' The Surgeon followed afterwards,
suitcase in hand, pausing only to give Hattie a curt nod.

The Sheriff's story was pleasingly dramatic. After
rereading the advanced bulletin and realising the
Conductor was the criminal described, he'd sprinted the
length of the train, only to find the final door was locked,
and that the man had managed to cut himself off with
any number of potential hostages. He'd glimpsed the
peaked cap through the window, taken aim, and –

Bang. End of story.

Nobody bothered to ask Hattie how she figured
it out. Nobody cared how she'd been alerted by the
Conductor's ill-fitting hat and the lack of a holster for
his gun. No mention was passed of the fact that heated
pistols have identical entry and exit wounds. It simply
wasn't important that she'd noticed the delight on
the Conductor's face when the Stowaway appeared –
the delight of a man who'd found his scapegoat. Also
forgotten was the fresh scorch mark on the rear door
that Hattie had sent the Stowaway to find. A scorch mark
that would, to a skilled gunslinger, tell the entire story of
the shooting without a word.

The villain was dead, and that was all that mattered.
Nobody cared. Except, perhaps, the Stowaway – but
she'd hung back when the Sheriff appeared. Silent, with
caution in her eyes. Only when everyone else had left did
she finally speak. 'Some Sheriff.'

Hattie nodded. 'Indeed.'

'That shot could have hit anyone.'

'He nearly hit *you*.'

'I hit the ground. Good instincts, I guess.'

Hattie looked at the Stowaway, who looked back at her with faint trepidation.

'Disgraceful,' said Hattie, shaking her head.

'W-what?'

'Look at this.' She grabbed the Stowaway's cloth jacket, lifting it to show where the seams had come undone at the elbow. 'Do you sleep in this thing?'

The Stowaway yanked her arm away. '*No.*'

'Liar.'

Hattie strode over to her handbag and pulled out her travel sewing kit: a small blue and white pouch, embroidered by hand. An old memento. She sat down, motioning impatiently to the seat next to her. 'Don't stand there like a turnip.'

The Stowaway sat. Hattie scrutinised the tear and cut a length of black thread with her scissors. 'I'd rather a more neutral colour, but we make do with what we have.' She held the needle up to the light and threaded it. 'Lift your arm up. Chop-chop.'

The well-worn cloth pinched between Hattie's fingers, supple and smooth as human skin. It took well to the thread. Her hands found the old rhythm and she let herself slip away into the simplicity of it. Pierce, tug. Pierce, tug. The Stowaway watched with mute fascination as the final line was pulled, tied and snipped.

'It looks like a machine did it,' she said, twisting her elbow to admire the mended line.

'It'll hold. But you ought to take better care.'

The Stowaway watched as Hattie slotted her tools back into place. 'I wish I had a skill,' she said sadly. 'The only thing I know how to do is shoot.'

'Lawman?'

'Sort of. I was a soldier. I gave it up.'

'Good.' Hattie sniffed. 'Nasty way to make a living.'

'It was.' She lowered her head. 'Yeah, it was.'

'*"We are more than the things we do."*' Hattie zipped the bag and slotted it back under the bench. 'My mother used to say that.'

'Condolences, by the way. For your mother.'

'Thank you.' Hattie paused. 'You're quite a long way from home, aren't you?'

The Stowaway went pale, but Hattie only laughed. 'Correct again!' She clapped. 'Another point to me! Don't worry, I don't mind. That's your problem. And God's, perhaps. But definitely not mine.'

'You're very perceptive,' the Stowaway said, shifting a little.

'Thank you. It was the boots that gave you away, if you're curious. Smoke?'

The Stowaway shook her head. In the folds of her dress Hattie had a cube-shaped pocket, sewn just to hold her cigarette tin. She drew it out, selected one, lit it up, and blew, watching the grey plume ripple against the window.

'You told me you were in a hurry,' she said. 'Where are you going? Back to your people?'

'Back to my person.'

'Oh.'

'But I don't know where I'm going. I mean – I'm going to the *New Destiny*. To find a communicator. But things keep getting harder…' She rubbed her eyes. Tired eyes, Hattie noticed. 'Like you said. It's not your problem.'

More rustling in the handbag. Hattie produced a pink stub, fresh ink blacking her fingers. 'Here.'

Holding it up to the light, the Stowaway read, 'Ad – admit – one. Where?'

'Wherever. It's a coach ticket.'

Her crooked face lit up: 'South?'

'Yes, as far as Wonderville.' She waited. 'If two people want to be together, they ought to be. Otherwise, the world just seems... a little uglier, don't you think?'

The Stowaway clutched it. 'Can I really have this?'

'Why not? I can always buy another.' Lifting the cigarette back to her lips, Hattie thought: *There I go again. Sticking my neck out.* But she felt at peace, strangely enough.

Outside, the passing hills rose and fell like the chest of a sleeping man.

…less than a month after the discovery of Tritium on Breton, primary planet of the Sovay-4 system, an Imperial inquiry was launched to investigate financial corruption in the Bretonian High Council. The Emperor ordered an interim trade embargo and motioned for Breton to be downgraded from colony to protectorate. This motion was enforced by a strong military presence at key warp tunnels throughout the system, and later on the ground at the capital city.

Better writers than I have already analysed the escalation in hostilities that followed, hostilities that culminated in the disastrous assault of Celestial Tower – so revoltingly described as a 'triumph' by the Centralian press. I could spend many paragraphs explaining why that framing is false. But the final death toll speaks for itself.

– 'Pattern analysis of the correlation between rare mineral deposits and the deployments of the Central Imperial Military, 2650–2810' Dr Noelle Daley, *Geology Today* (2811)

THIRD INTERLUDE

THE RIGGSBY SHERIFF'S office was an inconspicuous building on the right side of town, though the difference between right and wrong in Riggsby was a distance of only a few yards. Small windows like squinting eyes looked out past the tracks to the campers' district, a smattering of caravans with lace curtains and cinder-block wheels.

Inside the office, a shroud of moths fluttered around a naked lamp. There was the buzzing of the bulb, shouts on occasion from the caravans beyond, and, steady as clockwork, the tapping of an impatient heel on the floor. *Pok pok pok*. The heel belonged to Hattie Warbler. Every now and then she would let out a long, grandiose sigh, sometimes while studying her nails. But Deputy Seawall could tell she was frightened.

He was waiting for her to speak first, which at last she did with a sharp: 'Well?'

Seawall cocked his head, mirroring her. 'Well?'

He'd kept her waiting all day while he chewed out the

other passengers, drawing out the interviews until well after sunset. Now the station was empty, and they were alone. Him and his best witness. Best, and least favourite.

He paced before the table.

'Ms Warbler,' he began. 'You seem like a pretty smart woman to me. Nobody's fool, for sure. I'm gonna be honest with you, and in return, I'd like it very much if you were honest with me. See, as a principle, I—'

'Oh grow up!' she snapped.

Seawall was caught mid-sentence, slack-jawed. 'Huh?'

'This is childish. Just let me say my piece so we can both leave.'

The Deputy frowned. It was a good response, but he didn't like her tone. He tried to look genial. 'Go on then. You have a piece?'

'She's going to Wonderville on the six o'clock train. Gone, I should say,' she added curtly. 'God only knows how many hours ago that was. After that she's on to the New Destiny. She's a good few inches taller than you, wearing a check shirt, ranger's hat, and—'

'Alrighty, you can stop there.' Seawall forced a chuckle. Inside, he was furious. Six o'clock was long past. If only he'd started with the seamstress! From Hattie's petulant expression he could tell she was thinking the same thing.

He took the seat opposite her. 'I knew all that already,' he lied. 'I got some other stuff I wanna talk about.'

'Oh – well – in that case…' Much to his pleasure, she started to flounder. 'Why didn't you say so?'

'Because…' He hesitated. How much to say? 'Because, Ms Warbler, this is a delicate matter.'

'What's that supposed to mean?'

'I'm talking about state secrets.'

'Oh, is that what you're calling yourselves now? A

state?' Hattie looked appealingly at the ceiling. 'Goodness me. And here I thought you lot were a club of badge-collectors.'

'Cut the shit.' He leant a little closer. 'What did she tell you?'

'Not much,' Hattie admitted, fussing with the grey fabric about her lap. 'But I can draw my own conclusions. I'm not blind.'

A little thrill of horror played over the back of Seawall's neck. 'What'd you mean by conclusions?' he asked, knowing perfectly well. 'What do you suspect?'

No answer. Moths bickered overhead.

'I thought you were keen to leave, Ms Warbler.'

'I am.'

'Then I'll say again: cut the shit.'

'Fine. I suspect she's...' Hattie grasped for the right words, natural frankness struggling against a deep taboo. She jerked her chin slightly upward. 'From far away. Very far.'

'Where?' he pressed.

'Space!' she burst out. 'Space, you silly man! Outer space! God beneath me!' After a pause, she added sulkily: 'I hope you're happy. I feel ridiculous.'

'And you were planning to keep this suspicion to yourself?'

'It's not my business.' She sniffed. 'Besides, who would believe me?'

A fair point, thought the Deputy, reclining. Who *would* believe her? Nobody else in the carriage had even suspected the truth – he knew that much from his interrogations. Legally speaking, the whole incident had already been entombed in paperwork and buried six feet deep. All he had was one bad-tempered spinster with a hunch.

'I don't see why you care,' she said. The embarrassment of the outburst seemed to have riled her up: she was flushed, angry. 'We're talking about black space. Surely this is the Church's issue? Why aren't I talking to Ursula Ramirez?'

Ramirez. The name alone made Seawall grit his teeth. 'It's a legal matter,' he said. 'The Church has no power over the law.'

'Oh no?' Gradually, the seamstress began to look at him properly, studying him. It was as if she'd only just noticed he was there. 'You're rather sheltered, aren't you, Mr Seawall?'

'Am I?' He had to resist adding, *That's Deputy to you*.

'Oh yes. Out here in the real world, most people will trust a Preacher before they trust a Sheriff.'

He knew he was being goaded, and spoke with a concerted calm. 'Common sense ain't too common out here, sure. But that'll change.'

'When you're in charge, you mean?' She let out a sudden, spiteful laugh. 'Come *on*.'

He bristled. 'It doesn't matter what you think, ma'am.'

'Doesn't it?'

'No.'

'Look at yourself, Mr Seawall.' She seemed totally relaxed now, her beady eyes peeling him like fruit. 'Strutting around town like a headless chicken, bullying honest folk, playing like you know what's going on when you clearly haven't a clue. And for what? To impress the grown-ups? Well *I'm* not impressed, that's for sure. Nobody in their right mind would be. To me you're nothing but a spoilt little boy.'

Seawall suddenly felt very sick. The sight of her skin was repulsive to him, the hang of her neck, her leathering wrists. Just like his grandmother's. He thought: *Smug old harpy.* He thought: *Bitch.* He thought the pistol felt good in his hand, and then he saw that there was blood on the table and that was that.

It was the right call, he decided afterwards, gathering the body up, her ruffle-clad corpse like a great bird shot from the air. No sense leaving a witness running about.

Besides, she'd provoked him. He'd been deliberately provoked. It was only fair.

BAOZI

THREE THINGS WERE happening at once. A mile or so outside of Riggsby, midnight winds cooled the soil that would lie forever on the remains of Hattie Warbler. Her grave would never be found.

Far from that sad plot, on a well-kept track, a diesel coach carried a dozen-odd passengers closer and closer to the pulsing core of Earth's last civilisation.

And at the Eden Inn, a well-respected fourteen-room establishment on the road to Wonderville, a young woman appeared and asked to book a three-night stay. Her name was Ava Palava, and within minutes of her arrival it was clear to everyone that she was the most exciting thing to happen there in years.

Ava wore a sense of mystery about her like a fine perfume, moving noiselessly through the corridors with one hand clasped permanently around the handle of a gold-trimmed briefcase. Evening times she drank alone in the corner of the bar, her chin turned just so to catch the candlelight. Distant. Unspeaking. Once or twice, when she glided to the bar for a glass of wine, some brave young man or woman would ask what her business was in town. Her answers were polite and charmingly evasive. If pressed further she would lapse into a sad silence, her eyes vacant as she reflected on some personal disappointment from the past. Then she would turn the same questions back on the asker, who would inevitably become flattered and flustered, and speak about themselves for a length of time they would later recall with embarrassment.

The only person she ever spoke to at length was the inn's titular landlord, Mr Eden. Each morning she could be found lingering at the front desk to ask after his sick father, or share his despair over the latest tax rates. Ava was a landlord's daughter herself, it turned out; she knew all about the pains of the business and was full of excellent advice. Her sympathies had a positive effect on Mr Eden, too. He started growing out his sideburns.

It was considered a great tragedy when Ava left a day earlier than planned. More tragic still, she didn't have time to bid anyone farewell, but on her bed she left a note of thanks so sweet and touching that Mr and Mrs Eden had it framed and hung on the wall of their bedroom.

It took them a week to realise that she'd never actually paid.

WONDERVILLE: a kind-hearted traveller might describe it as a medley, or a collage. An honest one would call it a mess. Situated at the head of a crossroads just a half week's drive from the *New Destiny* itself, it was well placed for reputable and disreputable traders alike. The former occupied the domed buildings of wood and whitewashed cement with painted signs that creaked in the wind, while the latter were forced to set up stalls or move around on foot peddling their wares.

At peak hours the slim stretch of tarmac down Wonderville's centre became a cacophony of pedestrians, horses, motorbikes, and the occasional trundling car. Currents of humanity competed for directional dominance; whirlpools formed and were swept underneath, flows and counter-flows, voices barking with instruction, protest, all while the smell of food and manure and gasoline hovered overhead in a hot cloud. The older shops had constructed porches just so they could raise themselves above the chaos.

On one such porch a traveller sagged against the railings, watching the street with a glazed expression. Crowded, by Earth standards, but a ghost town compared to the megacity of her youth. Her fingers fiddled idly with a black stitch on her jacket's elbow. Through the corner of one eye she was monitoring the far end of the road – the edge of town, where the traffic bunched up against a dam of barricades and uniformed men. Every pocket was patted down, every boot opened and scrutinised, every hat removed to get a better look at the wearer's face. And every protest, met with the same barked response: 'Order of Deputy Seawall! No exceptions!'

They invoked his name like a holy mantra. One of the uniforms glanced up, sensing something, and the traveller quickly looked away.

Every road to New Destiny was blocked.

In her mind swirled the words of the Preacher's son: *You'll be sorry when he gets you.*

And she was sorry, gotten or not. Each fresh obstacle chipped a little more at her spirit, each new problem one problem too many, and what little good humour she'd had long since drained like blood from a stone.

From a slipstream below a girl broke off and climbed hurriedly up the steps, well dressed and clutching a gold-trimmed suitcase. She made a beeline for the traveller, started speaking as soon as she was in earshot and didn't stop.

'Pardon me, I'm so sorry, this is rather presumptuous I know.' The girl moved quickly as she spoke, setting the suitcase down and pulling loose a scarlet ribbon tied around her neck. 'I was just thinking how much you'd suit this little piece I'd picked up last month, really, it's so your style, you must trust me—' From the end of the ribbon hung a lace bonnet, which the girl swung smoothly around the Traveller's neck. 'I've always had an eye for people, you know, and to be frank you're not doing yourself any favours with *this* thing—' *This thing* was the battered ranger's hat the Traveller was wearing. The girl removed it, pulling the bonnet up into place. 'See, it's because of your facial structure really, so *striking*, really evocative, unusual, all the way up there, it suits you so well—'

The Traveller glanced at the blockade. She couldn't risk a scene, not here, not now. So she watched on in silent bemusement while the girl plonked the hat on her own head. 'There. I'm going to take this for you, okay, darling? You won't miss it. Ta-ta!'

She picked up her suitcase, leapt the railing one-handed and vanished into the crowd. The Traveller watched her go. Then she turned and stared at her reflection in the glass shopfront.

The girl had lied. The bonnet did not look good.

In fact, it looked grotesque – like someone had tried to make a doll out of a withered corpse. Stress had made her brittle, whittled her bones. *Stars,* she thought. *Is that really me?*

'There you are, you little shit.' A hand grasped the Traveller's shoulder, and she was spun around to face an older woman with an unflattering geometric haircut. 'Eh?'

Behind the woman stood a young man. He looked winded by exhaustion, half bent with his hands on his thighs. 'Wrong person, boss,' he said.

'Yes, I can see that,' the woman snapped. She scrutinised the Traveller, her lips scrunched tight as if pulled by a drawstring. The Traveller stared back blankly.

'It was the bonnet that confused you, boss,' offered the young man.

'No shit.' She let go of the Traveller's shoulders. 'Who the fuck are you then?'

The Traveller did not respond.

'An idiot,' the woman decided. She turned. 'Come on.' She grabbed the young man by the elbow and dragged him back into the crowd.

In a cheap hotel at the edge of town the Traveller lay staring up at the ceiling. A great canopy of mould had spread from a corner, coffee-brown, weakening the material so that the plasterwork sagged pregnantly downwards.

The window slid open. A suitcase appeared, swiftly followed by Ava, who eased herself over the sill and dropped silently to the floor. The red lace bonnet was hung on the back of a chair, and she lifted it free, setting down the hat in its place, thinking: *Gotcha*.

'Evening.'

Ava froze.

'It's alright,' said the Traveller. She rolled over, pulling the threadbare blanket over one ear. 'Leave the window open when you go.'

Ava stared at the bed. A leather holster hung from one side of the bedpost, an old cloth jacket from the other. She walked back to the window, then paused. She turned, swinging the bonnet from one finger. 'Awfully calm, aren't you?'

The Traveller grunted.

'Sorry about what happened before. I hope that old witch didn't bother you too much.'

'Not really.'

Ava leant back against the sill. 'What's your deal, anyway? Trouble with the law?'

No response.

'You've got a rather dangerous vibe.' Ava put the bonnet on, pulling the ribbons taut either side of her neck. 'I like it.' She nodded to the bedpost. 'Do you know how to use that pistol there? Or is it just a toy?'

The Traveller rolled over to face the ceiling and sighed. 'It's not a toy.' She glanced down at Ava. 'Do you want something?'

'Your name would make a good start.'

The Traveller rolled onto her other side.

'No?'

The Traveller said nothing.

'I'll call you Darling, then. Darling, you can call me Ava.'

Ava moved from the sill to sit on the edge of Darling's bed. She crossed her legs, rested one elbow on the top knee, cupped her chin with her palm and drummed her fingers lightly on the side of her face. 'I'd like to hire you, Darling,' she said. 'You see, the last few years of my life have been taken up by a long, sad tale, and I feel it's high time that this tale was concluded.'

'Mhmm.' Darling's grunt was muffled by the blanket.

'I can pay well.'

'Mhmm.'

'Not just in money. For instance, with a letter of recommendation that would get you past that pesky blockade. That's why you're stuck here, right? I saw you staring at them before. Of course it's none of *my* business why—'

Darling sat up. Her face was gaunt in the half-formed light. 'A letter?' she asked. 'That's all I need?'

'Yes. That, and a bribe. Which I can also provide.'

'How long will this take?'

'Just a day.'

Darling slumped backwards against the headboard, defeated. 'Fine. I'll help you. Just – not more than a day, okay? I need to get out of here.'

Ava stood, beaming. '*Wonderful.* I'll meet you at the stables tomorrow, okay?' She returned to the window, slung one leg over the sill, then paused. 'I assume you know how to shoot?'

Darling nodded.

'Excellent.'

She slipped out of sight.

Lingering on the ground below the window, Ava heard Darling sigh, and say to the empty room: 'Oh, love. What am I doing?'

EARLY MORNING. DARLING slipped away as soon as she could, keen to get the day's shenanigans over with, and found the main street quiet, almost peaceful. The tradesmen were still setting up their stalls – fold-out tables, crates pushed together, hand-sewn banners promising things like **Finest antique sunglasses** and

Rubber balls – they really bounce! Bleary-eyed officers leant against the struts of the southern barricade, yawning, swapping jokes.

A low whistle cut through the chatter. Darling turned and saw Ava standing in the shadow of a narrow alleyway, smoking tobacco from an arched black pipe. Her dress from the previous night had been swapped out for grey leggings and a high-collared black jacket. Darling went over to her, dodging an overladen crate that was dropped an inch shy of her feet, and asked, in a lowered voice, 'Where are you getting all these clothes?'

'It's my riding outfit,' said Ava, as if that answered anything. She turned the pipe over and tapped it on the side of the wall, loosening a small shower of ash. 'Come on. We're going to buy some horses.'

She took Darling by the arm and led her around the corner, into Wonderville's well-groomed backstreets. A block away, indicated by the jutting slated roof, was the stable yard. Ava added airily, 'And when I say buy, I of course mean steal. Would you mind lending a small hand?'

'With the stealing?'

Ava tittered. 'Oh, Gaia, no. What I need *you* to do is follow in after me and start eyeing up whatever looks expensive. There's a brand new saddle on the far wall – start there. Pretend you're checking the security.'

As Ava strode ahead, she called out: 'So – you just want me to *look* like a thief?'

Ava laughed. 'You already look like a thief, Darling.'

She slipped through the door without waiting for an answer.

The decor inside the stables was self-consciously elegant,

all wood varnish and framed portraits of the dead. The air was spritzed with a floral perfume that mingled unpleasantly with the scent of manure. Horses stood obediently in front of their tie-posts, heads bowed, ears flat, motionless except for the occasional feeble hoof scraped across the straw. By the door Ava spotted a pair of mares, older, but plenty. *You'll do,* she thought.

She walked over to the counter, where a squat man in a velvet cap was counting paper slips. First impressions were critical here. The man had not yet looked up, so Ava made an effort to step as loudly as she could. Success: the noise drew his interest, and he looked up to see her bearing down on him, spine straight, chin high, with the impatient air of one who does not like to have her time wasted.

'Good morning, I'd like to buy that stallion in the corner.' The salesman was accustomed to more build-up in something so monumental as a horse purchase, and while he fumbled, Ava added, 'Now, please.'

'Of course, ma'am, of course.' He stacked his papers and shoved them away, pulling the glasses from his nose. 'All of our adult horses go for a hundred, so—'

'Very good.' Ava took out her purse, popped the clasp and counted out five clean twenties, placing them down on the counter. The man's eyes widened by a hair, and he looked up at her, taking off his cap to run a hand over his hair.

'The saddle...'

Ava narrowed her eyes.

'...the – uh – the saddle is included, of course.'

'I should think so.' She rewarded him with a smile. 'I'm terribly sorry, but is it okay if I get him prepped now?'

'Yes, of—' The stablemaster's eyes alighted on

something behind Ava's shoulder. Darling had arrived. Ava, still smiling, shifted herself a little to block his view. '...of course, right away, ma'am,' he finished.

He led her over to the stallion, turning once or twice to look at Darling again. Ava saw her run a finger along the base of a copper stirrup. *How subtle,* she thought.

'Here he is.' Arriving at the stallion, the stablemaster turned to her, inclining his head slightly. 'Lovely beast. Healthy. Very obedient. Just the thing to impress your girlfriends down at the track.' He tightened the buckle, undid the bindings, and led the horse a few steps forward to Ava. It followed meekly. 'Would you like to have a little trot round the courtyard first?'

Ava took the reins and gave the horse a frank appraisal. It stared back apathetically, jaw working in circles to grind down some last scrap of breakfast. She chewed her lip for a moment. The stablemaster stared off behind her.

'Actually, no. Take this one back.' She thrust the reins into his hands. 'I want those two, over there by the door.' She pointed to the mares.

'Oh – uh, yes.' The salesman made a quick recovery. 'That'll be another—'

'I'm not paying you again.' Ava raised her voice, and a few of the stable hands turned to look. 'I've returned this stallion, worth a hundred, and I've already paid you a hundred in cash. Are you trying to double-charge me?'

'No, ma'am, of course—'

'I should hope not.'

'Yes, I—' His eyes flicked over to Darling again, who was making a show of scanning the nearest exits. 'Yes, of course, sorry—' He started to tie the stallion back to the post. 'If you'd wait just a moment, ma'am, I'll have them prepared for you—'

'I'll do it!' Ava snapped. 'I know how to buckle a horse. What do you take me for?'

'Of course, ma'am, go right ahead…'

Ava strode over to the mares, grabbing the twenties that still lay on the counter as she passed. She heard the salesman approach Darling, saying, 'You! Can I *help* you?'

Ava smiled as she led the mares out into the yard.

'Come on, Darling. Foot in, step up, sit down.'

'I heard you the first time,' Darling muttered. She stuck her left foot in the stirrup and made a pathetic half-jump with her back heel. The horse whinnied, tossing its head. Darling let go. 'I don't think it likes me,' she said.

'*She* is called Briar.' Ava trotted behind them in a brisk semicircle. 'And you're making her nervous. Try again.'

Nervous? Darling couldn't believe that. It was less like an animal and more like a huge angry wall. The feet were impossibly large and heavy enough to stamp clean through her toes – and the less said about its rear end, the better. Yet there was Ava, bobbing up and down the courtyard in perfect sync with the horse she'd decided to call Saguaro.

'Just lean forward,' she called down, 'and climb up. God's tits, you're not *nearly* as tough as you look.'

Darling clenched her teeth. She gripped the saddle, her eyes burning with a grim intensity. Then she stood. For a moment she swayed, tilting dangerously far back. Then she swung the other leg over and sat.

Ava clapped. 'There you go! That wasn't so hard, was it?'

But it *was* so hard. And being on top was even worse. She could feel every twitch and shudder of the alien thing beneath her. 'Ava, I don't think—'

'I've not hired you to think,' Ava interjected. 'Give her a nudge. Both heels. We'll run out of light at this rate.'

Darling obliged, and to her surprise Briar fell into a trot. She tugged the rein. Briar tugged back, still trotting. She tried again, harder this time, and they turned in a slow, resentful arc, back round to face Ava.

'That's the ticket,' said Ava. 'Now follow me. And *relax*, please. You've got a face like you're passing a kidney stone.'

Darling's knuckles were white around the rein. She forced herself to let go and lightly touched the hilt of her pistol. *It'll be fine.*

They rode eastwards out into the wasteland.

The last of Wonderville's buildings fell away, and they joined an unmarked track dappled with patches of broken tarmac. Ava would periodically snap open a compass and check their direction while Darling struggled to keep her feet in the stirrups.

'Are you going to tell me where we're going?' she asked.

Ava reached into the folds of her jacket and pulled out a slip of paper. 'Here.'

Darling tried to nudge Briar closer, but the horse only snorted and waggled her head, so she was forced to lean out and grab the pamphlet with one hand. Briar staggered irritably to one side. 'Bad horse,' Darling muttered. She held up the paper, a peach-pink fold-out map with *Visit Sunny Margit!* printed across the top.

'At the bottom. Where it's circled.'

Darling drew the pamphlet up to her face and read out loud: '*Nos... Nostalgia Tavern. Rare colle... ctibles – comics and fig-urines.* What do you want there?'

'Margit's a no-man's town,' Ava said, ignoring the question. 'Not even bandits have claimed it as far as I can tell. No roads running in or out – hence why we need more *upmarket* transportation.' She rubbed Saguaro along the side of her neck, and the mare snorted happily.

'Is it dangerous?'

'Perhaps not. But a town that large, this close to the city? There's likely a reason nobody's settled it. That's what you're here for.'

'Right.'

They lapsed into silence. Darling absorbed herself in the task of riding, which she was surprised to find herself enjoying. It had a rhythm that was almost musical, a swung beat from back to front, side to side – *thu-thump, thu-thump, thu-thump*. Even the sweaty boiled-soap horse smell, which she'd found so off-putting at first, had a pleasant warmth to it.

'*Darling!*'

Darling snapped to attention, hand rushing to her hip. 'What?'

'You were falling asleep.' Ava fell into step beside her. 'Sweet Mother Earth. What do you do all night? Lie there with your eyes open?'

'I used to take – I used to have things to help me sleep. But you can't get them here.'

'Herbal teas?'

'Mmm-hmm.'

Ava's gaze lingered a second longer. Then she turned forwards, clicking her tongue. 'You ought to learn to lie better,' she said. 'You smile every time.'

'What?' Darling blinked, nudging Briar on to catch up to her. 'No I don't.'

'You do. Just a little smile. I've seen it.'

Darling raised a hand to her face. *Where'd I pick that up?*

'Don't dodge – deflect. People are narcissists. Give them a chance to talk about themselves and they'll forget that they were ever curious about you.'

Darling pondered this.

'Aren't I right?'

'Maybe.' She paused. 'You're kinda cynical for your age, huh.'

Ava laughed. 'That's the ticket. Now follow it up with a question and I'll be all yours.'

'I wasn't trying—'

'I know, Darling, I know.'

IN EARTH'S ANCIENT times there had been a general understanding that when it came to architecture, age and dignity were natural partners. To say that your house had stood for a hundred years was a point of pride, signifying not just power but inherited power.

But since the Great Departure that notion had flipped. Earth was a planet without conservationists. What was new was natural and useful; what was old was crumbling and cursed, best left alone to crumble further and acquire more curses.

So it was with the ruins of Margit.

As the town drew closer the garbage of the old world began to rise around them – collapsed wire fences, a lone streetlight, half a bin. They passed a wall of rotting paper, then a faded green sign, announcing:

MARGIT 1 KM

A single gutted car became a queue, dotting the ground at intervals up to an empty intersection. Raised on a kerb, a squat red tube dribbled clear water onto the ground. Ava saw this, then turned around and called: 'Let's give the girls a drink, shall we?' She dismounted with a flourish, approached the tube, and removed one of the nozzles with a thrust of her heel. The dribble became a stream, and Saguaro, with a little encouragement, stuck her face in. Darling felt an excited tremor run through Briar.

'Okay. Okay.' Gripping the tip of the saddle, she slowly reversed the manoeuvre from earlier, inching downwards until she felt the ground connect with her heel.

'You two seem to be getting along better,' noted Ava, as Darling led Briar over to the water. She took out a handful of dried fruit chunks from a sack on Saguaro's side and offered them to Darling. 'Do you want to feed her?'

'Sure.' Inspecting Briar's mouth up close, Darling realised she wanted nothing less. It was a grotesque approximation of a human mouth, similar in the basic elements, but curved and hairy, with teeth stretching far back into the glistening gums.

'Keep your fingers flat,' said Ava helpfully.

Darling obliged. Briar started snuffling over her palm. She stood completely stiff, ready for the pain.

Briar started eating.

'Shit,' Darling whispered. 'Oh, shit. It tickles. Oh shit.'

Ava started to laugh. Briar finished eating and started sniffing up her wrist, looking for more. Darling leapt back, stifling a yelp, and Ava had to clasp a hand over her mouth.

Briar gave up searching for more food and stared expectantly at Darling, doe-eyed, still chewing. Darling extended a cautious hand and patted her on the centre of the forehead.

'Good horse,' she said.

The ride resumed. Soon they were penned in by tall, boxy buildings, almost all of them some variation on the colour beige. Cladding hung loose on rotten brickwork, peeled away like strips of flesh from bone, with lightless, shattered windows watching from all sides. Withered trees, their roots drowned in tarmac, stuck out from the pavement at precise intervals. A string of shrunken grey bunting hung overhead.

'Can't imagine why someone wouldn't want to live here.' Ava's voice was stifled by all the empty space. 'Let's take a moment – I need to check our bearings.' She began to dismount.

'Stop,' ordered Darling.

Something was watching them from the other side of the road. A scrawny creature, bandy-legged and snub-nosed, with a head shaped like a bullet.

'It's just a dog,' said Ava. 'Come on—'

'I said stop.' Darling heard Briar's nostrils huff anxiously.

Dotted around the street, on the corners, or crouching in doorways, she could see half a dozen pairs of yellow eyes. She'd have spotted them sooner, but they were pale with brick-dust and flakes of cement. Camouflaged by the rubble.

Briar pawed at the road.

'Why don't we look for another way in?' suggested Ava, with just the faintest tremor in her voice.

'Stay still. If we move—'

A snarl cut through the air. The closest of the dogs leapt forward, pelting down the road with a startling speed. Darling drew. She hit the dog's front leg, and it fell on its chin with a strangled yelp. Two more launched from either side. Darling aimed again, but the shot went wide. For a moment she couldn't understand (*I missed?*) but then she realised it was Briar, turning to run back the way they'd come at a frenzied gallop. Darling couldn't slow her down: it was all she could do to keep from getting thrown off. Each step was sharp enough to knock her breath out. She heard more snarling, then a shriek went up from behind her.

Shit, she thought. *Fine.*

Darling let go of the reins, planted both hands on the saddle and leapfrogged off Briar's back. A mixed success – she cleared the horse, but collided with the ground at an angle so that she rolled backwards in a heap, swearing, feeling something twist somewhere. She scrambled to her feet and sprinted back towards Ava. By some miracle she was still in the saddle, but one of the dogs had planted its teeth in Saguaro's leg. The horse stumbled back, braying in pain. Darling couldn't shoot – the dog was too close to Saguaro – so as she ran she stooped to grab a loose brick, raising it up to catch the mutt on the side of the head. It reeled around with a bloodied snarl, aiming a paw at Darling's midriff that swiftly exploded with a pistol shot. The dog fell back. Darling turned to see another pair approaching Saguaro's flank and fired two shots between the horse's legs. One dog was hit in the rear, another dashed across the eyes.

'*Behind you!*'

Darling turned. Not fast enough. She felt the dog collide with her knees and lost balance, solid ground slapping across her shoulder blades, managing to raise an arm and keep some space between the jaws and her face. Drool splattered on her forehead, teeth snapping an inch from her eyes. She found beneath the dog's belly with her foot and kicked upwards, lifting it free from the ground. It landed half a yard away, limp and silent. Darling breathed. Then she heard behind her:

'*Woah!*'

Saguaro had held up well at first, but the gunshots had sent her into a panic. Now she was rearing, her eyes wide and edged with white crescents, slender legs kicking outwards. The suitcase came unhooked and thudded into the ground. Ava pulled herself all the way forward in the saddle, yanking the reins back. As Saguaro's front legs thudded back into the ground she slipped off, jogging as she landed, one hand still gripping the reins. But Saguaro was too fast. She jerked her chin, ripping herself free, and took off after Briar, trampling over the suitcase as she went.

Then it was quiet again.

Ava looked down at her suitcase. It was dented. Her shoulders trembled for a moment. Then she said, with a forced brightness: 'It's okay! We can walk from here. It's close. I still have the map…'

Darling looked at Ava: panting, eyes bright, whorls of dark hair plastered against her forehead. Wired up like a firework, and visibly, painfully young.

'No,' said Darling. 'Sorry. We're taking a break.'

'A break?' Ava's voice crackled. 'Darling, don't be absurd. We haven't even—'

'Half an hour.'

Ava's jaw clenched, and for a moment Darling thought she was going to scream.

'Very well. The shop won't go anywhere, will it?'

'No,' Darling agreed. 'It won't.'

Behind one of the taller buildings Darling found an ascending tunnel of platforms and ladders they could climb all the way to the top. The roof was flat, with a hard-tack floor, and empty save for the rusting tunnel of an old air vent and a few scattered plastic deckchairs. Darling paced around the rim, pistol in hand, while Ava sat herself down in a chair with a shuddering sigh.

'Looks like we're safe.' She holstered the gun.

'Good,' said Ava, mopping her fringe back. 'If those little fuckers learn to climb ladders, give me a call.' She lifted the suitcase and set it down on her knees, undoing the clasps with a smooth *click*. Darling turned demurely away.

Ava rolled her eyes. 'You can look.'

Darling wanted to seem disinterested, but her curiosity had been building up for a while. She peeped over Ava's shoulder. Inside the suitcase – and in good mint, despite the deep dent to the outer casing – clear plastic folders were fitted in sideways, like the pages of a book. Each folder contained a vibrantly coloured paper pamphlet. Darling frowned. She looked closer, and recognised them for the relics that they were. 'Are those... comics?'

'You remember that long, sad tale I mentioned earlier? It wasn't about me.'

Darling grabbed another deckchair and pulled it over, brittle legs juddering across the rooftop floor. She sat down awkwardly on the edge. Ava flipped through the suitcase and selected a comic, drawing it out slowly with both hands. 'This is *Baozi #8*.'

She handed it to Darling, who held it in both hands, trying to look appropriately reverential. The artefact seemed out of place – not just in that drab town, but in the whole drab planet, where most artificial colour had long since worn away under the sun's glare. The cover showed a squat muscular boy breaking through a wall with his fist, the punch spewing out an arc of rainbow rays. Behind him a second boy with spiky hair cheered him on.

'That's Bao, the hero.' Ava's middle finger landed on the muscular boy. 'And that's his best friend, Gyo.' She pointed to the spiky figure behind him.

Darling held it closer. 'What's going on?'

'Oh, this is Baozi training. After he loses his power crystal in Issue #8 in the fight with Doctor Pierogi, he has to learn to create smaller crystals out of his own sweat. Which is significant because it requires flow magic, which eventually – we're not talking until the final issue here – eventually lets him punch a door through time and rescue his girlfriend Princess Empanada. She lives in the future.'

Ava said all of this with a completely straight face.

Darling lifted the comic, turning to the first page. 'So it's like… fantasy?'

Ava reached over and plucked it out of her hands. '*Baozi* spans many genres. It's more of its own thing.' She slotted the comic back into place. 'Have you been to New Destiny before?'

'No.' She shook her head. 'Uh, first-time visitor.'

'I'm from there. It's a rather feudal set-up, you know. Poor folk on the lower decks, rich folk on the higher. The rule goes that as one ascends in prestige and wealth, one ascends the city accordingly.'

Is this a metaphor? Darling wondered. She kept her mouth shut, afraid to give away her own ignorance. 'Sure.'

'I grew up on floor four. A cut above the average citizen, but in New Destiny – nothing special. But we had a family friend who worked on the top deck. The *very* top,' she added, with significance. 'On my sixth birthday she sent down a copy of *Baozi #5*. I loved it. Naturally. It's a work of genius, after all. Word got back to her, and the next year I got *Baozi #2*. And the year after that, and the year after that, out of order, but a different issue every time. I don't know how she kept finding them. We didn't see much of one another, but *Bao* was, sort of, I don't know, sort of our thing, our little joke.' She lifted the folders, running them through her fingers one by one. 'I've got every issue now except for #11. That's the second last.'

'So you just want to... find out what happens?'

It took Ava a moment to respond. She leant back into the deckchair, folding her arms behind her head. Far to the east the land clustered upwards in a range of hills, their blunt peaks hooded in dark shrubbery. 'You'll recall Gyo,' she said.

'Uh-huh. He's friends with Boo.'

'Bao.'

'Yeah.'

Ava took a breath. For the first time since they'd met, she was having trouble speaking. 'He...' She paused. 'He dies in Issue #11.'

Darling frowned. 'The missing one?'

'The missing issue, yes. And that wouldn't be so bad, only... so, let me explain—' She sat up. 'In Issue #9, Bao and Gyo are reunited after being away from each other for months. Because Gyo infiltrated Dr Pierogi's lab, right?' She spoke quickly, breathlessly. 'And he's been working as a double agent. But he gets captured, and Bao goes on this tremendous mission to break him out. And they meet up, and there's this whole double-page spread – it's very moving, honestly – but then at the start of Issue #12, Bao tells Princess Empanada that Gyo was the best friend he ever had and that he'll never forget him. There's no mention of what happened. He's just gone! You'd assume it was Doctor Pierogi, but Bao doesn't say anything to him about Gyo in their final battle, which you'd think he would if he'd been involved. So why? What happened?' Ava exhaled. 'It's pissed me off for years, Darling. I *have* to know.'

Darling nodded. She was trying so hard, it made Ava laugh.

'You think I'm crazy, don't you?'

'No…'

'It's fine. I quite agree.'

Darling scooched back, reclining into her chair. They both stared up at the sky. A frayed ribbon of cloud hovered overhead, anomalous in the pure blue atmosphere.

Huh, Darling thought. *That's the first cloud I've seen.*

Distant winds pushed the cloud's edges wide, until it wisped away into nothingness.

'Have you ever been in love, Darling?' Ava asked, after a while.

'I am in love,' she replied. 'Present tense.'

Ava turned. '*Really?*'

'Uh-huh.'

'And where's…'

'She's gone.'

'I'm sorry.'

'No,' Darling corrected, frowning to herself. 'No. Not like that. Not *gone* gone. Just missing. I'm trying to find a communicator. So I can send her a message. So I can find her.' Darling took a breath. 'What happened to your friend?'

'Oh—' Ava cleared her throat. 'Yes, she died.'

'Condolences.'

'Thank you.'

Darling paused. 'Do you... like Gyo? More than Bao?'

'I don't know. I suppose I liked the way they feel about each other.'

'I get that.' Darling yawned, stretching her legs out. 'Yeah. I think I get that.'

There was another moment of peace. Then Ava rose sharply up, briefcase in hand. 'Alright. Let's go find this comic, shall we?'

Darling hauled herself reluctantly to her feet. 'You got it.'

They moved through the town in tight formation: Darling ahead, fingers brushing the edge of her holster, with Ava following close behind. After some time they came to a deserted plaza dotted with planters of moulding soil and loomed over by a great palatial ruin.

'That's the town hall.' Ava scrutinised the pink pamphlet. 'Yes. We're close now. Take the road on the northern end.' They followed around the corner, to another avenue, wide and deserted. Ava stopped. 'There.'

Across the road stood the Nostalgia Tavern. It was a small shoddy shopfront squeezed between two larger structures. The logo, looping blue font on an orange background, was still readable, though the colour had all but faded. Paper comics drooped behind grimy glass. But neither of them noticed the logo, or even the display. Their attention was on one thing only.

Stuck into the ground in front of the shop were dozens and dozens of sticks, varied in length and material –

walking sticks, bits of railing, an old table leg. All of them had been whittled into sharp points and secured to jut upwards and outwards. It looked like recent work.

'What in Gaia's name…?' Ava went for a closer look, but Darling caught her on the elbow.

'It's been fortified.'

Ava scoffed. 'You think someone lives *there?*'

But Darling wasn't smiling.

'Fine. After you then.'

Darling stepped ahead. There was a path between the spikes leading to the doorway, but it was so narrow she had to turn sideways to get through. She pushed the door open with her foot. 'Hello?'

Dark shelves. Silence. 'It doesn't look like there's anyone here,' she called back. 'Hello?'

'Hello,' said a soft voice from behind the counter.

'Holy—' Darling stumbled back, half falling into a display table. A hardbound graphic novel wobbled on its axis. She caught it, set it up straight again. Her heart was thudding. It had been years since anyone had managed to catch Darling by surprise.

'Is everything okay?' Ava called from outside.

'Everything's fine.'

The counter was positioned in a corner directly parallel to the door, almost behind it, so that the shopkeeper could see the customers as they came in. The man behind the counter stared at Darling expressionlessly. He wore small wire glasses, a chequered shirt, and slacks. Jowls with a coating of light stubble sagged down the corners of his bloodless lips. He was neither fat nor thin, neither old nor young: if ever a person could have been a perfect medium, it was him.

'He-hello,' she said at last. 'Can we look around?' It

felt absurd to act like she was in a normal shop, but she couldn't think what else to do.

'I would not mind if you looked around,' replied the man tonelessly. There was a comic in his hands. He licked one finger, turned the page, and resumed reading.

Ava appeared in the doorway. She saw the man sitting there, and exchanged a look with Darling.

It didn't take long to conduct a full search. The shop was small, and many of the shelves were empty save for a handful of paper volumes pushed to one end. Most of them were sealed in plastic wrap. A few were out in the open, curled at the corners, speech bubbles yellowing. Darling found a shelf of tiny plastic women, crammed so close together that their twig-thin limbs and stiff, rippling clothes all overlapped. She turned back to Ava and shook her head. 'Let's go,' she whispered.

'Wait.' Ava glanced towards the man behind the counter.

Darling looked at him, then back to Ava. She wanted to protest. She couldn't think why.

Ava skipped over to the desk. 'Excuse me?'

The man looked up. A faint wrinkle between his eyes suggested irritation.

'I'm sorry to bother you so late in the day,' she began. 'You see, I'm looking for a particular issue of a particular comic. *Baozi #11*. It's by—'

'I know *Baozi*.'

'Oh.' Ava faltered. 'Oh, that's great.'

The man looked at her.

'Do you happen to have a copy?' she asked.

'I happen to have a copy.'

'Of-of Issue #11?' Ava placed a hand on the counter to steady herself.

'Of Issue #11,' the man repeated.

Darling could feel unease coming up in her stomach like bile, as Ava asked: 'May I purchase it?'

'No.'

'Oh, I don't mean for a regular price. I can pay—'

'No. I won't sell it for any price.'

He opened his comic and resumed reading.

'What if I traded it for the rest of my collection?' Ava set the suitcase on the desk, fluttering her fingers along the rim. 'I have them all, right here. Perfect condition.'

He looked at the suitcase with blank disdain. 'No.'

'But – can I at least look at it?'

The man locked eyes with Ava. 'No.'

'Have you read it?'

He nodded.

'Could you tell me what happens?'

Darling saw how the muscles in the man's face were working to keep him from smiling. 'Say please,' he said gently.

Ava swallowed. 'Please?'

'No.'

He turned back to his comic, but behind the lenses his pupils were still. He was waiting.

'Ava.' She jolted at the sound of her own name, and turned to see Darling by her side. 'Can we talk outside?'

They moved between the spikes and out onto the street, with some fussing, as the tail of Ava's coat caught on one of the spikes. She pulled it free, not seeming to notice how it tore. Darling was ready to speak, but Ava whirled on her before she could begin.

'What was that?' she hissed.

'Hey now, I didn't—'

'*Can we talk outside?*' she mimicked. 'Why didn't you step in?'

'And what?'

'And *threaten him,* you invalid. *With your gun.'*

'I'm – Ava, I'm not your goon. Anyhow, that wouldn't have worked.'

'And *why not?'*

'He's playing with you. He doesn't have a copy.'

'But what if he does?'

'He doesn't.'

'Well, I'm not leaving until we've turned that little *shithole* upside down!'

'I don't think he'll sit back and watch?'

'Then fucking *shoot* him! What did I hire you for?'

Darling chose her next words carefully. 'I am not gonna shoot anyone.' She almost added: *Again.*

'Yes, you are, or our deal is off. No letter. No bribe.' Ava's hands balled at her sides. 'Do this now, or you can stay in Wonderville and *rot.'*

'I just…' Darling sucked her teeth. *'I don't have time for this, Ava.'*

'You're not listening. I have been looking for Issue #11 for years. Literally, years. This is my final lead. If he has a copy, I can assure you it is the only copy on the continent.'

'So? Tough luck.'

'*No.* We just have to take it.'

Darling crossed her arms. 'I'm not hurting someone just to satisfy your curiosity.'

'You think I did all this out of *curiosity*?'

'Didn't you?'

'Do not talk *down* to me.'

'I'm not talking—'

'Yes you are, you're – you're treating this like…'

'Explain it to me then. Explain why it's so important.'

'I just – I just couldn't – I couldn't understand, I need *answers*. People don't just fucking *die* for no reason, it's—' Ava turned away. She was wiping her face furiously.

'Ava.' Darling placed a hand on her shoulder, but she shook it off.

Darling saw the man standing behind the shop window. He was watching them – watching Ava – with glittering eyes, slowly spooning something from a tin into his mouth.

'Stay here.' Darling walked back into the shop, found him sitting behind the counter again, comic in hand. The scent of tinned fish stink hung heavy in the air.

'I've got an offer,' he said.

'Do you now?'

'Your gun. For *Baozi*.'

Darling nearly laughed, but he wasn't kidding. 'What?'

'You can disable it before you give it to me.'

'Yeah, but – why?'

The man did not reply. Darling drew the pistol, watching the barrel glisten in the dust-pillared light. Behind the counter the man removed his glasses. His eyes were small and red-rimmed underneath, and they fixed upon the pistol with total reverence.

'It's new,' he said. 'I want it.'

Darling twisted the gun round. With a discreet flick of the thumb, she locked it into safety mode. Part of her knew that making the trade was madness. An empty holster: she'd be happier with a missing limb. But her heart hurt for Ava. For the weight of the unanswered question. It was a weight she knew too well herself.

The man held out his hand. His fingers twitched a little, like the spasms of a corpse.

'You're not seriously going to give your lovely pistol away, are you?' Ava was leant in the doorway.

Darling stuttered. 'I-'

Ava snorted. 'It's fine. We're leaving, Darling. I'm sorry for wasting your time.' The last line was directed at the man. He was motionless, one hand still extended.

'Are you sure?' asked Darling.

'Perfectly. Come along.'

Darling shrugged and slotted her pistol back in the holster. The weight of it filled her with a relief that was almost physical. 'Well then.' She looked back at the man, touched her hat. 'Bye.'

'*Wait!*' The man stood. His fleshy face was pale, trembling with – rage? Fear? Darling couldn't tell. 'We haven't finished.'

'You had your chance to negotiate,' said Ava. 'Good day.'

'But...'

'No buts.'

The bell above the door jingled as it slammed behind them.

They were perhaps fifty yards down the road when a noise came from the Nostalgia Tavern, a sort of wail, long and shrill, filled with self-pity.

Ava twisted around, staring down the empty street. 'Do you think he'll come after us?'

'Doubt it.'

'Good.' Tittering, she asked: 'Did you see his face? I wish I could bottle it.' She snorted. 'Really! A tragic specimen. What do you suppose he does with all those plastic dolls?'

Already Ava was rearranging the whole incident in her mind, casting it as a comedy. Knowing better than to break the illusion, Darling said: 'I don't want to imagine.'

'Oh Mother God, and that *smell*. How old do you

think that fish was? Must be Pre-Departure. Ugh! I'd have thrown up after another second.'

'Yeah. Gross.'

They rounded the corner back to the plaza. Wisps of black cloth shrieked warnings and rose in a wave.

'He didn't have any Baozi merchandise on the shelves,' Ava went on. 'Did you notice that? I bet he'd never even heard of it. Anyway, I had another thought about that line in Issue #12. See, *Baozi* has these things called temporal rifts, they're a phenomenon created by a special device Bao's mother passed down to him…'

'Uh-huh.' Darling's eyes were on a spot at the far end of the square, the place where the birds had been.

'It could be that Gyo got caught in one of those rifts and got transported to a pocket dimension. That's essentially another universe. He might have even jumped in to save Bao. It would make sense, wouldn't it?'

Ava realised she was being ignored.

'Darling?'

'Let's go another way.' Darling swung around. Her hat was turned down, shadowing her eyes. 'Come on.'

'Why?'

'It's not safe.'

'What are you—' Ava tried to peer ahead, but Darling stuck an arm out. 'For God's sake, Darling, I'm not a child! Let me see!'

Reluctantly, Darling stood aside.

It took Ava a second to put together the identity of the thing splayed out on the pallid flagstone. The thing that was half open, burst like a sack and speared with four legs, dark and sodden and unmoving.

It was Saguaro.

To be more accurate: it was her corpse.

'Uh-huh.' Lips moving silently, the officer read down the letter. 'Yep. Uh-huh.'

Three of Ava's twenties had been folded up with the paper. The officer had pocketed them without comment, then set to reading the letter as if it were a relative's will.

'Right. Hmm.'

Darling was like a cat in a bath, every inch bristling with nerves. Behind the two of them was the press of the crowd, their impatience a background hum, a sonorous, ambient grumble. In front of them lay the barrier. If anything went wrong they'd both be trapped.

Tongue poking out of her lips, the officer turned the letter to the other side. 'Right. Mm. Okay.' Folding it down, she frowned at them both over the rim of her spectacles. 'Yes. Hmm. I see. Which one of you is the city resident?'

Sheepishly, Ava raised her hand.

'Hmm. Long way to go for a bit of shopping.'

A helpless shrug.

'As for you…' Sweat beaded above Darling's eyebrows, right below the brim of her hat. 'What's your vocation?'

She grinned. 'Tourist.'

'You're well-armed, for a tourist.' The officer swapped a look with her partner on the other side of the barricade: just a second's glance, but Darling caught it. A slight rising of the elbow; the partner's hand rose, resting on a hidden grip.

Shit, she thought. *Shit shit shit.*

'Would you mind if I asked you a few more questions?'

'About what?' asked Darling. 'This old thing?'

With a big motion – almost *theatrical* – she drew her gun and pointed it at the officer: Ava let out a shriek.

Heads began turning with that rising, sickly lightness of sudden panic that spreads with a drawn gun in a crowd, the adrenaline spike of impending violence; but it was too late, she was too fast, it had already –

Click.

Nothing came out of the barrel.

'It doesn't work,' she said. 'Just a toy. I only carry it to look cool.'

'*Haaaa!*' Braying laughter. Across the barrier, the officer's partner pointed at the three of them, doubled over. 'I saw that, Suzie! You totally jumped!'

Indignant, Suzie yelled back, 'Like *space* I did!'

When the barricade was safely behind them, Darling drew the pistol again, showing a clasp concealed along the barrel. 'Still in safety,' she said, with just a sprinkle of conman's glee. 'Did I fool you?'

'Of course not,' said Ava huffily.

'*Really?*'

'Shut up.'

They bid farewell by the roadside, brief, affectionate, awkward. After the final handshake Ava stood a moment, watching Darling's lanky form recede into the distance. A strange anxiety fell upon her – not for herself, but for Darling. She nearly sprinted after her, nearly grabbed her by the arm. Nearly said, 'Who are you, really?' and, 'Don't go. It's not safe.'

The feeling passed. Ava talked her way back through the barricade and returned to the hotel. The next day she woke early and began combing Wonderville, asking at every shop and stall until she found what she was looking for.

A heat pistol.

Not as new as Darling's, but better than standard issue. She wrapped it in cloth and rode back out eastward to the ruins of Margit, accompanied by a few assistants, procured through more official routes this time. On the way there they saw only a single dog, which one of the assistants shot on sight.

They crossed the old footsteps, down the highway, through the streets, taking a longer route to avoid the plaza. They came to the street where the Nostalgia Tavern stood.

But the comic shop was gone. Every square inch had been burned to ash.

I.S.S. NEW DESTINY, IMPERIAL LINER.

*LAUNCH SCHEDULED AT 06:00 HOURS
ON THE FIRST DAY OF THE YEAR 2515
FROM PLANET EARTH (SEE 'FINALISED
EVACUATION SCHEDULE')*

DESTINATION: SYSTEM 7769.Q (UNNAMED).

*ARRIVAL DATE PASSED BY THREE YEARS. NO
CONTACT. PRESUMED ENGINE FAILURE.*

ALL HANDS LOST.

REPEAT: ALL HANDS LOST.

– Memo, Imperial air force, 2518

MR SANDWICH

NEW DESTINY WAS a city with another city in its shadow.

One huddled on the ground.

The other rose into the air.

Both lay at the centre of a great plain, surrounded on every side by acres of fields. Corn and wheat, turnips and squash; plant life genetically adapted for difficult terrain. They were spaced out evenly behind barbed wire fences, straining upwards, stems like fingers reaching for the sunshine that cooked them brown and yellow until they sagged back into the soil.

Where did the seeds come from? From the coffers of the *New Destiny*. And what of the water? Piped in from far below, by the grace of God.

No, not God. By the grace of the High Sheriff.

Those seeds were his. Those fields were his. The *New Destiny* was his.

Finders keepers.

Crossing through the farmlands – the high stalks buzzing with hidden insects, bric-a-brac road levelled by hooves and tyres and human feet – the *New Destiny* itself could be seen for the first time. It began as a smudge on the horizon. A mountain, maybe? But no. No mountain could be so *geometric*.

Then, closer, as dusk came on, the city would flicker to life. Only in the dark could it be seen for what it really was: the shape of it, the lines, hard angles, grids of yellow light stretching up to touch the moon. And at the furthest end – and the highest point – a flash of red. It came and went, once every two seconds. Faint but unmissable. A beacon. The top floor, the seat of power.

The mind buckled at such a sight.

It longed to get closer.

But to even touch the *New Destiny*'s hull you had to cross the city that surrounded it. Underland, it was called: a scrap metal ghetto with roads of hardened earth, living off siphoned energy from the engines of the old ship – engines that were meant to carry the great vessel to the galaxy's core. Because the ship lay in a crater, the roads in Underland were all sloped downwards. From the outer edges of the town one could look out over a descending wall of tin rooftops, strung between with laundry and naked electric cables, converging around the sheer wall that was the *New Destiny*'s base. Gates inside were well-marked – and well-guarded, with steel barriers and bulletproof tollbooths to keep out non-residents.

Most inhabitants of Underland were folk who either wanted to move into the *New Destiny*, or had been kicked out and couldn't afford to return. It was limbo; a waiting room, a rubbish heap. Nowhereseville.

Naturally, the only businesses that flourished in Underland were the bars.

The Scavenger was a rathole of some renown. It had much to commend it: proximity to the *New Destiny* (so close that customers could go out the back door and piss against the hull), no fewer than seven different types of spirits for sale, and a fully working set of lights, advertised by the flickering pink sign that hung above the street and spat at passers-by.

It was a typically dismal evening in the Scavenger – tense and half empty. In one corner a record player warbled feebly. *Rumours*. Again. It played to a resentful silence, punctured occasionally by the hollow *poc* of a ball colliding into one another on what proprietor Dara Liu called 'the stickball table'. Nobody knew the rules of stickball. All they had to go on was a poster Dara had hung on the wall of some serious-looking men bending over the table with the stick angled lengthways. People invented their own ways of playing. Nobody ever seemed to win.

Dara paced up and down behind the bar, working at a stain on the base of a wine glass. He was nervous. Dara was usually nervous. He rode through life at the crest of a great tidal wave of anxiety. It had made him bald early on in life, though he still took pride in the handlebar moustache that pulled his lips down into a permanent walrus frown.

He came to the counter's curved edge and turned on a heel to survey the room yet again. Nothing had changed. He was still there, the bastard, reclined with his bourbon in the booth on the far wall, merry as the new day. Dara couldn't understand it. The Deputy had access to all the luxuries New Destiny had to offer – there were restaurants on the upper levels where you could look out the window and see the curvature of the Earth, or so went the stories – but he slunk down to Underland more often than not, to shoot stickball and watch the record skip and stutter. Deputy Seawall seemed at home among the grime.

For the barman, Seawall's presence posed a problem. There were certain people in Underland who would always get their drinks for free: that was to be expected, for business bows to power above all else. But the Deputy was on another level. Seawall was the kind of man who could take out all the money in the till, spit in the nearest glass, give Dara a quick kick in the testicles, and still expect to hear '*have a good night, sir*' as he walked out the door.

But all he did was sit and watch the room.

It boded ill. Oh, it all boded ill.

At the other end of the bar sat another customer who was starting to trouble Dara, a man he was mentally referring to as 'Mr Sandwich'. He had a thick neck and eyes like a basset hound, bloodshot and watery, sagging into his cheeks beneath a jutting brow. The physique of a thug, but the clothes of a wealthy trader – a crisp suit shirt, cuffs linked in silver. He'd ordered sweetened water and a meat sandwich and had enquired about the sandwich no fewer than three times since he'd ordered it. Every time, Dara told him the same thing – the chef was working on it, she'd send it through soon – and the man smiled and nodded. A minute later he'd ask again.

To top it all, some homeless woman was throwing up in the toilet.

Dara rubbed his brow with the back of his wrist.

Spacemen, he was sure, never had to deal with such things. *Heathens,* he corrected himself. *Sinners.*

On the wall behind the bar, sealed in a plastic case,

Dara displayed a memento from Saint's Cradle – a beer bottle, chipped, murky brown, picked up on a month-long pilgrimage many years ago. It felt like an appropriate token for a barman. He prayed every day that Gaia would deliver him a better job.

'Excuse me.'

It was Mr Sandwich. Dara held back a sigh.

'Look, pal, it'll be ready when it's—'

'I need to pee.' There was a whining keen to his voice that reminded Dara of a child. 'The cubicle door is locked? I can't get in.'

Dara gave the glass one last wipe and set it down. 'Sit tight. I'll clear it out.'

He circled around the bar – Dara was not a fit man, but he could move like a demon when annoyed – came to the toilet and hammered on the door.

'Excuse me,' he called, as impolitely as he could. '*Excuse me?*'

There was a pause. Then the door swung open, and the homeless woman loomed over him, wavering on her feet.

'All done,' she said.

She brushed past him, almost colliding with Mr Sandwich as he dashed towards the open cubicle, with more half-muttered apologies. Mr Sandwich ignored her. He leapt into the cubicle and slammed himself in.

Dara watched the homeless woman place herself at the bar. The cracked plastic cushion on top of the stool sagged as she sat, sighing dust. She picked up her glass, found it empty save for a dribble, drank the dribble, smacked her lips loudly, and resumed staring at nothing. She'd been far along when she came in, and had then sunk herself deeper into the amber over the course of a steady hour. Enquired about *veteran's discount*.

'We don't keep pets here,' he told her. She'd only hung her head.

From the boots – well-fitting, modern in make – Dara guessed she was another former city resident, kicked out for non-payment of rent. From the look of the rest of her, he guessed she'd been kicked out a while ago.

He felt a chill like a loose draught and turned to see if one of his loutish customers had propped the door open. But it was closed. Then he turned some more, and saw that he was being studied by the flint-chip eyes of Deputy Seawall.

Seawall raised a hand in Dara's direction. He curled one finger. Dara moved towards him as if pulled by a hook.

'Yes sir?' he asked, coming to his side. 'Everything alright?'

'Everything's dandy, thank you, friend.' The Deputy had the look of a strip of worn leather, and when he smiled, he did it with all his teeth. 'Say, can I ask you something?'

'Of course, sir.'

'Your customer with the stomach trouble.' He indicated the homeless woman with a slight glance. 'How long's she been here?'

'Oh – uh—' Dara worked his apron into nervous bunches as he spoke. 'About an hour, sir, since before you arrived. She's not local to this part of town.'

'She's a lot less local than that, if you ask me…' Seawall rubbed his chin. 'Do you know where she's headed?'

'Same old story – tried to get inside the *New Destiny*, couldn't pay the toll. Seemed quite upset about it.'

'And now she's eating her troubles, eh?' He took out a slip of fives and tucked it into Dara's pocket. 'Okie dokie. Thank you, friend. Much appreciated.'

'Of course, sir. Thank you, sir.' Dara paused. 'Wait, did you say eating?' He turned. *'Mother God!'*

The homeless woman had two hands wrapped around a sandwich – *Mr Sandwich's sandwich* – and was biting into it with mammalian relish. The chef stood opposite, wiping her hands on a cloth.

'Is it good?' asked the chef.

'So guh!' she replied, mouth open.

'Vic!' Dara beelined for the counter. 'Vic, what are you doing?'

'Serving food.' Her hands went up on her hip. 'What are *you* doing?'

Dara was reaching around to try to grab the sandwich away, but the woman moved well for a drunkard, and could evade his every reach with a jerk of his head, still eating the whole time.

'Ma'am – ma'am, that isn't – *ma'am*—'

Too late. The last corner of the crust slipped between her lips and was gulped down in one.

'Gaia, she's like a python,' mused Vic.

The homeless woman beamed with tipsy pride.

Pounding steps announced the arrival of Mr Sandwich at the bar. He looked at the crumb-scattered plate, and then at the homeless woman, who froze, licking one finger.

'My sandwich,' he said.

'I'm so sorry sir.' Dara glided to Mr Sandwich's side. 'It was our mistake. We'll make you another one, double-time.'

Vic cleared her throat. 'Actually Dara. That was the last of the bread.'

Between his temples, Dara could physically feel his blood pressure mounting. 'How about some soup?' he offered. 'A lovely bowl of soup, sir?'

Mr Sandwich said nothing. Rage had made him white from the hollow of his collar to the crown of his head. His eyes were fixed on the homeless woman with hate and disbelief. 'Why did you do that?' he asked her. Again, that childish rising tone. It almost sounded like he was holding back tears. The woman, who was lagging behind everyone else by a few seconds, finally realised what was happening.

'Oh my stars. I'm so, so sorry. So so sorry.' She was making a concerted effort to be sincere, but there was a part of her that wanted to laugh. It shone through her eyes. 'I couldn't say no. Just couldn't say no. It's been so long since I had a sandwich, you know, I...' Mr Sandwich did not look consoled. 'Look. I'll pay you back, see?' Drawing a ten from her back pocket, she lifted his hand and pressed it into his palm. 'That's it. That's all I've got.' She turned back to Dara. 'Could we get another—'

'Get out,' he said flatly.

'Okay, okay.' She picked her hat up and set it back on her head. 'Okay.' She nodded to Vic. 'Thank you. Best cook on the *planet*.'

Vic's cheeks reddened a little. 'Now, now.'

'Literally.'

'Get out!' Dara almost shrieked.

'Okay, okay, okay.' She zigzagged towards the rear door, humming tunelessly.

'Now, sir.' Dara turned his attention back towards Mr Sandwich, who was standing like a pillar. 'About that soup.'

Mr Sandwich was staring downwards. He relaxed his hand, and the slip, crumpled almost to powder, floated to the floor. Then he lurched out of the back exit, following the homeless woman.

'Ho, ho,' came a voice behind Dara. It was Seawall, who had moved to one of the stools without a sound. He lifted his bourbon, inhaled gently. 'I love it when this happens.'

Dara took a napkin from the counter and dabbed at his forehead. 'When what happens, sir?'

'When a problem solves itself.'

THE STARS IN Underland were split between the real and the fake. There were more of the real stars, but the fake ones shone brighter and closer. When she stumbled out of the bar the homeless woman was met by a wall of this false night sky. An endless inverted horizon, arching up to the edge of the world, and she stared up at it, speechless, wondering if the vertigo would make her throw up again. It didn't.

Then she brought her gaze down, down, to eye level, to the place where the spaceship was half buried in the ground. Graffiti writ with knives, like the scratchings of a dozen mad animals, covered the *New Destiny*'s hull – curses, praises, calls to action, or even just the author's name, for posterity. She placed her hand on the cool surface.

Where are you, love?

There was a blare of scratchy music, and she turned to see the man from before emerging, as wide as the door frame he walked through. She sensed violence in him even before he slipped off his cufflinks, even before he rolled his sleeves up over swollen forearms, up to the elbow that struggled to poke out amid the heap of pale flesh.

'Hey, now.' She raised both palms. 'I said sorry, right? Didn't I say sorry?'

He shook his great hands loose one by one, raised them in fists.

'Fine. But before we begin, can I just say—' She finished the sentence by kicking him between the legs. He let out a hoarse cry, instinctively dropping his hands to his groin, and she took the opening and thrust two fingers into his throat.

'You hit—' The man's voice came out half strangled. '—my soft bits.'

'I sure did, starshine. And you know what else? I—'

The man's face scrunched into itself, reddening, mouth open and warped like a rubber band. His big eyes shone with hurt and confusion.

She lowered her hands a little. 'Hey. Look. I was only—'

Then she was on the ground. It was raining. It was raining in one ear. Wetness down the jawbone. The large man was above her.

And

His

Foot

Was

Coming

She rolled.

Down, and lifting again, and in the acrid soil he'd left a crater, much like the crater the town was built in, a small Underland if you will, a small disaster zone, and moved away again and thought

I'm not high. I'm drunk, I'm not high –

Nothing, no pill popped from a mottled shell, was twisting her vision, meaning that the foot she had dodged – just barely even *thought* to dodge – would have made a grisled cavern of her head if she'd been just a mite slower.

Just a mite slower.

She sprawled back, up, onto her feet. Naked static cut her brain in half. But look, here, another opportunity – because he was pausing in shock, pure disbelief, that someone he'd hit had gotten up again. *Finish it now*. A hit to the chin would do it. She threw. But his arm was up already, impossibly fast for someone of his bulk, and her fist glanced off his elbow, ripping pain up to her shoulder blade like she'd punched a wall. That hand was ruined. She could feel it, even through a haze of whisky, the knuckle fractured and sunken back into the flesh.

One arm whipped out. That *speed!* She dodged backwards, but –

Oh God –

His reach was long, she'd miscalculated. A clip of a connection over her right eye. The skin split. One half of the world was static, the other drenched in red.

It was time. Her hand went to her hip.

But the holster was empty.

No.

But that wasn't possible.

How?

She'd never once –

The fall.

Time to run, then.

But the scratched-up hull was at her back, and the man was in front, stepping closer, raising his hands again, jaw wired shut. Buzzing with the energy that hate can give. She would have to pick a side and dart. No time to consider – she went left, towards a clear path. Through the curtain of blood on her right eye another blow came rushing. It sank into her abdomen, into the ribs, which snapped like matchsticks – one, two, three, four.

She keeled.

Oh my stars oh emperor oh fathermotherallthegods that HURTS.

Pain, no matter how many times you feel it, is always the worst it's ever been.

No time like the present.

Blood in the mouth, lapping against clenched teeth like liquid rust. His hand was on her shoulder, for leverage. The physics of it were so simple a moron could understand. The hand was a hammer. The hull was an anvil. And between that, she was just butcher's stuff – what was left of her, anyway, being lifted up one-handed like she was a child –

But even as a child she never lost a fight –

How absurd, she thought. How absurd, after everything that had happened, to die over a sandwich. But she'd started it, hadn't she? She'd hit first. Even after she swore off the whole business of hurting people.

Clarity, now.

This was punishment.

Of course it was.

Not just the pain and the death. The whole hilarious unfairness of it, to have come so far, and then have it end with her squished like a bug at the bottom of a wrecked cruiser. Like a pointless dream. Like a bad joke.

Stop punishing yourself.

A memory like a gasp of air.

Oh, Noelle.

She looked at the man who was about to kill her, at his pupils so large and black she thought she might see galaxies floating in there.

Then she spat blood.

He cried out, more in disgust than distress, free hand rushing to wipe his eyes. But it worked: the grip relaxed, and she was down, stumbling free – where is it – *there!*

Winking out at her, a shard of pure silver in the blackened muck. She stooped to pick it up and her legs gave in and she fell, but still her hand took it up – a thin line of blood trailed down the stock – and now she was on her side, panting, pointing it up at him.

The man took a step. Saw he was at gunpoint. He dropped his hands with a doleful air.

'No fair,' he said.

In that moment she wanted so badly just to kill him – more than she wanted anything, more than she wanted to not be in pain, more than she wanted to be home again. Not out of rage, but just so she could feel, even for a moment, like she was in control. Like she was safe. Just so she could say, *I shot the monster and then I went to sleep, the end.*

She held the pistol steady.

The man waited for her to shoot him.

When she didn't, he rolled his sleeves down again. His huge body was shivering, because the centre of Underland was a damp and airless place, especially at night. He looked around the alley as if he'd woken up from a daze. Some other emotion was taking him now: hunger again, most likely. He raised his head into the air and breathed, nostrils dilating, searching the evening currents for the next thing to pull him along.

He was not as pitiable a creature as you might assume. His only real fault was that he could feel just one emotion at a time. When that feeling was gone, he let it go entirely; there was no resentment in him. And as she watched him lumber away, the side of his face glowing a soft yellow with light from some distant window in the ship-city above, the woman found it hard to resent him too.

She hurt so much it hardly mattered either way.

FOURTH INTERLUDE

Deputy Seawall followed the trail of blood until he found the woman from space passed out in a bin. He nudged her with a steel-capped toe. 'You alive?'

There was a long pause, long enough that the Deputy got his hopes up. Then she groaned and cringed away – perhaps from his prodding foot, perhaps from a phantom somewhere behind her eyes.

'Hmm.' He rubbed his chin, surveying the street around them. No witnesses. He mused to himself: 'Alrighty then. No time like the present,' and drew out from his chest holster a six-shooter revolver. Lovely piece of kit: jet handle, floral engraving on the cylinder. Made a proper *click* when you cocked the hammer. Deputy Seawall had a complex relationship with the Church of Gaia, but he held a zealot's love for the tactile and the analogue, especially when it came to guns.

He pointed it at the woman's head.

A voice, mottled with age and static, buzzing from a clip on the back of his belt: 'Aidan. Come in, Aidan.' For a second he wavered, pulled almost physically between his options. *Shoot or answer? Shoot or answer?* The voice piped up again: 'Damn it, boy, you pick up this second or so help me God...'

He holstered the revolver and unclipped a compact transceiver from his hip. 'Sorry, sir. I was just heading somewhere quiet.'

'Where are you now?' it demanded.

'Downtown.'

'Downtown? Since *when?*'

'Only a couple days ago.' Seawall bent his head, massaging the bridge of his nose as he spoke. 'I'm just – chasing up some leads. Didn't have time to come up.'

'Uh-huh. Sure you didn't.'

'Oh, give me a—'

His raised voice disturbed the woman in the bin. She muttered something, jerking her fingers. Unkeen to wake up his quarry, Seawall paced over to the street's end, asking, 'Are you gonna bust my balls about this all night, sir? I'm kinda busy.'

'Maybe I will! If I feel like it! I'm...' The voice on the line collapsed into a scorched, rattling coughing fit. Seawall held the receiver away from his ear in faint distaste. When it was over, the voice sounded wearier, older. 'Sweet Mother beneath me. That was a bad one.'

'Sounded it, sir.'

'Listen. Forget those leads. They can wait for today. Just come up and see me, alright? We're having problems with the Project. I need you up here.'

'Okay, sir.'

'*Tonight,* Aidan. Not tomorrow.'

Only with great effort did Seawall keep from audibly grinding his teeth: 'You got it, sir.'

'Thattaboy.'

The line went dead. In a hurry now, and very much in the mood to kill someone, Seawall stalked back to the bins, revolver in hand.

But she was gone.

He swore. Searched. Ran down to the opposite end, where the road split into four, no, five different alleyways, all of them dark and crooked.

No sign of her.

Anger nearly took him, then – anger like shrapnel that he had to expel from his body – but there was nothing there for him to spend it on, nothing to transfer it to, except a few rubbish bins and a stretch of pavement. So instead he sighed. Smiled. Tucked that shard away with the rest.

'Fuck me,' he said lightly. 'Talk about a charmed life.'

DANCERS UNDERGROUND

IN THE AGE of interstellar travel, the foremost task of any space-faring individual was to acclimate themselves to the hum. Gentle, but omnipresent; you felt it as much as you heard it, in your feet and hands, nestled gently in the back of your skull. Some pilots claimed the hum helped them sleep at night. Farmers leaving home for the first time were known to wake up screaming, convinced that they were being hunted by a swarm of insects.

The smaller the vessel, the greater the reverberations. So the hum on the *New Destiny* was faint, almost imperceptible. It hovered at the edge of audibility.

Still, she could feel it.

With one hand splayed on the wall, the woman – listed in the discreet bureaucratic language of the craft's computer system as *'unclassified guest'* – could feel the ship's vibrations all the way up to her first finger joint. So different to the last vessel she'd travelled on, where the corridors thrummed like the arteries of a great heart...

This was no trick – or if it was, it was a trick

indistinguishable from reality. The engines were on. The ship was running.

There was hope.

Her face was turned outward at the window, towards a panoramic ocean view. A brisk morning, from the looks of it: the bruise-coloured waves moved restlessly into one another, trimmed with spittle foam under a glowing grey sky. She ran a finger lengthways across the glass. The ocean vanished. Now she was looking down a mountain pass, chalk-white cliffs falling down into a glittering stream hugged by shrubs and golden grass.

Swipe. A valley of snow-capped pines.

Swipe. A grove of olive trees.

Swipe. A jungle.

Swipe. A garden.

Swipe.

The screen went black, and the room shrank into the airless box that it truly was. Now she could see her reflection in the empty screen: two eyes smudged in violet, a fresh set of stitches on the forehead. For the last half an hour she'd been rising back up through a gauzy wall of whisky and painkillers, and now she was sharp enough to feel herself ache with each inhale. But the pain was good. It kept her awake, kept her focused.

She'd sold the gun. Sold it to an 'onboarding officer' – some spotty kid inside a tollbooth with a stamp and a rifle slung over his shoulder, yawning enormously at the top of the dawn shift, who snapped to attention when he saw what she was offering.

'You sure?' he kept repeating. 'You sure sure?' When she confirmed that she was indeed *sure,* he'd stuck his head over the counter to make sure nobody was watching. 'Okay.' A flurry of ruffling papers, the clacking of a keyboard. 'New residents need ratifying, but I can put you in as a petitioner. Gets you a room and lower-deck access. Will that work?'

'Yeah. Whatever.'

'Okay, okay.' Two-fingered, he slid a yellow card over the counter. She went to take it. 'Nuh-uh.' He pressed the card down with one finger. '*Give it.*'

So she did. She handed over the gun. The boy whispered something embarrassing, '*Come to Papa*' or something similar, and stroked it up the side, looking admiringly down the barrel. She said, flatly: 'Can I go?'

'Uh-huh. Your room is on deck three.' Without taking his eyes off the pistol, he added: 'And go to the med ward. You look fucked-up.'

At the med ward, a dark-suited and irritable young surgeon – somehow different from the dark-suited and irritable young surgeon she'd met previously – stitched her up and made her swallow two doses of a substance she knew from field hospitals, a foul-tasting fluid called knitbone.

'Mind your ribs,' she'd said. 'They're healed, but they'll be tender for a while. And drink some water.' It was an enormous room lined with oval beds, most of them empty.

'Where'd you get that stuff?' she asked. 'Knitbone?'

'Do you have insulin?'

'Yes.' Then, with suspicion: 'Why?'

'Just curious.'

From there she moved a floor upwards, to the promised room. It was tiny, coloured yellow and white, and sparsely furnished with a few robust-looking objects – a bed, a table, a chair. The bed in particular made for an intoxicatingly tempting prospect. But there was no telling how long she'd sleep for if she let herself, how much time would be wasted. And she had no time; her ears were primed for the sound of pounding boots, the command to throw her hands in the air. Without that pistol she'd be forced to comply.

So instead she sat on the edge of the chair and held her head in her hands.

What now? she thought. *What next?*

Signal. I need to send a signal.

Then she went to the window, to see if it could be compelled to turn into a map.

Close inspection revealed that the blank screen was not entirely blank. In white letters on the top right were the words

YOU ARE NUMBER: 776.

The Guest touched the number, and a pop-up appeared in the centre.

WELCOME TO THE NEW DESTINY!
THE TIME IS NOW: **07:29**
YOUR PLACE IN THE VISITOR QUEUE IS: **776**.
THE HIGH SHERIFF THANKS YOU FOR YOUR PATIENCE.
MAY GOD HOLD YOU DOWN.

There was a scrolling menu along the side, with a list of banal options: entertainment, map, inbox. At *map,* her heart jolted. She touched it, and was presented with a cartoon icon of a spaceship hovering over a 3D rendering of Earth.

Flight map, she thought sourly. *Right.*

Entertainment led to an empty scroll wheel. And the inbox, was of course –

Inbox (1)

She pressed a finger to the message, and words filled the
screen:

LOUNGE. LOOSE WINDOW. 10 A.M.

There was no sender listed.

'Huh.'

The door slid aside at a press from the card. Outside, a
crowd of people was sweeping past, chattering excitedly.
She cast another glance back at the window. Ocean
waves. There was no time to second-guess herself. She
ducked outside, into the streets of the *New Destiny*.

Corridors, more accurately. But they were wide enough
to feel like streets, and busy enough, too. People brushed
around her, talking, clutching handbags and suitcases,
absorbed in one another. There was a busy, jubilant
atmosphere. Every now and then a note of song or a
raised voice rose above the chatter. Many of them wore
monochrome outfits – pale grey, whitish-blue. A few
strolled around in suits and dresses and were given a
respectfully wide berth by the others.

Caught in the stream and afraid to raise notice, she
moved with the crowd, passing a dozen doors like the one
she had emerged from. The walls and ceiling were all the
same shade of wan anaemic green, and she was sure they
were twisting, sliding clockwise and counterclockwise,
like a tunnel of cogs. Was the floor strictly level, or was
there a gravitational generator pulling them all down?
Which way was west, east? Which way was up?

Water, she remembered. *I forgot to drink water.*

The crowd flowed and grew under its own momentum,
and the Guest found herself lost in the centre, unable to

see the sides. Like a swollen dam they burst out into a huge chamber. She recognised it as a hangar; docking tubes dangled empty along the side. One wall was taken up by a vast aperture – an airlock – which was open just a fraction, so a thin beam of natural light shone down. Positioned in the path of this beam was a hydraulic lift, raised well above the crowd, upon which stood a woman in shimmering robes of green and brown, her wiry white hair cut in a half-dome, her neck overhung with half a dozen rings of beads. The Guest, who had been carried close to the front, gazed up at the Preacher and was reminded of a mushroom.

The crowd went quiet.

The Preacher raised her hands.

'When the waters run dry?'

The Guest turned, startled. The Preacher's voice, high and clear, rang out from a speaker in every corner.

The congregation murmured in obedient unison: *'Drink dust.'*

'When the floods rise?'

'Breathe water.'

The Guest lowered her head, tried to move her lips in sync with the others.

'And when the fires burn?'

'Bathe in the ashes.'

The Preacher's hands lowered, and she smiled warmly down at them. 'Thank you. Just checking we're all awake.'

Chuckles in the crowd. This was a well-worn joke. The Preacher held a scrap of paper high above her head. 'I want to talk to you about this today. Can everyone see?' Craning necks. The Guest could make out a splodge of colour, some rough writing. The Preacher went on. 'This artefact was recently discovered, hidden away in a chamber on the second level. I will describe it to you now: a crayon sketch of a purple planet with a house built on the surface. The caption reads *Our New Home…* It is not the work of a great artist.'

Rumbles of laughter. The Preacher folded the drawing up, squeezed it in her hands. 'But it inspired me to some interesting thoughts,' she went on. 'The child that drew this was, of course, a sinner – a child of sinners. And we can see that sin even in something so simple as a drawing. The desire to abandon our Mother Gaia is the greatest evil. It is unforgivable. It is dirty. Foul.'

Agitated shuffling. Somebody coughed.

'But doesn't it seem cruel, too?' she asked. 'This child never made it to their new home. They died, along with their family and everyone else, when the ship malfunctioned. Doesn't that seem unfair?'

Silence.

'It's easy to think that way. It's easy to feel sorry for this child, this innocent. But remember that their death was an act born of love. It was love that made Gaia call this ship back from the sky – love for Her children, even as they tried to escape Her embrace.'

The Preacher raised her arms again, now to indicate the walls of the hangar, the domed ceiling. 'We live every day surrounded by the detritus of sin, in the shell of a poisoned dream. But this ship is also a reminder of the natural forces that even our most advanced ancestors could not escape. The forces of love. Of justice. Of gravity.' She folded her hands on the railing. 'When our Lord High Sheriff discovered the *New Destiny*, he saw in these ruins not just shame, but hope. For it is evidence of the one redeeming quality of our species – that ultimately, we are powerless. Praise Gaia.'

It was just two words, spoken flat, but it issued forth a roar from the crowd that scared the Guest out of her skin.

'*PRAISE!*'

'And praise her son, our Lord, the High Sheriff.'

'*PRAISE!*'

'Praise them. Work hard. And pity—' The Preacher held the drawing up again, creased and battered. 'And pity the Departed souls, who were not worthy of being called back to fertilise our Mother's skin. May their corpses rot in the great black vacuum.'

And though she knew she was being paranoid – and knew that she was near the front, and that she stood out in the crowd, tall as she was – for the final line of the sermon, the Guest was convinced that the Preacher was looking directly down at her.

Afterwards the congregation dispersed into streams. The Guest followed a group heading the way she'd come, and then split away at a random junction. She strode around in circles, ignoring the curious gazes of the passers-by. Signage in the *New Destiny* was a mixture of original – embedded into the walls, directing towards stairwells, accommodation, storage – and new, painted sheaths of tin, announcing WHOLESALER or CHEAP REPAIRS At last, faded and half hidden in the wall, she saw an etching of the word *Lounge*.

This directed her to a low-ceilinged room filled with squat, uncomfortable-looking furniture, where people buttoned up in brightly coloured aprons sold food hot and cold. There was a general clamour of cutlery and muted conversation.

Along the wall were circular windows – real, this time,

small and thickened, built for travel. The Guest strolled alongside them until she found one prised away from the casing.

She looked around. People were knotted together in groups, talking quietly, enjoying a kind of public privacy. She pressed gently on the glass, and it swung to the side. She rested both elbows on the sill and leant out, squinting in the sudden sunlight. Underland stretched out beneath her like a carpet of wet moss, seeping into the patchwork fields beyond, which themselves melted into the hazy blue hills.

'Morning, Darling. Got a cigarette?'

It was a voice that seemed to float out of nowhere. The Guest recognised it with a jolt.

'No,' she replied.

'Shame.' A sigh. 'It makes good cover.'

From above her head the Guest heard a few light taps, and then a cloud of tobacco-ash poured down and settled in her hair. She twisted, trying to look up. 'Hey! Watch—'

'Eyes forward.' The voice was curt. 'This is all strictly incognito, understand?'

She twisted reluctantly back around. 'What are you doing here?'

'I live here, remember? When I'm not chasing some dream.'

'Huh.' The Guest mused over this, stroking the ash out of her hair. 'Did you follow me?'

'After a fashion. I pulled some strings. All under the radar, don't fret.'

'Uh-huh.'

'You slipped onboard quite quickly. I'm impressed.'

'Yeah, but…' *I lost my gun.* The Guest couldn't bring

herself to say it. 'The preacher woman. I think she might have noticed me.'

'The High Preacher?' The voice was aghast. 'Ursula Ramirez? She *saw* you?'

'I don't know. Maybe. I was near the front.'

'Mother of— That woman is one of the most powerful people in this city. Do you understand? If she of all people knows that you're—' There was some anxious fumbling, the click and re-click of a lighter, and a long exhale. Warm pipe smoke floated loose in the air. 'Look,' the voice said. 'It wasn't wildly easy to track you down. I'm not expecting payment, but – I need you to answer this question honestly. Can you do that?'

'Yes.'

'Why are you here?'

'I want to see the High Sheriff.'

A snort. 'Yes, Darling. You and everyone else.'

The Guest hesitated. She took a breath. The air was thinner and cooler than it had been on the ground, and she could feel an unsteadiness in her lungs, a tremble. When she spoke again, she started slowly. 'This ship still works,' she said. 'The networks are running. The engines are on. So the communicators must work, right? If something crashed somewhere on the planet – you could signal them from here, right? So if I asked him…'

No response.

'Right?'

'You're looking for your ship.' The voice was quiet. It wasn't a question.

The Guest's throat felt like a hollow reed.

'You'll need to get higher. Right to the top.'

She exhaled, still trembling. 'So you think there's a chance?'

'I don't know. I don't like this. If there was a crash it'd be big news around here. They'd be selling the scrap at a premium. But I've not heard anything – the High Sheriff could be hiding it. But I don't know...'

'Just tell me how to get upstairs.'

A sigh.

'Well, you can't take the lifts with a petitioner's pass. And the stairs are not an option. The higher you go, the stricter they get. So that leaves the guts. The good news is the High Sheriff doesn't control the guts. But the people in there... they do things their own way. They've been here longer than he has.'

A klaxon sounded.

'*Shit,*' said the voice. 'I have to go.'

'I don't—'

'Find a vent. Follow the heat.'

'What do you mean?' The Guest had to restrain herself to keep from yelling. She leant out further. 'Wait. *Ava!*'

But she was gone.

Finding a ventilation shaft proved easy. Being alone with one, not so much. The Guest was starting to get surreptitious glares in the lounge, so she left, turning down increasingly smaller corridors until she came to a dead-end hallway, grimy and underlit. Here the sterile smell that swamped the rest of the *New Destiny* vanished, and left in its place a greasy, mechanical odour. There was nothing there except for a door marked **stuck** and a metal grille on the base of the wall with creeping rust around the edge. The hum, when she touched the grille, felt just a fraction stronger.

For a while the Guest switched between slamming the edge of the ventilation shaft with her heel and, when pedestrians passed in the adjacent street, leaning against the wall: nothing here to see. If anyone stared, she'd stare back until they hurried on. At last the casing came loose enough for her to wrench it free. She peered inside. It was nothing but a lightless maw.

She dropped to her elbows and crawled in.

It was roomy enough. A short person might have managed on hands and knees; but she was forced to shuffle, squinting, groping along, stubbing her fingers on the segmented metal. Each slight bump sent low, hollow vibrations down the vent.

Her hand met resistance. She thought it was a wall, but feeling along she discovered a branch in the path.

Follow the heat.

She pressed a palm to either side. One felt warmer. She twisted around the corner and shuffled onwards, repeating the process at the next junction, and the next. If there was a pattern, she couldn't follow it. Deeper and deeper. Soon she was moving just to stave off panic, thinking that if something happened nobody would know about it for many weeks, and even then just because of the smell – which would be made all the more pungent by the stale, warm air that tickled her face…

She didn't hear them approach. Even their breathing was silent. All she knew was an increase in heat, the closeness of another presence, and then something sharp pressed up against the skin.

'*What do you want?*'

Their voice was high and lilting. There were no threats in the question. Nevertheless the Guest shot up in terror and smacked her skull against the top of the vent, sending a baritone chord singing down through the shaft.

They both waited patiently for the note to stop.

'I'm trying to go up,' she whispered.

'*What will you do?*'

That question was easy enough to answer. 'Anything.'

Scrambling. Something was pressed into her hand – an ink-stained slip, though it was too dark to read.

'*An invitation to the Mouth,*' they said. '*Do you accept?*'

'Y– yes?'

'*Then come.*'

The figure slid back soundlessly into the chute and the Guest scrambled to follow, turning down bend after bend until they emerged into the place called the Mouth. She stood up and took it in, wiping her hands down on her trousers. It was a tall spherical cavern, run around with walkways and ladders, the walls pockmarked with dozens of jutting shaft-mouths and sluggishly spinning fans. Grubby red lights appeared at intervals in the floor, dim enough that they revealed only vague textureless shapes in the place of objects, half-blinding the untrained eye. She couldn't see how high it went – maybe the very top. Heat lay over everything in a sickly film. The friend from the shaft was revealed to be a slim, long-limbed youth with sandy hair and moony yellow-white eyes.

'I am Byker,' they said, looking towards, but not quite at, her. 'I will take you to the Queen.' Byker started around the chamber at a light step, gesturing towards the centre. 'Mind the Throat,' they warned. 'It has a way of swallowing outsiders.'

She looked to where they were indicating and felt a touch of nauseous vertigo. There was a hole there. Easy to miss in all the crimson shadows, but wide enough to fit a car. The surface inside looked odd – covered in smooth ridges that seemed to glisten, almost, like some kind of meat –

But Byker moved fast, and she couldn't slow down for a better look.

They came around to a recess, a place where the circular wall fell back into itself, allowing space for a structure – a sort of dais, not an original part of the ship but made up from loose material, crates and pipes and bits of sheeting. Several dozen people were huddled around. Like Byker they were big-eyed and lean, and almost all of them were whispering, with short words and large loose gestures like they were painting with their hands. Everyone seemed to be arguing.

On top of it all, in a high-backed velvet throne, was the Queen: reclining like a fat silkworm in a dress woven from the shards of a broken mirror. He was addressing one of his subjects, who was standing before him in a purplish suit, hands clasped tight behind their back.

'You're quite sure?' The Queen sounded bored. 'Not one note?'

'As if I haven't tried them all a hundred times!' the subject burst out. 'Again and again. I'm telling you, this is down here. We have been *sabotaged*.'

Excited murmuring from the onlookers. The Queen's lip curled. 'Don't take that tone with me, child.'

'I'll take the tone till *you* take action.' They stood tall, shoulders flung back, and aimed an arched finger up at the throne. '*C'est faible!*'

The Queen rolled his eyes. 'Enough. Go to your rehearsal.'

'With my throat cut?' The subject threw their head back, barked out a single, bitter laugh. '*Ha!* I'll try, your Majesty.' They turned and stalked away, watched at all times by the crowds.

'Now, Byker,' the Queen said. 'I see you've tracked down our little chute slug.'

'Yes, your Majesty.'

'Step forward then, o stealthy one. Tell me why you decided to come through from the body beyond, and make such a cacophony in my vents.'

Soft sniggering. The Guest looked back at Byker, who nodded, and whispered: *'Make it good.'*

The Guest stepped up onto the dais, feeling moon-eyes trained on her from all sides. This was beyond surreal, now; she wanted to slap herself, to get back to reality. But there could be no returning. She had no choice but to ride out the dream. The Queen gazed at her down the length of his nose. His eyes were heavy-lidded, painted in a thick, rainbow sheen.

'Your Majesty,' she said, smiling as broadly as her nerves would allow. 'I'm – uh – I'm most grateful to you for agreeing to see me. I need to get to the communications tower on the top of the ship. I was told you have a way up. As I said to Byker, I'll do—'

The Queen cut her off with a theatrical yawn. 'I'm literally falling asleep. Look at me. I'm falling out of my throne.'

More sniggering. The Guest stuttered. 'I-it's—'

'Child.' The Queen gripped the side of his throne and leant down. 'I don't care where you're going. Just tell me what it's all *for*. Hunger? Greed? Rage?' He raised a sculpted eyebrow. 'Or even love?'

'L-love.' She shifted from one foot to the other, a live wire, buzzing with embarrassment. 'It's love, your Majesty.'

'All for love.' He sat back, dagger-long nails gliding over the soft folds of his chin. 'True love?'

She nodded.

'I don't believe you.'

'What?'

'I don't believe that you're in love. Convince me.'

Suddenly the Guest understood something of Earth's religion. It was tempting to pray to the ground, *please, please, swallow me up.* Instead she asked, 'What do you want me to do?'

The Queen sat in expectant silence.

The Guest pressed her lips together.

'I knew—'

She took a deep breath.

'I knew I was in love the first day we met,' she started. 'I saw her and I thought – oh, shit, not now…' She trailed off. 'But I couldn't stop it. It had already happened.'

The Queen considered this.

'We are dancing tonight. But our singer tells me the Throat is cut. We cannot dance without music. Go down the Throat. Undo the cut. If you make it out in time – passage is yours.'

She bowed her head. 'Thank you.'

The Queen snorted. 'Thank me when you're back. *Lover.*'

Byker was tasked with sending her off, and did so with such a grim look that she almost had second thoughts. 'You'll need these.' They passed her a thick-handled wrench and a torch. 'Climb down the Throat. Look for a valve. Turn it. Once you're sure it's open, go up as fast as you can.' As they spoke they mimed it fluidly, climbing, searching, wrenching.

She held the tools in each hand. They felt weighty. 'How dangerous is this?' she asked.

Byker shrugged. 'The Queen has willed it.'

Hardly a comforting answer. In the hugeness of their

pupils, the Guest noticed a diverted gaze. They were looking up, towards her hat. It was a distinctly covetous look.

'Do you want this?'

Startled, a little flushed, they said: 'I was thinking it is likely to fall off. That is all…'

She pulled the hat from her head, held it in both hands, looked at it. *I'm giving away everything today,* she thought. Then she handed it to them. 'Here.'

Wordlessly, reverently, they took it, pinching the frayed lining of the brim.

Their business concluded, she stuck the wrench in the loop of her belt, gripped the torch with her teeth, and approached the rim of the Throat.

'*Wait—*'

Byker's shout was wince-inducingly loud after all the whispering. She turned to see them twisting and wriggling free of something.

'I can't take your shirt,' she protested, but to no avail – Byker draped it around her shoulders like a wreath.

'For your hands,' they said, and then slipped away, leaving her alone at the side of the chasm.

She could see now how she'd been given the illusion of a meat-like surface. The interior of the Throat was lined with pipes – thick and thin, humming and still, overlapping one another like feral black ivy as they fed in and out of the body of the ship. As with the cavern above, there was no way of guessing the depth. She clicked the torch on with her tongue – a candle would have been less feeble, but never mind – and crouched on her haunches, feeling around until she found a pipe suspended low enough from the network to wrap both hands around.

She shuffled closer, and then slung herself over the

edge, ignoring the vehement protesting from her aching midriff. Climbing was easier than she'd feared; the pipes were old and cased in grime, but solid enough, and her hands found joints easily in among the metalwork. When one clumsy foot slipped, it quickly found fresh purchase on some other outcropping. After a while the light of the chamber receded to a distant haze. Still the cavern beneath her showed no signs of ending. Her hands grew sore, and she forced herself to relax them. Torchlight wavered between her teeth.

Probing down for a foothold, she was surprised to find a solid surface. She released one hand, then the other, and finally stood, breathing, shining the light around.

The base of the Throat was a bowl. Pipes ran down from the walls, along the floor and into a malformed growth at the centre, an uneven dome perhaps half a metre high. All of them were connected to this one stem, miles of entrails flung out from a single body. There was a low door on one end – thick as a blast-shield, and locked, when she tried it.

'Okay,' she said, hoping that the sound of her own voice would lift the sense of being in a tomb. It didn't.

She found the dome's valve, a metal disc at the top, about as wide as her hand. It had been secured in place by a fresh plastic zip-tie. She remembered the cry of the singer: *We have been sabotaged*. They'd been right.

Beneath the valve was a faded yellow-black stencil of the word **DANGER**. *Helpful,* she thought. The Guest slid out the wrench and yanked at the zip-tie until it snapped. Immediately the valve started to waver and loosen; she turned it around with little effort, tugging until she heard a sinister hiss emitting from the centre of the dome.

Recalling Byker's warning, she slipped the wrench back into her belt and started to climb again.

A few yards up, the Guest became aware of a warmth under her fingers. Nothing punishing; it was the pleasant temperature of fresh bread. But the pipes had been crevice-cool on the descent. She moved higher, and the heat relented. But as she stopped to get her bearings, she felt the temperature rising again. Not just in that pipe. In all of them.

Dread tightened around her chest.

She tried to climb faster, but she was awkward, laborious. It was becoming almost too hot to touch the metal. Heat was rising from directly below, from where she'd turned the valve. And still the exit was only a smudge.

Her palms tingled with the promise of pain.

But how to hold on?

Byker's shirt. She'd forgotten she was wearing it. With teeth and fingers she ripped it in two, wrapping it around both palms as thick as it would go, and climbed onwards, feeling heat rise like an angry dragon. She knew the bowl-shaped floor would be throbbing with it by now. If she fell she'd be like a steak dropped on a sizzling pan from great height. But there was the light of the exit –

– how long till she let go?

There was no caution in how she moved. She just swung hand to hand, feet scrabbling, arms heavy and numb with exhaustion. A hole burned through Byker's shirt, and the pain made her yelp and she dropped the torch. It pinged below from wall to wall.

– was that her skin that she could smell?

Then a new light filled her eyes, and someone grabbed her by either elbow and hauled her, shaking and panting like a reeled fish, over the lip and onto cooler ground. She spat out every curse she could think of, against the stars, against her ancestors, against the Emperor himself.

'You're back.' It was Byker. They were wearing the new hat; it looked quite fetching.

She shot them a withering smile. 'Surprised?'

They shook their head, then looked mutely down towards her hands. She looked as well. The rags of their shirt had cooked away to a shrivelled husk, her exposed fingertips shiny with blisters.

'You did say anything.'

The Guest's return was met with neither reverence nor gratitude, only muted surprise. On the balconies above they pointed down at her, digging into one another's sides. The Queen, of course, was unimpressed.

'Back by the skin of your teeth, *mon amour,*' he said, slouched back, cheek resting softly on one fist. 'Now, child, don't give me that look. You'd have done it either way. I was only saving you some anxieties on the way down. Now, Byker...'

Byker had been standing to her side with the stance of a person waiting to be dismissed.

'Well done. You may lead the dancing tonight.'

Byker's whole body went rigid, hands slapping soldier-like to their sides. They radiated pure excitement from every pore. 'I'll send this ship soaring,' they declared, quivering. '*Dans le soleil*. I'll burn your eyebrows off.'

'See that you do.'

The Queen fluttered his plump fingers, and Byker spirited away. Before they vanished the Guest saw them leap, spin in a full circle, and land again without breaking pace, fingers clutched tight on the brim of the ranger's hat. Just for the thrill of it.

'Now...' The Queen swept gradually up to his feet, his dress glittering like a clear lake. 'I'm a monarch of my word. You may follow me...' A few members of the crowd stepped forward, but he held up a hand. 'Stand down. Lovers are a danger only to themselves.' He fixed her with a wry look. 'Isn't that right?'

She looked down at her hands, throbbing in time to her pulse, still burning away under the surface. She nodded.

'Come on then. And don't touch anything. I don't want pus on my things.'

The Guest followed the Queen through an archway behind the throne, up a staircase, through a curtain of soft fabrics, and into his personal chambers. It had been an engineer's office in a former life – one wall was taken up by a window of reinforced glass that looked down over the Mouth. There was also a sloped counter of buttons and dials and a dark glass monitor that, judging by the powders and brushes littered around the keyboard, had been repurposed into a cosmetics mirror. Strewn around on the floor were trunks overflowing with clothes, plastic shoes with screwdriver heels, slippers with soles of welded tin; a noticeboard with several dozen earrings tacked to the surface like the scales of some gigantic fish.

'I hope you don't consider me callous,' said the Queen. He swept through the room, bending down over the monitor to admire his face from either side. 'It's a good thing to have the Throat clear. Those tasteless parasites in the Body beyond like to amuse themselves from time to time, trying to hurt us, trying to stop our music.' He swabbed his pinkie in blue powder and dabbed it gently on the top of one eye. 'When I was Byker's age I lost a companion of mine to the Throat. And one does hate to see history repeat itself, *ce n'est pas bon*, not good for the humours. Now, where is it…'

He moved around the swathes of scarves and necklaces draped over the counter until he found, buried deep, a box glued all over with plastic jewels. From inside – he had to pinch it lengthways on account of his nails – he took out a white plastic card.

'Here it is – the skeleton key. It is a gift from my ancestors, unfortunate people, they were…' He looked down at the card, a nostalgic glaze to his heavy-lidded eyes. 'I had a thought when I was younger that I would go up to the top and shoot the man that runs this place. But I was continually getting distracted, you know, keeping my little children in check, and before I knew it I had grown too old to be a martyr.' He held it out to her. 'You can go upstairs, *mon amour*, but be careful. Remember that it is always better to live…'

She took the key, squeezing it hard. 'Thank you. I—'

There was movement in the chamber below, and the Queen turned his head sharply, looking down through the glass. Bodies were forming into rows. 'Ah, they are getting ready to start. I must go. Without me presiding it will be chaos.' He gestured to a second door, opposite the one they had entered from. 'Keep going up and you will reach a lift. It will open to the card. That will take you to the uppermost levels.'

The Guest nodded, half listening, half entranced by the movements below.

'*Je suis désolé*. It is not for outsiders to see.'

She nodded, struggling not to look again. As the Queen made his way to the exit she blurted out: 'Why not?'

The Queen paused, one hand lifting the fabric curtain.

'True beauty,' he said, with a smile like a brush-stroke, 'is a delicate thing.'

With that, he let the curtain drop.

The Guest longed to run to the window and watch the dancing, but she forced herself to leave. *I'll tell her about this someday,* she thought.

The door led through to a walkway, another of the ring-shaped platforms that circled the chamber, connected at intervals by ladders. It was deserted. Everyone was at the dance.

Except –

Across the chamber, a flash of purple caught her eye. She recognised it as the one from before, the person called the singer. She could see the singer's back only, that form-fitting velvet suit stretched taut over the shoulders. They were sitting in front of something – a machine? If that was the right word. It was as if a segment of the Throat had been cut away, revealing a cross-section of delicately fluted piping many yards wide and high. They spread like branches from something over which the singer was hunched, fiddling with something she couldn't see.

Being a born performer, the singer had a sixth sense for a curious gaze, and they whipped around, fixing on her instantly. On seeing her face, they broke out into a grin that was almost manic, and clapped their hands together.

'BRAVO!' they yelled. Each clap boomed across the empty space. '*BRAVO!* Now go, lover, before we change our mind and SHOVE' – they gestured brutally – 'you back down our THROAT!'

There was no need to tell her twice. She hurried up the staircase two steps at a time, and the next, and the next, until her legs and lungs were burning. Each platform had its own clutter – bedrolls, boxes of clothes, food, scattered tools. Only when she was sure she was out of sight did she permit herself to look down.

The effect was like looking through a kaleidoscope. A mass of colour, specks of life swirling in perfect, ever-shifting coordination. Were they dancing yet? Or just assembling? It was too far to tell.

But still. The effect was mesmeric.

Reluctantly she resumed her climb, trying to fix her focus upwards, back to the goal that had been, for so long, the source of single-minded pursuit. She was almost close enough to permit wild fantasies – like what the message would say, if she was able to send one out: *I'm here. I'm okay. Where are you? Are you okay?*

Also, if she had the space: *I love you.*

Also: *I miss you.*

Also: *The last time we said goodbye, I wish I'd held on just a little tighter. I wish I'd stayed there just another second. I wish I'd buried my face in your neck and told you how much I love you. I wish I wish I wish.*

With each new level the circumference of the chamber shrank and shrank, until the platforms grew to cover the whole floor, connected by a spindly spiral staircase at the centre. The Guest paused again here, resting a hand on the rail and looking down at the layers of metal mesh and emptiness beneath her.

It started as a single note, delicate as an eggshell. Then another, firmer, richer, deeper. Then another. The scale trickled down, a melody that built momentum until it paused to touch the base of the octave. There was a pause like a breath. Then they came together and made a chord.

A *chord!*

So rich it turned her blood to wine, every hair lifted,

skin going up in a wave of prickles – with so many disparate parts it shouldn't have worked, but it did, somehow, like some strange animal lost to time. The chord sank into the minor like an exhale, an inversion that was also a perfect fit.

The strangest thing of all was that she wasn't hearing it. Not really. It was physical music, reverberating through the ship and into her as if she was a human tuning fork. She touched both hands to the rail, and the effect was doubled. She laughed out loud, lit up by the pure joy of it.

All the ships she'd travelled on, and that was the first time she'd heard music in the hum.

FIFTH INTERLUDE

It was a worn and defeated Deputy Seawall who moved through the officer's mess that afternoon. Everything slumped on his shoulders; weeks of travelling, a belligerent chewing-out from the old man, and the cock-up from the previous night, grievously stupid and mostly his own fault. Part of him still blamed the High Sheriff – ignorant to his plans, but still finding a way to ruin them. Hounding him on the communicator day and night as if he were still a little boy. Seawall belonged to a sad class of person, a phenomenon that has repeated since the first king was crowned: the embittered, ageing heir apparent.

When the yoke of Deputyship grew too heavy he liked to come down to the mess, the place where his authority was strongest. Formerly an engine bay, it was now a stale-smelling pen of benches where low-level officers and unscrupulous sub-deputies came to eat trays of mash and beans in the gargantuan shadow of the portside thrusters. The ceiling was high, the humour low. Most of the surfaces were sticky. It did him good to go down there and listen to sentences trail away unfinished, to watch faces pale and spines straighten as awareness of his presence rippled through the ranks. However long the old man clung to life, there would always be a number of people who considered him the boss.

But today, with Seawall's spirits so low, even the underlings didn't notice him; he moved around the walls like a passing shadow, chewing tobacco, his mind idle. He was mulling over the High Sheriff's latest scheme, the so-called 'Project', how much it *riled* him, grinding his teeth until the tobacco was reduced to a bitter pulp. He stopped to spit out what remained. A wise decision. Had he taken another step, that would have been the last moment of his life.

It went by in a flash, the colour of smouldering coal, snatching a few fine hairs from the tip of Seawall's nose. He looked, first at the welt of glowing metal on the wall, and then towards the person who had fired the shot: a marksman of some nineteen or twenty years, sat among a huddle of admiring co-workers. This young officer had been showing off his new weapon when a jostle from a passing diner had caused him to fire it by mistake, and now he and his friends were arranged like an oil painting, all of them paralysed with acute terror as they realised where the bullet had gone. Where it had *nearly* gone.

Seawall picked his way through the tables, bringing stillness, and a grin. By the time he arrived the whole hall was so engulfed in silence that you could have heard a baked bean drop. He planted both fists on the table and asked in a genial tone: 'Beg your pardon, son. Mind telling me where you found that pistol?'

The elevator had two buttons only – *up* and *down*. The

Guest selected up, and as the floor hauled upwards she felt a familiar sensation in the base of her gut, a tug like she was leaving orbit. Bracing herself on one wall, she took note of her injuries – the tender area around her lungs, a cut above the eye, several fingers lacking in the right amount of skin. Bone-deep weariness and unvoiced dread. And the pistol, missing from her hip: not technically a wound, but worse, in a way.

Bing. The doors slid open. Shapes rushed in, and she leapt back, raising one leg ready to kick. Her assailants clattered to the ground – brooms and mops. She emerged, sidestepping buckets, into a cluttered maintenance cupboard. The elevator doors rolled shut behind her, stuck all over with faded hazard tape.

Beyond the broom closet she found a tight network of sparsely populated 'streets', curved and spotless as a new toilet, with a subdued and focused atmosphere that made a marked contrast to the busy throngs downstairs. Dapper-looking people passed by, some of them shrouded in lab coats. She returned their stares.

'Excuse me?' As the Guest was knocking on an unmarked but important-looking door, a thin man with a precarious comb-over sidled up to her and asked, politely, 'Who are you?' There was a pause as the Guest tried to formulate an answer, which he took for confusion, adding: 'This is the *top* floor. Are you lost?'

'Yeah. I'm a petitioner.' She held up the yellow card, then affected an embarrassed laugh. 'Here to see the High Sheriff. But I can't find the office.'

'Oh!' This seemed to placate him, though he still looked puzzled. 'So late in the day?'

'I, uh – I got lucky. Skipped the queue.'

'I see. Very well.' He motioned for her to follow with a

jerk of the head. As they walked, he added, 'It amazes me that he's still seeing people in his condition. Generosity beyond belief.'

She nodded eagerly. 'Yeah?'

'Yes. He's not a strong man, you know. Be patient with him.'

'I will.'

They came to the correct doors, and he stood aside, sweeping his hand. 'Good luck.'

'T-thanks.'

Another slight nod that said *you'll need it*.

The doors slid shut behind her, and she was alone, facing an upward-sloping corridor. The featureless porcelain walls gave way to panes of glass, flooding everything in a serene natural light. The Guest felt oddly buoyant. Maybe she could reason with this man, the High Sheriff. Clearly he was more enlightened than the average zealot, even if he did have a peculiar way of doing things. *Generosity beyond belief.* Perhaps he'd extend some of it to her.

The glass corridor ended abruptly with a brass-trimmed door of varnished mahogany. It was so incongruous with the rest of the ship that it looked like the fragment of a dream, but the wood felt real under the surface of her fingers, the burnished copper handle smooth and cold. It opened with a faint creak, and she entered a small, boxy antechamber. Sterile air gave way to a cloying warmth, tinged with the musk of trapped bodies. Thick carpet, faux-marble walls trimmed in carved oak, a crackling fireplace – a projection, surely, but it *felt* real – chairs with puffy cream cushions that looked like they'd never been sat in; solemn oil portraits of unfamiliar families. It could have been a set, but there stood idle a station of medical equipment – a trolley hung with an empty IV drip, trays of syringes and tubes.

At the back of the room was a man. He said, 'Show's over.'

As she approached he lifted a lazy hand, training the barrel of a heat pistol at her chest. She stopped.

'Is that – my gun?'

He nodded.

'Oh.'

'Normally I'd use a revolver,' explained the man, 'but I'd hate to spill blood on the carpet.'

Raising her hands, keeping her voice level, the Guest said: 'Just let me talk to him.'

'No.'

'I'm unarmed.'

'I know you are.'

She considered this. Considered him. 'Are you the Deputy?'

'Sure am. Seawall. A belated pleasure.'

'Whatever you think I did, Seawall, it wasn't me.'

That raised a dry chuckle. 'You're not guilty of anything but shitty luck.'

'Uh…' She paused again, lost. 'So why… why can't I…'

'Lots of reasons.' There was something unassuming about him: the rumpled shirt, the dry skin, the easy way of speaking. But she could tell he wasn't bluffing. 'Trust me, you wouldn't want to see him either.'

'Why not?'

'Because he's the one that shot your ship out of the sky.'

A long and agonising silence. When the Guest spoke again, it was slowly, each word extracted like a tooth from her mouth: 'That is a lie.'

'It's true. We've got cannons on this old tub.' He gave the marbled wall an affectionate pat with his free hand. 'I've been busting my ass for the last month trying to track you down. Had to clean up a few folks – Du Cream, and the woman from the train, what was her name…'

'What do you mean, clean up?'

But she knew what he meant.

An '*ah-hah!*' snap of the fingers. 'Harriet. That was it. Seamstress.'

Seamstress. A fusty woman with a needle and thread, tutting as she patched up her jacket. *You're quite a long way from home, aren't you?*

'Don't blame me, friend. Wouldn't have had to do it if you'd minded your business.'

'Where's the crash site?'

A slight rise of the eyebrows: 'Why? Got someone you're worried about?'

She took a step closer.

'Where is it? How many survived?'

'*Nobody,*' Seawall almost spat. 'That was the whole idea. You're the only one left.'

She looked at him.

'Ah, for fuck's sake. Nobody *asked* you to come here, friend. It was your choice.'

'It was an aid mission. We came to help.'

'Maybe. Either way, it was dangerous. Can't have outsiders rocking the boat right now. So…' He rubbed the back of his neck. '…yeah.'

'Yeah,' she echoed.

'It wasn't my call.'

She watched in bewilderment as his eyes shifted uncomfortably from corner to corner. 'Why are you saying this?' she asked.

'I don't know.' Seawall barked out a bitter laugh. 'I thought it'd be less cruel. It's not, really, is it? He always tells me I'm a son of a bitch.'

He raised the pistol.

'Don't be sad, Captain,' he said. 'You'll be joining her now. It's for the best.'

Then –

As the bullet tore through, her mind was visited by a strange thought:

I've never been shot before.

Shot *at*, yes; run over, tasered, bitten, battered, burned to blisters. But never shot. Not once in her long career as a soldier. Not once, even on this wasted Earth.

The first sensation was of a sudden and incalculable loss. Like grief. One moment you have something: a living person, a working body. The next moment you don't. And there's that space, that moment where you feel almost giddy, as reality keels from the blow. It's a magic trick. Things that seemed impossible a moment ago are suddenly real, suddenly happening, and now anything could happen; a whole galaxy could be sucked away in an instant, stars stuttering out like fairy lights. Anything is possible. Nothing is sacred. Nobody is safe.

Now there's a glob of molten glass where her kidneys used to be. Dribbling the way liquid will, spilling over those soft hidden organs, searing them crisp.

No time like the present.

Curtains, grey and moth-ravaged, sweeping in from either side of the stage. Dim the lights. You heard the man: *Show's over.* And it's a tragedy, she thinks, the unbloodied carpet rising towards her, because in all these years she's only had a few months of proper living, of genuine happiness. So much life wasted in the wrong place. Wasted without *her*.

Human history makes up less than 0.5 per cent of the history of Earth. Noelle told her that. Just a tiny fraction. But oh, *what* a fraction! What a mess we made on that planet, she'd said, what a wonderful disaster, what a sublime calamity. Just think what we could do with a little more time.

Just a little more time.

THE FALL OF THE LADYBUG

'Wow. IT REALLY does look like an insect, don't you think?'

'Mmm.' Awkwardly, the foreman cleared his throat. 'Perhaps – just a little. But it's a sturdy model, I hear – you've only got a small crew…'

'Quite,' Noelle replied, wondering why he didn't see her remark as a compliment.

The trans-solar departure bay was in chaos as usual. A nasal voice read announcements from a suspended audio speaker, ignored by the crowds that moved in tight streams between the hulking bodies of the cruisers. Every now and then the air would be ripped apart as one of them fired up and began its ascent towards the distant ceiling. Noelle had to carry her notes under her arm to prevent an updraught from blowing them away.

Between two of these monstrous cruisers the *Ladybug* nestled, so small in comparison that she and the foreman had passed it three times before realising it was there. She was three floors high, cherry red, with a domed hull built for stability over speed. Noelle swelled at the sight. You couldn't have designed a less aggressive-looking ship if you tried.

But there were soldiers on the gangway plank.

Her first thought was panic. Had her father changed his mind? Had she made a mistake with the release forms? Was the Imperial government interfering, despite their promises? Then she recognised the Captain, and the fear cooled. This was a scheduled inconvenience.

An armed escort had been the first of Duke Daley's conditions in funding the project. The second was absolute secrecy. The third was that when Noelle came home she would take up a lecturing position in some minor university and never darken his doorstep again. She'd tried to persuade him that an aid mission was no place for soldiers, to no avail:

'Retired soldiers,' he'd responded from behind a touchscreen. 'They're on my payroll now.'

The Central Galactic Empire was not total, but it was dominant. Every war it waged was one of conquest and aggression, 'liberating' dissident planets and buying out their natural resources at a cripplingly cheap rate. None of this devastation would be possible without the willing compliance of the army. Noelle didn't want to share air with these people, never mind work with them.

It was the Captain who stood out the most, standing as she did a full head and shoulders above the rest. She was physically striking in a way that the broadcasts hadn't quite captured: tall and jagged, with an actor's easy confidence. The soldiers hemmed her in on every side, clamouring for attention so much that Noelle had to raise her voice to be heard.

'Good morning, Captain.'

The soldiers stood back, falling resentfully into step.

Grow up, Noelle thought. *I'm in charge here.* Only the Captain seemed unaffected by the change in atmosphere. She turned to greet Noelle with a broad, condescending grin, her hand outstretched.

'Morning!' she said. 'Have we met?'

'No.' Noelle ignored the hand. 'I'm Doctor Daley. The project leader. Do you have everything you need?'

'Sure do.' She dropped her arm as amicably as she'd raised it. 'If you don't mind, I wanted to go over some details with you before we—'

'It can wait.' She shouldered between two of the soldiers and strode up the plank, the foreman trotting after. 'We've got six months to plan, after all.'

'Of course, Doctor,' the Captain replied, still jovial. 'Whatever you say.'

In the sour aftermath of Doctor Daley's arrival, Captain Marshal was heard to say, very quietly, 'Ah, shit.'

'What was that, Captain?'

'Nothing, nothing. And call me Kei. I'm retired, remember?'

THE *LADYBUG* WAS a private vessel by design. It had been passed down in the pilot's family, through three generations of steadily decreasing wealth and standing, until the ship was all they had left to prove their former glory. As they toured from chamber to chamber, Noelle noticed little scraps of the ship's former life. The kitchen was outfitted with a luxurious stone-tiled floor and a long window with a row of built-in herb pots underneath. Patchwork cushions plumped the seats of the canteen, old coffee-rings were sunk into the tables. There was a rear chamber that smelled faintly like wet dog. Even the lab, which had been totally refitted for Noelle's team to use, had a smiley face carved crudely at knee level into one of the door frames. They went in a ring, each door circling around the central chamber that looked down onto the shuttered ceiling of the cargo hold.

'My grandfather believed that a room without a window was just a trumped-up prison cell,' the pilot explained. 'You can see the stars from everywhere – even the toilets.'

All in all, the crew numbered nineteen: six people to run and maintain the ship, eight humanitarian scientists of various disciplines, including Noelle, and five private soldiers led by Captain Marshal. It was a small team, and they could all fit around the four welded benches of the canteen with room to spare. They had their first briefing there while the *Ladybug* was still docked. Noelle had to stand on a chair.

'Our status at present calls to mind the ancient example of Schrodinger's Cat,' she began. 'That is to say: if we succeed, we were always going to succeed, and acted under the benign wisdom and foresight of the Emperor himself. And if we fail, we were never anything more than a splinter group of idealists who departed of our own accord. Some might say this is a foolish endeavour—'

One of the soldiers leant forward and whispered something in the Captain's ear. Noelle carried on.

'—but looking at history, I find the people I most admire were declared foolish at one point or another. To make progress we must look hard at the things we choose to ignore, the things that we try to bury. We'll find the future there. A toast, then, to our forgotten home, and mankind's new frontier: to Earth.'

Applause. Some of the scientists cheered. The Captain,

leaning back with legs splayed out, languidly slapped her palms together a few times before the noise died down.

'Beg your pardon, Doctor,' she began.

Immediate hush.

'I want to get some facts straight. Just for my benefit, okay? So one—'

She spoke slowly, ticking the points off on her hand.

'One, this is the first visit to Earth in maybe three hundred years,' she said. 'And two, we don't know anything about the situation on the ground, because the Earthlings cut off all contact at the time the planet was evacuated. Three, what we do know is that *they* don't like *us*, because our whole existence goes against their religion. Am I right so far?'

'Is this going somewhere, Captain?' Noelle's voice was thin.

'It is.' With one elbow, she pushed herself up a little higher. 'I think it's great, really. What you're trying to do. And I want to help any way I can. But my, uh…' She gestured to her holster. 'My skill set is kinda narrow. So I guess what I'm saying is, you and your team should prepare for the best-case scenario – me and mine will prepare for the worst.'

This time only the soldiers applauded.

LESS THAN AN hour after the speeches had been concluded and the last of the cans had been drained, the *Ladybug* quietly slipped free of the gravitational pull of the Imperial Capital and began aerial manoeuvres for the first leap. The ship's red shell shifted to flank the sun, triggering a nanotechnical shaded layer to materialise on all of the portside windows.

Noelle's quarters fell into darkness. *Perfect*, she thought. *Suits my mood.*

She was sat cross-legged on her bunk, with microfilm star charts spread in a semicircle around her. From one end to the other they tracked the *Ladybug*'s projected route out of the densely populated galactic centre and towards the furthest reaches of the spiral's arm, zigzagging from system to system in a series of jumps that, from God's perspective, just about made a straight line. At least, they did until the end. There the journey became more abstract. Unlike most populated planets, Earth had no beacon to aid the ship's computer in tracking their approach. Getting there required good old-fashioned navigation – the same slow process by which the human race had carved itself a path through the barren wilderness of the Milky Way.

All of this Noelle knew in theory. And as the project leader, she felt a duty to know it in practice as well. But the dots, lines and labels were swaying before her eyes, spreading into formless constellations, endless fractals, NS decimal points –

She let herself fall back, hitting the pillow with a thud. She was thinking about the Captain again.

It had gotten to the point where the mere fact that she was irritated was irritating her. Never mind the obvious moral objection to having a mass murderer swanning about on board. It was the little things. The way she sat. The way she smiled. One of the humanitarians had made some simpering comment about turning the other cheek – but six months of cheek-turning sounded like a long time.

We'll just have to stay out of each other's way, she thought. She stretched her legs out, spilling star charts across the ground. *Focus on the mission. Focus on what matters.*

*   *   *

ON THE FLOOR below, in her own quarters, Captain Kei Marshal was also awake, lying with her feet jutting out over the edge of the tiny bed. The red and white capsule moved easily between her fingers, spinning from joint to joint. Taking it would place her in a solid and dreamless sleep for exactly eight hours, as indicated by the number '8' printed on the front. Stored neatly in the compartments at her side – alongside her pistol – were similar pills for five hours, three hours, even one hour. But she wasn't ready to sleep just yet.

It was the Doctor's eyes that were troubling her most: large, serious eyes that had fixed on her not with contempt but with an open and angry frustration, as if Kei was the latest in a long line of obstacles that she'd had to overcome. It was that detachment which really got under her skin. She could accept that the Doctor would never like her, but she wanted the animosity to at least be personal.

There were other details to mull over. The blue overalls she wore (Kei had not met many scientists before, and had been imagining lab coats), the trio of metal hoops that pierced the top of her right ear (a lapsed punk?), the streaks of white hair at her temples (the rest of it was thick and black), the well-chewed nails (nervous? thinking?). The way her voice shook when she spoke about Earth.

Kei stared at the ceiling.

Stupid woman. She's going to get herself killed.

She swallowed the pill and killed the lights.

*   *   *

A SCHEDULE IS an invaluable tool on the side of sanity on a long-haul space flight. Every morning, at 07:00 hours Central time, the overhead lights flickered on one by one, and the window shaders clustered briefly into an image of a cartoon sun before dissipating into nothingness. The passengers of the *Ladybug* would rise, blinking and groaning, and set about their tasks for the day.

Territorial lines were quickly drawn. Due to the secrecy involved in the mission, a lot of the humanitarians had been recruited quickly with minimum time to prepare. They spent their days on the upper floors, divided between the lab and the 'seminar room' (a converted entertainment deck). There was a perpetual chatter and rustling of paper and piling up of stained mugs.

The soldiers, by contrast, occupied the lower floors, running rings around the inner balcony, blasting music out of the walls of the gym, tearing up shelves in the storage closet they were trying to convert into a weapons room. Often they'd be called upon to help out the understaffed flight crew with basic maintenance. The *Ladybug* had to make overnight refuelling stops at least once a fortnight, so there was always discussion of the fun they could get up to next time they went shoreside. At mealtimes the factions split off into separate tables.

Noelle avoided the Captain just like she'd planned. If they did speak, it was brief, such as their meeting on the stairs on the fourth day.

'Uh, Doctor, excuse me…'

Noelle felt herself being yanked out of what had been an excellent mood. She formed a neutral expression. 'Yes, Captain? Can I help you?'

'Some of my team are looking to blow off a bit of steam. I thought it'd be a good idea if they did it in the canteen – a few drinks, maybe one night out of seven? It helps keep discipline, you know.'

Noelle bristled with indignation. She wanted to make the Captain sit down and file a formal request, along with a full risk assessment and an estimated budget, and have that request put to a vote, and personally rubber-stamp it with a big '*No*' on the base – but being a hardarse somehow felt like playing more into her hands. Instead she said: 'That's a communal space, Captain.'

'You'd all be welcome to join us.'

They both knew that would never happen. Noelle's lips formed a smile.

'Of course,' she said. 'Just don't leave a mess.'

They never did.

A FEW WEEKS later, Noelle found herself in the kitchen during one of these sessions, brewing some late-night tea. Her first instinct was to hurry out as fast as she could, but a snatch of conversation made her pause. She could see them through the pass-through window, gathered around the furthest bench, cans in hand.

'Come on, Kei.' One of the soldiers – a redhead – crowded the Captain's side. 'When are you gonna tell us?'

She was feigning innocence. 'Tell you about what?'

'About *Breton*. When you stormed that fuckin' tower!'

The name whisked a slip of breath from Noelle's mouth. She crouched closer to the window, watching as the Captain drained her can and set it down. 'Maybe another time.'

'Ahh, come onnnn.' Chummy exasperation from the redhead. 'You at least have to tell us if the numbers are true. On the news it said three hundred, but I heard—'

'Funnily enough,' she cut him off, 'I wasn't keeping count.'

The soldiers sniggered, but Noelle was positive she'd heard a strained note in the Captain's voice. She glanced up, and their eyes hooked on one another for a moment before Noelle broke free. As she hurried guiltily back to her room, she heard the Captain saying: 'Alright, that's enough. Let's call it a night.'

AFTER THAT INCIDENT in the canteen, the Captain started to spend more and more time in her quarters. At least, that's where everyone assumed she went. It was hard to find privacy on the *Ladybug*. The soldiers – out of respect, or perhaps just bored of her evasiveness – carried on without her, drilling in the workout room, whooping into the night.

At mealtimes Noelle would glance over to her empty section of the bench and feel a formless anxiety pooling at the back of her mind. But such worries proved easy to ignore – or at least, easy to bury in distraction. Professionally, this was turning out to be the most exciting period of her entire life.

After years of private theories and trashed papers, Noelle was finally able to share her ideas about Earth with other minds: similar in intelligence, but different in focus. The results were electric. She was chiefly interested in climate science, but the atmosphere of Earth was tied to its past in a way that was utterly unique to that planet. Anthropology was just as important as ecology, history as insightful as oceanography. In the beginning she'd dreamed only of making a place where the leftover people could live sustainably. But with each day, with each new breakthrough, her ambitions grew a little more. It was never acknowledged in any meeting or report, as if saying the dream out loud would curse it into impossibility. But over the course of the first month the goal of their work slowly shifted. She and her team were no longer satisfied with patching Earth up for human usage. They wanted to restore the planet completely: with glaciers and rainforests, blue whales and wildcats. A pre-industrial paradise. A marvel of cutting-edge geo-engineering. An ancient world, made new again.

A miracle.

IT WAS A tiny, dirty, frost-shocked moon in the middle of an underpopulated solar system, with little to commend it outside of a fuel station and a few subterraneous dives in which a passing traveller could get blind drunk. Noelle had a view of the town from the control deck – a collection of curved white rooftops huddled tightly against the blizzards that howled down from all sides. Here and there were signs of human life: a golden pinprick from an unshuttered window, a snatch of music. Laughter.

Noelle was pacing. She had no intention of staying the night, but the crew had wanted to stretch their legs, even through two feet of snow. Which was fine. But it was getting late, and the soldiers still hadn't returned.

'We'll be grounded if this storm gets any worse,' said the navigator, Jules, swiping at an onscreen model of the moon's swirling cloud system. She turned her chair around, looking sympathetically at Noelle. 'Why don't I go down there and haul them out by the earlobes?'

'I'm half tempted to order a take-off without—'

On the ground below a group of figures emerged, struggling on each other's shoulders. Noelle sighed. '*Finally.*'

'Hallelujah.' Jules swirled back to her screen. 'I'll lower the gangway, shall I?'

As she trotted down the stairs, Noelle became aware of a mounting excitement. The Captain had gone groundside at her crew's insistence, shrugging sheepishly and promising to have them all back in an hour or two. *Promise broken!* There was no way she could wriggle out of this. They'd *have* to confront each other.

It wasn't clear to Noelle when exactly she'd gone from wanting to avoid the Captain to wanting to talk to her. It had happened slowly, like so many other things.

The wind cut razors across her face as she stepped out onto the platform, stinging her lungs, snapping at her hair. When she saw the security team, a quick headcount revealed only four swaying bodies. Noelle brushed ice out of her lashes and yelled over the wind –

'Where's the Captain!?'

They squinted back at her. 'Huh?'

'Captain Marshal! Where the hell is she? We need to leave now!'

The soldiers exchanged wary glances. 'We – I mean – uh—'

'Oh, stars above!' Fastening her coat to the top notch, Noelle brushed past them, heading for the soft golden lights below.

The town – Noelle hadn't bothered to learn its name – was tiny, and seemed to be made up entirely of bars. Most of them spiralled down many floors deep, burrowing around a vertical furnace that radiated heat from a source much further below. She ploughed up and down each of them, scanning crowd after crowd of bleary-eyed punters who leered at her face and scowled at her accent. Never mind insubordinate. This was *absurd*. Dangerous, even, in that kind of place, in those kind of weather conditions. If she didn't show up on her own Noelle would have to get the local police involved, which would mean questions and delays, and possibly imperil the whole project—

'Doctor?'

Noelle stopped. The raucous laughter of bar number five had been silenced with a slammed door, and the snow-covered street was soft, insulated, quiet. She turned. The Captain was sitting on an upturned bottle-crate around the building's side, hunched against the wind, with a half-unconscious man propped up on her shoulder. And was that tar on her forehead?

Noelle blinked, and then held back a gasp. The Captain's face was covered in blood.

'What're you doing out here?' The Captain's words carried just the hint of a slur. 'I thought y' were st…' She paused, pressing her knuckles to her mouth to suppress a burp. 'I thought you were staying on the ship?'

Noelle was too cold and tired and angry and worried to bother with any pleasantries. 'What the fuck happened, Captain?'

Roused by her voice, the unconscious man murmured, 'Lemmie go, y' bitch… I'll kill y'…' making motions of what in his head was probably a series of devastating punches. They glanced harmlessly off the Captain's chest.

'Bumped into him at the bar,' she said. 'Seems he had a cousin or something from Breton.' The man pawed vaguely at her face, and she lifted her chin away from his grasp, still talking. 'Would've been fine, but this arsehole of a bouncer stepped in – called him a traitor to the Emperor – smacked him right on the sharp end of a table.' She held up a chipped grey comms tablet. 'I just got off the line with his wife. She's on her way.'

Noelle looked from the Captain's bloodied face and back to the man, who'd dozed off again with snowflakes in his moustache. 'He did that to you?' she asked.

The Captain nodded.

Noelle pulled her sleeve back, checked the time, permitted herself one quiet sigh. Then she trod across the snow towards them.

'Move up.'

'Huh?'

Noelle ignored her, taking a space on the edge of the crate. She tucked her arms in and waited.

After a few minutes, the Captain said: 'Thanks.'

Noelle's hood moved in the notions of a nod. The snow fell soft around them.

As they made the way back to the ship – slowly, as Captain Marshal was more than a little unsteady on her feet, and was using Noelle as a human cane – the Captain leant down and said, conversationally: 'Y'know you're really gorgeous. Did you know that? Has anyone told you?'

'Okay, Captain, back up.' Noelle steadied her. 'You stink of booze.'

'That'll be the booze. Are you blushing?'

'Actually, I'm experiencing the first stages of acute hypothermia.'

'You're a cute... a cute...' The Captain abandoned the pun, or perhaps forgot that she was speaking at all.

Noelle stared firmly ahead. She could feel her soul sliding out of her body.

The Captain liked her. So what? What was she supposed to do with that information?

Noelle had been down this road before. People formed attachments based on ludicrous one-sided fantasies, and then decided that *she* was responsible for dealing with the way they felt – why? Why did the emotions of others, that she had no power to control, suddenly have to be her problem? It was –

It was –

It was so *inconvenient!*

But the Captain had never said anything. She'd bent like a willow to Noelle's every demand, given her all the space she needed, asked for almost nothing. No doubt she'd forget this in the morning, and if she did, she would never bring it up, except perhaps to apologise. There had been no searching silences between them, no strained moments – at least, not *that* kind of strained.

Had there?

'Have I been very stupid, Captain?' Noelle asked, with a suddenness that even she found surprising.

'Nah.' She chuckled sluggishly. 'You're smart. You got a degree. If you were stupid you'd be in the *army.*'

'Is that what you think?' Something connected in Noelle's mind – some hypothesis she had been moving towards without her own conscious knowledge. She turned her head to look up at the Captain, at that sleepless face still encrusted with blood. 'You're not proud of yourself, are you?'

The Captain smiled sadly. 'No.' She tilted her head back, towards the black lowness of the heavens, and when she spoke again her voice had thickened: 'Tell you the truth, Noelle, I don't much like myself at all.'

This confession, and the sound of her own name,

somehow stumped Noelle. There were a thousand things she could have said, but suddenly all of them seemed insensitive beyond measure.

They drew a little closer. It was impossible to tell who was pulling who.

A few hours later the *Ladybug* was back in orbit and the two of them were sitting alone in the canteen. There'd been no spoken agreement, but when Noelle returned from her room with an empty mug she'd somehow known she'd find Kei there. She was staring blankly out at the window, legs stretched wide before her, the gash still bright and ragged on her forehead. The lights were dim. Most of the ship was asleep.

'I let him hit me,' Kei said.

Noelle sat opposite. 'I guessed as much. And I understand, I do. At least, I can try to. But you need to stop punishing yourself.'

'It was supposed to be just me on this mission. I was told beforehand that if I signed up I'd be the only soldier on board. They lied to me. You get that, right?'

Noelle reached across the table and knitted their fingers together. 'I understand.'

'I enlisted when I was fourteen. They encourage it, when you're – when your other prospects aren't so good.'

She nodded. 'I know.'

'And I liked it, you know. I was good at it. But Breton changed things. After the tower was secure I had to walk back the way I came. Past all the bodies.'

'I'm sorry.'

Kei took a deep, steadying breath. 'It's not your fault.'

They left it like that for a moment. Then Kei pulled her hand away. 'Can I ask you something?'

'Of course.'

The Ladybird hummed. Outside the window was a pool of nothingness.

'Why Earth?' asked Kei. 'I'm sure there's still a thousand planets that need your help just as bad.'

Noelle frowned. She did this when she was thinking, Kei noticed: glared at empty space, as if she was trying to intimidate the problem.

'I had a picture book when I was little,' said Noelle. 'A very old one – my father bought it at an auction. It was written on Earth, way, way long ago, in ancient times. It was about these ducks living in a public park in the middle of a big city. When it comes time for the ducks to move home, the citizens work together to create a path for them through the ground-cars. And nobody complains about the disruption. They just do it as a matter of course. Because they understand there are some things more valuable than, than just *grinding away at life* –

'I know – well, I know now – that the book is a fantasy, that the ground-cars were poisoning the air, and the parks were hardly a replacement for a true symbiotic ecosystem. But still, there's – there's just something about it.'

Noelle's frown turned suddenly on Kei. 'I know you think I'm naive,' she said. 'But I've seen this Empire. Seen how it runs. It's not just a system that creates victims. It *needs* victims to survive.' She pressed a finger down on the tabletop, hard enough to whiten the nail. 'It's as if someone made a terrible mistake long ago, and that's tainted everything that's come after it. If only we could get back to the source of the wrongness and patch it up, the rest of the galaxy will heal. Earth is the stem. It's the root of all our problems. If I can save that place, I can save everybody.'

Noelle's cheeks were tinged with pink. Kei looked at her steadily for a second. Then she laughed: a real laugh, bubbling out brilliant as lava.

'Noelle Daley, that is the stupidest thing I've *ever* heard.'

A FEW EVENINGS later, a young soldier by the name of Okroj was chopping vegetables in the kitchen with a botanist called Jobson. After ten minutes of quiet chopping, Okroj posed: 'You know, I've been wondering... our Captain and that Dr Noelle... are they... a thing?'

Jobson put his knife down in an expression of deep relief. 'I thought I was going *mad*.'

They went on to talk animatedly for thirty minutes.

Similar incidents were occurring all over the *Ladybug*. The meticulously separate factions of scientists, soldiers and crew found themselves speculating together on an item of gossip that was, after almost a month of travel, a thrilling and much-needed distraction. Odd words and moments of physical contact between the two women were analysed to the point of redundancy – older members of either group were called upon to espouse their romantic wisdom – younger ones discussed the logistics – when they were seen sitting together for breakfast, the entire ship almost burst into flame.

'I'm surprised it didn't happen sooner,' said Jules.

'No you're *not*,' scoffed the Oceanographer. 'You didn't hear Noelle in those first few weeks. It takes a lot to make a pacifist that angry.' He laid his cards down. 'I fold.'

'That's how it *ought* to be,' insisted Private Eze, 'that's proper romance, man. *The course of true love never did run easy.*' She spread her deck upwards on the table. 'Full house.'

'*Smooth,*' corrected Jules.

'Thanks.'

Gossip laid the groundwork for cross-pollinations of a different kind. Now the anthropologist was discovered to be the ship's most accomplished cook, and the ship's mechanic started attending seminars after shyly admitting that he found it interesting. There was book-swapping, and storytelling, and avant-garde activity in the kitchen.

And still nobody could figure out the full extent of the 'situation' between the Captain and the Doctor. After a while they didn't really care.

As for the couple themselves – their segmented lives flowed easily together, and soon Noelle was conducting late-night research while Kei did push-ups in the corner. And when Noelle swore and threw her tablet across the room, hopelessly frustrated with the imperialist bias and general intellectual impotence of whatever paper she was struggling through, Kei would grab it in a practiced flash before it hit the wall.

'Pigs. Philistines!' Noelle would fume.

'They are,' Kei would agree, handling the tablet back, or kissing the top of her head.

As a student of climate, Noelle was intimately acquainted with the seasons. She knew their underlying causes, of course, but also their sights and smells, their colours, their moods. Many planets stayed locked in endless extremes: here it is always cold. Here it is always hot. But a truly liveable planet was one that changed

– because renewal, everybody knows, is the strongest imperative for life. She started to give seminars on death, birth and regrowth, and how this majestic cycle was once the crown jewel of Earth's ecosystem. The lectures were vigorously intellectual as always, but some of the older attendants detected a dreamy note in Noelle's bullet points. Springtime always held a special interest.

And Kei?

She was happy.

She didn't know how to be happy, but she was learning.

It was like a kind of poison she had to immunise herself against bit by bit, to keep it from being rejected out of hand.

She told her team the truth about Breton. She tried to do it kindly, but none of them could listen like Noelle did. They had questions, objections. Specifics were requested and given in short order. It wound up being a rather brutal conversation.

Afterwards there was a period of quiet. Each soldier retreated into themselves for a time. But none of them were introverted by nature, and one by one they came back. Okroj was the first, with a breezy nod in the corridor.

'Morning, Captain!'

'Morning, Okroj.' Then, cautiously: 'How're you feeling?'

'Good, Captain. Lots to do.'

She carried briskly along towards the gym. The other two emerged not long after.

Later, she said to Noelle, 'I'm still not sure I did the right thing.'

The remark on this occasion came after a long interval of ceiling-staring.

'Of course you did,' said Noelle. 'It'll take them a while, but they'll figure it out.'

'Figure out what?'

'How brave you are.'

At night they would dance in the cargo bay.

THE SECOND MONTH whipped past, and then the third. The Ladybird hopped from beacon to beacon, from buzzing city to crack-dry hamlet, moving inexorably closer to the edge of the map – a score of nothing drawn through the blackness that marked the Empire's furthest reach, beyond which lay the past in all its menace and mystery.

On the wall in the seminar room they'd stuck up a two-metre-wide map of Earth. Handwritten annotations were pinned up around it like petals, connecting here and there by lengths of twine. More were added every day.

The weapons room grew dusty.

MONTH FIVE. It had been a few days since their final pit stop, and the ship was crammed full of supplies.

'Attention, crew.' Jules's voice echoed through the tannoy at six on the dot, as the floor was still trembling from the force of the last leap. 'Attention, crew. This is an announcement. The *Ladybug* has officially departed Imperial territory. I repeat—'

The rest of her words were drowned out by cheers.

They gathered in the canteen. Someone rigged up the touchscreen to play music, which provided a thudding undercurrent to all the chatting and laughter. For once, Noelle immersed herself totally in the fun. Though everyone else spoke of ambitions, and what they were going to do, her overriding feeling was one of relief. Pressure had been lifted; a pressure that had been there so long she hadn't even noticed it.

She caught sight of Kei, hanging on the edge of another circle with detached eyes, and excused herself.

Kei started at the feeling of a hand on her arm. It was Noelle.

She spoke quietly. 'Need a break?'

She nodded, thinking: *I love you.*

The problem of privacy had long since been solved by Kei. Through a hatch at the back of the lowest deck, the two of them could access a place that they called the 'den'. It was where Kei'd gone to hide from her crew in the first month of the journey: a metal pod, windowed at either end, with a row of padded chairs welded to one wall.

The ship was too small to house a second vessel, and hardly needed a row of ready-to-launch escape pods in the time of the Emperor's peace. The den was there as a contingency in case of some dire, but very unlikely, emergency, like a fire, or oxygen failure, something that required an immediate evacuation. In that instance it could be boarded, sealed, and shot out into space to await rescue. The pilot had called it a lifeboat.

Someone before them had thought to use it as a hiding-place. Kei found a trove of pillows and blankets stuffed in the emergency supply crate, along with basic medical supplies, breathing masks, and a sealed packet of dried food. When one or both of them needed a break, the den was invariably where they wound up.

It quickly became Kei's favourite place in the entire galaxy.

'Can I tell you something?'

Behind her head, Kei could feel Noelle's torso rise and fall.

'Okay.'

'I never want this ship to land.'

Noelle paused. 'Huh.'

'You don't feel like that?'

'No. This is wonderful, but – getting to Earth, doing my work there – that's – important to me. I need to do that.'

'Can I tell you something else?'

'Okay.'

'I don't care about Earth. It's a madhouse.'

Noelle looked down at Kei. 'Things aren't going to stop between us when we get there, if that's what you—'

'I know. But there'll be changes, right?'

'Obviously.'

'I don't want changes. I just want you and me, on this ship, forever.'

'That's a very selfish sentiment, Captain.'

'So what? I am selfish.'

'Are you? What about me?'

'What *about* you?'

'Aren't I selfish?'

'No.'

'Isn't this whole mission just an ego trip for some – shallow, spoilt rich girl trying to feel good about herself?'

'Who told you that?'

'My father.'

'That's stupid. It's obvious how much you care about this. Not just to me – everyone can tell. Everyone.'

'But he's got a point, doesn't he?'

'No, he doesn't. Just because he's spent his whole life licking his own arse doesn't mean you're obliged to.'

'He told me I was an embarrassment.'

'Yeah, well… if my kid was a better person than I was, I'd be embarrassed too.'

Noelle ran her fingers over the fuzz of Kei's hair.

'I think you'll like Earth,' she said. 'In fact, I think you'll love it.'

Kei snorted. 'If you say so, Doctor.'

Kei had convinced herself that it was never going to happen. But still, the day arrived. Even as she stood on the observation deck, looking down towards the whorled clouds and yellowing coastlines, she still couldn't take in the reality of it.

'We'll descend into the upper atmosphere,' Noelle was saying. 'Send out a general signal, see if there are any working transmitters down there to receive it. We can formulate our strategy from there.'

Half of the crew were listening intently. The other half were by the window, noses flat against the glass. The mechanic was listing off the names of every ocean she could see, and Jobson and Okroj were hugging one another, practically dancing.

'We're not landing today, are we?' Kei asked.

'Not for a week at least.'

'Right.' She tried not to let the relief show on her face. 'In that case I think I'll take a nap.'

'Alright. I'll come see you in a bit.'

They kissed, quickly, sweetly; Kei pulled away, aware of the watching eyes. As she did so, something flashed on Noelle's face. Disappointment – in her?

They could talk it over later. 'See you soon,' she said.

Kei dreamed that she was falling.

She was falling gently from a great height. Her guts rose, but it was a pleasant feeling. A buffer against gravity's grip. There was noise somewhere, but it was far, far away. In all Kei's life she couldn't ever remember feeling so safe.

The noise was getting closer.

'Noelle?'

She spoke the name as she awoke. The den was in a terrible mess – things scattered everywhere – and she was alone, and she was still falling.

Falling faster and faster.

This wasn't the artificial pull of the ship. It was a new gravity, foreign, hungry, pulling everything into itself with reckless greed. Sirens screamed through the walls.

Kei struggled to the window and saw the familiar space blackness being consumed, first by white, and then by a crisp, clear blue.

The truth sank in at last. They were falling to Earth.

Kei shoved herself away, dashing across to the exit. It was sealed tight. She braced one foot on the wall and tried again, swearing viciously, bargaining with every god she could name. It didn't open.

Casting around for a switch, she instead saw the tiny screen to the right of the hatch. Before then it had always been dark. Now it read:

Please fasten your seatbelt.

Kei was suddenly thrown against the wall. A new momentum had overridden gravity just for a moment: a tremendous push to the side, sending everything spinning around. Had they hit something? Why couldn't she hear the siren anymore?

A flash of orange filled the window.

Kei thought, *please, no*.

Gripping the handles, she wrenched her face up to the glass, and saw everything she'd prayed not to see – the *Ladybug*, engulfed in flame.

The pod twisted. It was travelling sideways. Carrying her away –

further –

and further –

and –

NANA

WITH EACH NEW year that passed, fewer and fewer
scavengers went out to the city. It was a cursed place.
Through a mountain pass you reached it, beating ponies
or groaning engines, up, down, and then up again, until
the hideous thing unspooled beneath you in all of its
crumbling glory.

People swore that it was Gaia's doing. While all the
lands stayed dry and bleached and salt-ploughed, the
city was forever veiled in grey. Cracks of thunder like
snapping bones echoed down the concrete cliff sides and
into the shadowed streets below. There was no life there.

At first she thought that she was home.

Wrong word.

At first she thought that she was on the planet where
she'd been raised.

Buildings submerged in cloud stretched up on every
side, repeating forever. Wind wound through.

But, no, this wasn't right. The scale was off. Hundreds
of storeys only, rather than thousands. And where were

the bridges, the tramways, the contrails carving white scars in the sky? Where was the smell of fried food, the blare of the tannoy, the swearing match from the open window, the flickering billboard?

No ships to block the sun. No movement.

This was Earth.

The realisation stumped her.

Earth? The homeworld? The decaying mental asylum at the end of the galaxy? Why had she come here?

Why would anyone?

The chain of cause and effect that had led to that moment stretched out behind her – corpses, books, a handful of pills, a sewing kit, a sandwich, heat, dust, stars – and though she could understand individual links between each event, the pattern of the whole thing seemed utterly meaningless. These things had all happened to someone else, or a dozen other people. A dozen strangers. But not to her.

She might as well have been born on that slab of tarmac. Might as well die there, too.

Might as well. Kei closed her eyes, and the last thing she felt was a pinprick on the lids – a single spot of rain.

Something sharp was scrabbling on the ground near her ear. It moved up to her jaw, prodding, nipping at the skin. Kei winced reflexively, her mind swimming up from the bottom of a swamp. The thing pecked her again, this time at the top of her forehead, and she felt a second beak start to investigate her other cheek.

I'm dead. I'm dead, and these vultures are picking at my corpse, she thought.

'Get away, girls!' A voice approached rapidly from the side, and then there was panicked squawking, and the brush of something soft. 'Get away! You're awful! You're all awful! Get off!'

Kei opened her eyes to see a face perhaps two inches from her own, square and shrunken like a slice of stale bread, scrutinising her with bright green eyes.

'Forgive my girls,' said the stranger. 'They see the world as being made up of food, and not food. And the only way to tell one from the other is to try and eat it.' She let out a crackling, wheezy laugh. 'They're still deciding on you!'

Kei lifted her head, a gesture that rolled pain, or the awareness of pain, all down the length of her body. The air around her was close and warm and filled with the moist scent of greenery, enclosed by the soft sounds of rain falling against tarp. Strutting globules of quivering feathers, half dignified, half absurd in their dignity, nosed about between overflowing plant boxes. She was laid out on a bedroll in the corner.

The old woman vanished through a curtain of beads, and then reappeared, holding a bowl of something steaming. 'Soup,' she said, setting it down at Kei's side. She went back through the curtain – her movements were stooping and crablike, but she had the spry energy of a woman half her age – and returned with a second bowl. 'Tea.'

Both liquids tasted much the same. Kei's limbs were weak as paper, and her voice sounded alien as she tried to murmur a thanks.

'No thanks, no thanks,' she scoffed, flapping her hands. 'I like fixing things, eh? Fun for an old peanut shell like me, eh? Call me Nana.'

'Where'd...' She paused to swallow a lump of soft turnip. 'How'd...'

'We found you on Main Avenue. That's where they go to dump the things they want rid of.' Nana seemed incapable of standing still, and moved from plant to plant as she spoke, checking them, feeling the leaves, squirting water from a plastic bottle. 'Ken thought you were another corpse, but I knew better. I knew straight away, no, that one's not done just yet, not just yet.' She cupped her hands around her mouth and hollered, 'KEN! Get in here!'

A man ducked in through the curtain, broad-chested, with a mop of dark hair greased to hang over his forehead in a limp spike.

'This is Ken,' said Nana, still moving. 'He thinks he's mysterious. Don't you Ken? Ahh!' She cackled again. 'Yes, the waif is up, she's not talking much, but she likes my soup, doesn't she? Don't you like my soup?' She looked eagerly at Kei, who felt she had no choice but to nod. 'See, Ken?'

'Everyone likes your soup, Nana,' Ken said quietly.

'They do! They do!'

'Are you feeling alright?' Ken asked. 'What is your name?' There was an awkward, solemn air about him.

'Kei,' she said.

'Kei!' Nana cried it out. 'Good name. Solid. Easy to remember.' She squatted down, yanking the empty bowl from Kei's hand. 'You got it pretty good, eh? Shot right through, weren't you? Who was the culprit? I bet it's a good story, eh? Lots of twists and turns, eh?'

'She probably doesn't want to talk about that right now, Nana.'

Nana sucked her teeth, which made her face look like it was collapsing in on itself. 'Okay. I'll get it out of you soon!' She pinched Kei's cheek and wiggled it vigorously.

'Now go back to sleep!'

It was strange to be ordered about so firmly – stranger still to have no will to resist. Her head touched the mat and she was gone again within moments.

For a while time became porous, half-dissolved. Chickens went clucking, and Nana went clucking after them, and Ken walked in and out, and the sun came and went, and there was a constant stream of hot, flavourless soup.

Sometimes strange people appeared, exchanging things for eggs. They seemed friendly, though Ken always stood in the corner, arms folded, watching.

'Is she safe?' one of them whispered, glancing warily at Kei.

Nana exclaimed, 'Safe!? She's got a hole in her you could run a wire through. Whistles like a sailor when the wind blows! Safe. Ha!' She added knowingly: 'That attitude's why your tomatoes keep dying.'

There was one night when Kei woke up and couldn't breathe – she was going into shock or having some kind of seizure, or she was blind – but then she blinked the wetness out of her eyes and realised that she was sobbing. Nana was already squatting at her side.

'There there,' she said, cooing in the same voice she used when putting the chickens away. 'There there.'

A few hours later, when morning shone bright as a diamond through the blue-green tarp, Kei woke up and found her head was clear as a rung bell, and felt for the first time that the pain was not everywhere in her body but relegated only to a few manageable places. Nobody was around, so she rose quietly, took the plastic bottle, and started spritzing the plants.

'You're overdoing it on the kale. But if you want work,

I can give you plenty of that.' Kei turned to see Nana, watching from the doorway.

'KEN! COME HERE!'

Ken appeared, stern as a statue, with a frilly pink apron tied around his waist and a spatula in his hand. 'I'm cooking, Nana.' He saw Kei standing, and his mouth made a circle. 'You're up.'

'Yeah, she's up, wants to help already. Good attitude, eh? Give me that—' Nana pulled the spatula from Ken's hand and patted him impatiently on his backside. 'Go show her round the garden, I'll cook, you go.'

'Okay.' He turned to Kei. 'Follow me.'

He led her out of a plastic door at the end of the greenhouse, her first glimpse of the outside world in many days and nights. Somehow she'd assumed they were a way out of the city, in a dilapidated cottage. She couldn't have been more wrong.

Nana's garden was a shelf cut into the side of a skyscraper.

They were in the central district, surrounded by vast buildings, their windowed sides beaming with reflected light. Above them the sallow grey sky had morphed into a soft white canopy, cut with shafts of gold.

Kei staggered over and gripped the edge, gazing down at the street below where cars lined up like beetle shells. She could see other gardens, patches of colour on buildings above and below.

'How many people live here?' she asked.

'Perhaps a thousand,' Ken answered. 'Nana has been here the longest. She showed us how to survive.' His deep voice grew deeper with pride.

On a distant rooftop a windmill spun, blades glittering with dew.

Ken showed her around the garden – the water tank, the solar panels, the towers of old tyres stacked high for growing potatoes, and the tin basins lined with grains and greens. There was a tunnel on the coop leading to the outside, and as they walked the chickens weaved between their feet, preening in the sun.

They came to the far corner, where the winding fingers of a runner bean clung delicately to a rusted wire trellis. The sprouting pods were nestled in among broad, thickly veined leaves, tapered at the end to a perfect point. They looked, Kei thought, like an illustration of a leaf, rather than a real one.

'I don't get how this is possible,' she said. 'This rain. All this life.'

A sheepish look came over Ken's face. 'You aren't religious?'

She shook her head.

'You see that tower there?'

He pointed to the tallest building, right in the centre of the city. A slender mess of wires and dishes jutted up from the peak into a minor vortex of swirling mist.

'At the very top there is a machine. People built it a long time ago. It generates particles with a special charge, which causes water to gather around them. The water becomes clouds, the clouds make rain, the fallen rain evaporates and is caught up by the particles.' He made a circular gesture with his hands. 'Around and around.'

Kei's eyes widened in disbelief. 'Incredible. If only...'

If only Noelle could see this. The thought came into her mind uninvited, and with it a swoop of grief so destabilising she nearly fell.

'Kei?' Ken put a hand on her shoulder.

'It's fine,' she managed, heart aching at the memories.

Nana's voice came from inside: 'EGG TIME!'

There was a long interlude while Nana ran around, scooping up the chickens so that they could be introduced one by one – Daisy, Haisy, Molly, Polly, Becky, Freckley, and the red-gilled rooster Jack, twice the size of the others, who subjected himself to Nana's cuddles and kisses with affected disinterest. Then, more touring. Ken took her around the shelled-out remains of an apartment: slapshot kitchen with a rigged-up burner stove, the door to the stairwell, fortified with an iron lock, and finally his room, where he shyly showed her his collection of sketches. They were mostly charcoal and pencil, drawn on bits of scrap paper and cardboard.

Kei lifted free a portrait of Nana. She was drawn from the side in thick lines, and hastily, as if in secret. Still, he'd captured her well – she was shouting.

'It is hard to train without paper,' said Ken, frowning at a bare patch of carpet. 'But I believe I will improve if I work hard.'

Kei held the sketch up to the light. 'You're talented, Ken, you could trade these for stuff.'

'You cannot eat a picture,' he replied, blushing.

From that day forward Kei took on a role as a makeshift gardener's apprentice. She was still slow on her feet, but it hardly mattered, as the pace of the days was so unhurried. The more she healed, the more responsibilities she took on: weeding, feeding, watering, mucking out; in the gently mechanical tasks she was able to slip away from herself for hours at a time, to forget everything that had happened, at least for a while. It felt wrong to have nothing on her hip, so she took to sticking the trowel and the plastic spritz bottle on either side of her belt, a habit that moved Nana to tears of laughter every time she noticed.

Ken was happy to let her take over the garden work. It left him more time for foraging, which was his true passion, leaving in the early dawn and returning late at night. He always came home with something practical – batteries or light bulbs or strong rope – but Kei suspected it had more to do with his friend Shin, who grew wheat on the top of an apartment block two streets over and would usually come along to 'watch his back' as they were out in the city. From the garden Kei could see them walking side by side, dwarfed by the monolithic buildings, their linked hands just a speck between them.

Despite the tufts of life in the little rooftop gardens the city remained staggering in its emptiness, a picture of pure desolation. Storms came often, and they would wait them out inside the flat, watching the window shake in its casing. But Kei found this was a comfort. Grief to her was an apocalypse of the heart, and for the external world to be lively and normal would have felt nothing less than grotesque.

It took a few weeks before she was ready to talk about what had happened. The story came out in little fragments, some parts to Ken, who would listen in silence and occasionally nod, and some parts to Nana, who would interrupt regularly to bemoan the flaws of all the groups involved – the dogmatic faithful, the feckless young, and men, especially old men, especially old men in power.

'And they've got the cheek to call my city cursed! Eh?' Ken lifted his bowl up just as Nana's hand came slamming down on the table, rattling it right down to the floor. It was late, and they were gathered in the kitchen eating fried-tomato stew, their faces lit in soft amber by the moth-fluttered lamp. 'Acting like a bunch of bloody warlords out there with their big ship. Where's the humility in that, eh? I'd like to know!'

'I wonder how he keeps the farms watered,' Ken mused, as Kei wiped spilled stew from her lap.

'Pumps it up from some deep reservoir, I'll bet you. It won't last! The water'll run out, and then the people will get hungry, and mad, and then boom.' Nana slammed the table again. 'Heads on spikes. That's always how it goes! Isn't that how it always goes, Ken?'

'Yes, Nana.' Ken looked a little sad.

'So don't get yourself worked up about revenge,' she said, waggling a crooked finger at Kei. 'Those people will get plenty of punishment, in good time. In good time, they will.'

As she put the chickens away that night Kei meditated on the idea of revenge. It made sense for her to want it, but she found the idea physically repulsive. What happened on the *New Destiny* was like a gelatinous sack roosting at the centre of her brain. All day long she moved carefully through the space around it, frightened to touch the surface in case it burst.

There were never any questions raised about how long she would stay, or if she would find some way to repay them beyond chores and stories. Nana fed her unquestioningly, the same way she fed Ken and the chickens and the wild cats that sometimes climbed the long staircase to mewl at the door.

It was an unusually clear evening, and the three of them were sitting outside, in the fold-out 'nice weather' chairs that Nana kept in the back for those rare occasions. On a rooftop below another group was having a party, and the sound of the warbling accordion echoed from the building's side. Nana prowled along the precipice, tutting and glaring at the dancing figures below.

'Those fermenters, they're crazy. What a waste of grain.' A kick-drum was added to the band, and she leant over the edge and yelled, 'KEEP IT DOWN!'

In response one of the fermenters dropped to a knee and cried, 'MARRY ME, NANA!'

Laughter rose up into the warm air.

'Let them have their fun,' murmured Ken, smiling faintly beneath his sunglasses. He was in a good mood, having found an untouched sketchbook and some pastels downtown. Kei was resting her feet on an upturned bucket, leafing through a book on agriculture that Nana had given her to read. The impenetrable ancient text meant almost nothing to her, but she was enjoying the illustrations.

'They're crazy, I tell you. One of them's going to fall off the side one day.' Nana dropped herself into her chair with a huff. 'Well, serves them right, that's what I say. It's for the best!'

It's for the best.

The words were like a pebble dropped to the bottom of a dark well. A distant splash, and a soundless ripple.

Kei bolted upright. She walked to the edge of the garden and stared down at the party, eyes wide and unseeing. She heard Ken ask, 'Are you alright?'

Nana scoffed. 'Tell that boy he can't play for a slice of cheese!'

You'll be joining her now. It's for the best.

'Ah, I miss cheese,' Nana went on, speaking mostly to

herself now. 'We didn't know how good we had it, let me—'

'Nana.' Kei cut her off. She could feel an excited tremor developing in her hands, and she struggled to keep it down. 'Nana, you remember I told you about my…' She wasn't sure of the word to use. '…about Noelle?'

'Mm, yes, rest her soul, yes,' Nana said, nodding to herself.

'Before he shot me, Seawall—'

' If I had him here, I'd tell him a thing or two, yes—' Nana interjected.

'—he said, *You'll be joining her now. It's for the best.* It was the last thing he said.' Kei turned and looked imploringly at them. 'That's odd, isn't it?'

Ken's brows were furrowed deep with concern. 'Are you feeling well, Kei?'

But Nana was leaning forward in her chair, and her eyes were sparkling. 'Something on your mind, eh?'

'It's just – there is no way Seawall could have known about us,' she said. 'There was no – no physical evidence anywhere on the ship, we never sent notes. But he knew about it. How?'

Ken was on his feet. 'You are sure?' he was saying. 'You must be certain about this, Kei.'

'I knew it wasn't right, but I wasn't thinking straight—' All those untouched memories were blooming back into view all at once, so fast and vivid it made her skull ache. 'There were other things, too. He called me Captain. How'd he know my rank? It's not possible. Unless…'

'Unless somebody told him,' finished Ken.

He looked at Nana, who was pressing her lips tight together. Slowly, she rose up from her camp chair and moved towards the kitchen. 'I'll go put the kettle on.'

Ken gave her one last worried look before following Nana inside.

Kei stayed out long after the sun had set, pacing, pausing to stare up at the unfamiliar constellations. Her wound was throbbing. On the fermenters' rooftop the music grew slower and lazier, the laughter more intimate. Eventually Nana shuffled out, wrapped in a wool shawl, clutching her nightcap. She stood at Kei's side and for a while neither of them spoke – the longest she'd ever heard Nana be silent. She took a long draught of her tea, and then asked, 'When are you leaving?'

'First thing.'

'Ken'll offer to go with you.'

'He can't.'

Nana nodded.

'You must think I'm crazy.'

'Oh yes, you can be sure of that. Crazy's the word.' Nana squeezed her hand.

Something in this little gesture made Kei's guts revolt, and she bent down, clasping a hand over her mouth. She broke away and ran to the edge, holding her face over the precipice. But nothing happened.

'Shit,' she said, with a choking laugh, and then added, 'Sorry,' because Nana didn't approve of swearing.

'Mm, you can have that one, I'll allow that.'

Kei sighed. 'I'm not scared of getting hurt. I'm scared of the disappointment. I think it would kill me.'

'You survived the first time, didn't you? Don't see why you wouldn't again.'

Kei put a hand around Nana's shoulders – so narrow, she realised with a slight shock, and so small – and pressed the old woman against her side. The accordionist played his final chord out with inebriated grandeur, to the sound of equally inebriated applause. Nana cupped her hands around her mouth.

'God damned ruddy...' She paused to inhale. 'TERRIBLE! *BOOOO!*'

When Kei tried to leave early the next morning, she found Ken tying his shoes, expression glum.

'Ken,' she said, her voice low. 'I'm sorry, but you can't come.'

'I know. This is not about that.'

She followed him down the many flights of stairs – the first time she'd been down to the ground level ever since she arrived – through a fire door, and into an underground car park, a dingy cave of yellow paint and squat concrete pillars, linked to the road by a sloped entrance ramp. Leaning against one of the pillars, spit-shined and glittering from end to end, was a motorbike.

'It works perfectly,' he said, placing a hand on the saddle. 'I have not ridden it in many years, but I have been doing maintenance. It is ready to go.'

'Ken, I can't take this.'

'I would like you to. It reminds me of my old self. That is not a man I am fond of.' He took the handles and wheeled it out to the ramp. 'It is very easy to drive. Push to start. Twist to accelerate. Pull here to slow down. The fuel will not last the whole way, but—'

'I'm telling you, Ken, I can't—'

He placed the key in her hand and folded her fingers around it. 'Good luck.'

There was nothing more to say. They shook hands – he had a grip like a pair of boulders – and she climbed onto the bike. The engine came instantly to life, trembling with an energy that rattled her teeth.

She took off with only a nudge of the pedal, up the ramp and out into the bluish dawn, sprinkled with soft, tentative rain. She turned cautiously eastwards, moving through the debris, blinking away the rainwater that wept down into her eyes. Buildings peeled away to either side, and the broken white lines slipped faster and faster beneath the front tyre, summoning the rising mountains and the glare of the unshrouded sun.

THE MIRACLE

THERE WERE NO rankings in the Church of Gaia. It was a fact that Ursula Ramirez often had to remind her colleagues of – and, if she was being perfectly candid, herself. Theirs was a faith of submission, not dominance, and it had no need for the hierarchical structures that had characterised the churches of the old world. 'High Preacher' was simply a name bestowed upon her by a few worshippers here and there, grateful she'd united the wasteland parishes. And while she had long aligned herself with the High Sheriff, Ursula considered herself neither his supervisor nor his lackey. Her position was that of a spiritual advisor, a holy word in the old man's ear. It was not her job to enforce laws. She was simply a wind vane, pointing her vast flock towards enlightenment. They could choose to ignore her if they wished.

Man has always been free to choose damnation.

Ursula felt faintly sick as the elevator rose through the *New Destiny*'s body, a nausea, she was certain, that came from being separated so far from her Mother

250

God. But that was just a physical sensation. It held no bearing on the cold rage that gripped her heart. Ursula's wisdom was much sought after by the people, and since she preferred to take meetings in person, her schedule was often crammed. So it was only that morning that she had found the time, reclining in her study with a cup of herbal tea, to read the letter she had received from a remote parish to the north.

And now her anger burned like the fire at God's core.

The doors slid wide, and she stepped out into the pale smoothness of the top floor, greeted with a nod by a pair of armed officers. In the last month she had noticed a marked increase in city security; on the corridors of the lower levels they strutted to and fro like cockerels, some of them hardly older than children, with their rifles and polished badges glinting on their puffed-out chests. Seawall's handiwork: Ursula bristled at the sight. But she still gave them a smile, for it was the wayward ones who needed her light the most.

So much to fix. But today would be the start of it.

When she arrived at the upper chamber Seawall was already waiting in the parlour, sunk deep into a plush armchair. Hate was unbecoming of a Preacher, but Ursula could not help the way the Deputy made her feel. His smirk, laced with contempt and amusement, made her wish for a fissure to open in the Earth's surface and swallow him whole. A fitting end for the likes of him.

But she had to be professional.

'So you were summoned too,' she said.

'Sure was.' He was picking his teeth. 'We just got done.'

'That's convenient. I was hoping we could discuss your behaviour.'

Seawall's eyebrows shot up, but he did not ordain to

respond. This was another habit of his that she loathed: leaving long silences, knowing that she would fill them.

'Saint's Cradle,' she said at last. 'When were you going to tell me?'

The Deputy rolled the toothpick to the other corner of his mouth, and grinned. 'Never.'

'Never?' She could hear her voice rise with indignation. 'You threatened one of my – one of the most valued members of the Church!'

He leant forward, hunching with an elbow on each knee. 'I was just reminding him who's in charge. Is that so wrong?'

'Each Preacher must be free to act according to their conscience.'

'They act according to their interests, Ursula. Much like the rest of us lowly mortals.'

Her nostrils flared. 'You understand I shall have to tell Levee about this.'

He cocked a thumb over his shoulder. 'Go ahead. He's waiting.'

Ursula swept past, feeling Seawall's eyes bore into the back of her skull.

The High Sheriff's bedroom smelled as it always did: like congealed food, and body odour, and strong sanitiser, and dust. The respirator hissed in the far corner, and the overhead light was dim. He was sitting up – a good sign – but physically he looked more emaciated than ever, skin like dead leaves and mottled with liver spots, eyes milky and permanently encased in film. But even as his body crumbled he had not lost the sharp inquisitiveness of his younger years. When he looked at her she felt seen.

'I heard you bickering,' he said, his lips pulled into a smile.

'I'm sorry, Levee.' She took her place at his side. 'After all this time, he still loves to wind me up. How are you feeling?'

'Like shit. Now spit it out – what's the problem?'

There was no point trying to beat around the bush with him. 'Saint's Cradle. Do you know what he did?'

He glanced away, still smiling. 'Poor Aidan. Sometimes I think he never grew up.'

'God's tits, Levee!' Ursula burst out. 'The man *threatened* a highly respected Preacher! When will you stop treating him like an errant child?'

'He's just restless, that's all.' Levee's voice was soothing, untroubled. 'If he ever does something real bad, I'll take care of him myself.'

'He's up to something, I swear.' She shuffled closer, just in case Seawall was listening at the door. 'We should bring the Project forward. Before...'

'Before I kick the bucket?'

She winced. 'Yes.'

'Ursula...' He looked up at her. 'It's ready.'

'You're not serious.'

'Oh, I am, I am. One last round of double-checks, then everything's good to go.' He was gleeful.

'Sweet – Mother of—' Ursula leapt up and started to stride, robes swishing, gripping a swathe of beads in her fist. 'Should I call a sermon? No, that might raise suspicions. When is it happening? I've not...' A sudden pause. 'Aidan won't be happy.'

'Hush, now, relax. He'll come around.' At his motioning, she returned to Levee's side. 'I've got it covered. Just kick back and watch the show. And afterwards, when people come to you and ask what happened, make sure to tell them...'

He relaxed backwards against his pillows and let out a long, dreamy sigh.

'…make sure to tell them it was God.'

KEI HAD BEEN riding for so long that she had merged with the mould of the seat, her hands shaped into permanent gripping claws. The crumbling slopes of the mountain pass were behind her, and now she could see the outline of the *New Destiny* nudging up from the horizon, tauntingly close.

But the gas was running out. Already the bike's engine was beginning to stutter, a guttural coughing that shook through the padded seat every time she pressed the accelerator. Ahead of her on the road, a red pickup truck was trundling its way eastward. Kei was determined to overtake it before her fuel ran out for good, and she urged the bike on, crawling up until she was parallel to the truck – which, now she was close, was moving faster then she'd thought. She edged the speed up notch by notch, squinting against the airflow.

Something struck the front wheel. The handlebar careered in her hand, swaying drunkenly towards the truck. A horn blared behind her, and she tried desperately to steer back the other way, teeth clattering, the front wheel shaking side to side in vehement disagreement. She stomped on the brake and, feeling the motion lift her from the saddle, turned as sharply as she could. Both wheels slid, screaming, lengthways under her, until she finally came to a stop and fell off sideways in a heap.

She heard the truck screech to a halt, and then the slamming of a door. The driver leapt out onto the road and marched towards her, yelling, *'Are you crazy?'*

'I'm sorry, I—' Kei staggered upwards, wiping dirt out of her eyes. She looked at the driver, who looked back at her. '—son of a bitch.'

It was Amber Keeper.

A handful of months had not much changed the librarian's appearance, though her dreads were bundled behind her head rather than on top, and she looked a touch better-rested around the eyes.

'It's you,' she said.

Kei shrugged with the air of a criminal caught in the act. 'It's me,' she agreed.

There was an interim of silence. Kei coughed. 'Where's your library?'

'Sold it.'

'Okay.'

Amber shifted her weight, hands housed in her pockets. Her gaze flicked down to Kei's hip. 'Where's the gun?'

'Lost it.'

'Lost it? Are you stupid?'

Kei tried a half-hearted laugh, which broke against the wall of Amber's contempt like so many waves against a granite cliff. She remembered well how things had ended last time, and she hurriedly tried to haul the bike back upright, keen to move on. But when she turned the key, the engine only groaned. She turned back to Amber, grinning with embarrassment.

'I'll push it out of the way—'

'Goddamn it. Just get in.'

She turned and walked back to the truck.

Kei found her around the back, picking up books that had been spilled loose in the near-crash. They were stacked in the open boot, boxes and boxes of them. Salvage.

'You know something funny?' Amber asked. Her tone

was stiff, and she didn't meet Kei's eyes as she spoke. 'I was actually hoping I'd get to see you again. Dunno why.'

'Oh yeah?' Kei started picking books up as well.

'You ever find that thing you were looking for?'

'No,' she said, dusting off some pastel-coloured pamphlets. 'I mean – not yet.'

'Shame.'

Most of the boot space was taken up by a plastic crate, open at the top. Kei took out a book, a picture of a smouldering cartoon planet with the title *A Study in Decay*. Further below were science journals, a weather-beaten atlas, a pamphlet with the slogan THIS IS NOT A DRILL. Earnest, hopeful, blunt: they reminded her of Noelle.

'Why'd you have these?'

'I'm working on commission now,' Amber responded. 'Got given a long list of titles to try and find. It's been a bitch, I tell you.'

Kei flipped through a few pages of a journal called *The New Survivor*. Every other image was a wildfire, or a flood. 'Are they all like this?'

'Mostly. Say…' Amber leant casually against the desk. 'You're not still heading for the *New Destiny*, are you?'

Kei smacked the book shut. 'As a matter of fact, I am.'

'Uh-huh.' Amber studied her nails. 'See, I'm understaffed at the moment. I lost my last guy to an argument about *Lord of the Rings*… he said it was too long. Stupid son of a bitch. Anyway, if you wanna do security on the handover, I'll drive you up for free. I'll even throw in a Lee Child. One of the good ones.'

Kei raised her eyebrows. 'Without my gun?'

'Doesn't matter. I've seen what you can do with a paperback.'

'Was that a joke?'

'No.' She almost looked offended.

Kei looked down at the crate, at the litany of blue-green planets, some of them burning. In the corner of her mind she could feel hope taking root like a gnarled weed.

She closed the lid with a click. 'You've got a deal.'

They approached the ship-city from behind. Kei watched it grow from the passenger seat, eating away at the sky, running her hand over the seam in her jacket elbow.

'You're looking kinda pale,' said Amber. 'Need a pit stop?'

Kei declined. Keen to change the subject, she asked, 'Who ordered the books?'

'Dunno. Someone from high up. They weren't big on details. Not surprising – most of that stuff is borderline hedonistic.' Discomfort flashed across Amber's face. 'If – if you're the religious sort, you know.'

'Are you? The religious sort?'

'Ahh…' Amber shuffled deeper into the seat. A loop of beads hung from the rear-view mirror, rattling with every bump. Kei thought she'd touched a sore spot, but to her surprise the librarian went on: 'Thing is, I was raised by the Church. Would've probably died if it wasn't for them. And I feel – inside of me…' She pressed a fist against her chest. 'I feel like the Earth is more special than your average hunk of rock. But the older I get – the more I *read* – the more the whole Gaia thing feels like just another story.'

'Right.' Kei rested an elbow on the windowsill, fingers trailing the roof handle. They were driving through farmland now, blocks of colour rushed past one at a time – low rustling greens, high billowing yellows.

'Shit, I love this planet. I just – I'd like to think that it loves me back.'

'Of course,' Kei murmured. Her mind was on the *Ladybug*. 'It's home.'

The nose of the truck dipped dramatically as it rolled down into Underland, slowing to a crawl as they inched through the jumbled streets. They came at last to the docking yard, built around the cavernous maw of the *New Destiny*'s rear loading bay. It was a picture of controlled chaos, with vans and wagons flowing perpetually in and out, honking and heckling for space. Amber rolled up alongside a brown-vested guard and leant out.

'Book delivery,' she declared.

The guard glanced down at his clipboard. 'Ramp 14,' he said, waving them on through. There was an odd tone to his voice. In the mirror Kei could see him stare as they drove away. 'Looks like we're special,' she said. Amber just shrugged.

Ramp 14 was at the furthest end of the yard. It took them past a long logjam of food trucks and up into the spacious gloom of the ship's interior. The passage narrowed, and the clamour of human activity fell away behind them. Amber kept glancing behind, fiddling with the rear-view mirror.

'Too damn tight. If I get so much as a *scratch* on these hubcaps...'

Up ahead was a dead end, with a small pile of crates and a lone guard. She wore sunglasses, a tank top and – strangely – a pair of long black gloves that stretched up to the elbow. The gun at her hip was an old-style mechanical pistol, grey, compact, efficiently built.

'Looks like a mercenary.' Amber made a small gesture, first over her own chest, and then over Kei's. 'Mother God preserve us. Please let me get paid. Amen.'

'Amen,' Kei agreed.

The librarian hopped out, and Kei followed.

'Morning,' said Amber. 'Book delivery?'

'Uh-huh. Let's see them.'

That voice. She had a rasp like she'd swallowed a set of keys. But that wasn't the problem – Kei knew it. From where?

'Give me a hand,' said Amber. Kei was certain that the mercenary was staring at her, though behind the glasses it was impossible to tell.

At the truck's rear, Kei spoke with a low voice: 'Do you know her?'

'Dunno. I know the *type*.' She paused, panting as she tried to haul the crate away. Kei lifted it free of her hands.

'I feel like we've met,' Kei whispered.

'Fan-fuckin-tastic. Go intro…' She paused to take a breath, and slapped Kei across the back. '…introduce yourself then, Casanova.'

Back around the front, the mercenary had not moved, and only a slight turn of her head indicated that she was watching. Kei carried the crate over, glancing surreptitiously towards the pistol. Late twentieth century. She'd not seen a model like that before.

The mercenary pointed to the ground, her face impassive. 'Down there.'

As Kei set the books down, Amber asked, 'Will that do?'

The mercenary kicked the crate with her toe. 'Was this all you could find?'

'Uh-huh. Nearly all of it.'

The mercenary hesitated another moment. Then she took out a wad from her back pocket and counted out a number of slips, pinching them between black-gloved fingers. 'Five hundred. As promised.' She held them out. Kei felt her shoulders tensing as Amber got closer, missing more than ever the weight of her heat pistol on her hip. But the exchange went fine, and when Amber thumbed through the money her eyes glowed.

'Pleasure doing business with you,' she said, slotting the money into a compartment on her belt.

The two of them were turning to go, when – 'Wait.' The mercenary's face was turned in Kei's direction, and she was holding a single paper slip. 'Don't you want your cut?'

Kei held her hands up. 'Oh, I'm – I'm not—'

'Take it.' For the first time Kei thought she could hear a note of feeling in the other woman's voice, though what the feeling was, she couldn't tell. 'Come on,' she added. 'You rich or something?'

Kei looked uncertainly at Amber, who shrugged. *Why not?*

The mercenary was equal to Kei in height, so that when she stepped closer she could see her own anxious face reflected in the domed black glass.

'You don't remember, do you?' she asked.

Kei went still.

The mercenary reached over, grabbing the rim of her glove. She peeled it down slowly. Lengthways along her forearm, knuckle to elbow, dozens of staples held together the nastiest scar that Kei had ever seen.

'How about now?'

Kei yelled for Amber to run as she leapt in, wrapping her hand around the pistol, to wrench the muzzle upwards. The mercenary grabbed her by the shoulder, digging her fingernails through the skin, trying with her full weight to wrestle it back down. Someone hit the trigger, and a bullet rocketed up in the slim space between their faces. The mercenary grunted in surprise, but that was all she had time to do before Kei grabbed her two-handed by the collar and slammed their heads together. She fell back, and would have hit the ground had Kei not held on to her jacket. Instead she hung limp, nose bloody, glasses askew.

'Stand back! You lousy stinking...' Kei heard Amber trail into silence mid-threat, and turned to see the librarian wielding a sawn-off shotgun. 'You okay?' she asked, lowering it.

Kei nodded.

'What was that about?'

'Doesn't matter.' Kei laid the mercenary down on the ground. The shades remained miraculously intact save for a dent at the nose, and she lifted them free, bending them back into shape.

'Stop pissing around,' Amber urged. 'Let's go!'

'You go. I'm heading in.'

'*What?*' For half a second Amber looked ready to argue, hands still clutching the shotgun stock, her face twisted into the unlikely shape of a concerned scowl. But she relented. 'Shit. Fine.' She stomped back to the truck, threw open the driver's-side door, and then paused, one foot on the step. 'If you make it... look me up, alright?'

Kei smiled. 'Sure.'

There was some muttering about crazy heathens, and then she vanished, reversing back towards the yard with a squeal of rubber.

Kei slipped on the gloves as well as the aviators, but resolved, after some hesitation, to leave the gun. She knew it was a weapon that had been ill-used – remembered the musician on the highway, murdered from behind – and couldn't imagine how a device with such a nakedly violent design could ever do anything except kill. She lifted the crate and kicked her way through into the back corridor.

It was narrow, painted all over in yellow with black arrows along the floor, and busy with silver-badged guards who leapt to the side at her approach. One young officer broke into a jog just to get past her, so she stuck her foot out and said, in as gruff a voice as she could manage, 'Stop.'

He stopped, staring up at her, rigid with fear. 'G-good afternoon?' Kei looked him up and down. 'Love the new hair,' he added faintly.

'Where do these go?' She indicated the crate with a jerk of her head.

'The books? Oh! The new order, yes. That's lab storage, back of floor two. But mind that no ordinary folk see you' – Kei watched him blink away sweat – 'if – if you can – please.'

Kei grunted affirmatively and moved her leg, so the sweating officer could catapult himself down the corridor. She hoisted the crate up an inch higher and strode on, trying not to let the pleasure show on her face. It felt like being back in the old days, all the prodigious arrogance of an unkillable young soldier.

As if a run of good fortune could obliterate everything that had come along since.

URSULA RAMIREZ WAS having a crisis of faith. She had written and rewritten her sermon for the afternoon, trying to find an organic way to introduce the concept of miracles. But it was proving hard. It wasn't that she didn't *believe* in them per se. Childbirth was a miracle. A spiderweb was a miracle. Gravity was the greatest miracle of all, the ultimate evidence of God's love. Everything about the physical world around them was miraculous – so what was the point of expecting something impossible, when the possible was enough?

Discarded rolls of paper littered the study floor, and her tea had long since grown cold. Cramped and irritable from too many hours at her desk, she took to the balcony. This was the one indulgence that she allowed herself – a loop of metal out in the open air, where she could stare out at the curving majesty of God's body and let the awe run like clear water through her mind.

When the door slid open behind her, she assumed it was the usual girl coming to collect her cups, and ordered, 'I'll need a fresh pot, on the double, thank you.'

'Right away, ma'am. Anything else?'

The voice ran cold iron down Ursula's spine. She turned to see Deputy Seawall, hands in his pockets, kicking at the mess. 'What's the matter? Horseshit not coming out as smooth as usual?'

'What do you want, Aidan?' Ursula tried not to look as unsettled as she felt. Seawall's presence was always an ill omen.

He strolled up beside her, gripping the rail, and inhaling deep. 'What a mess,' he said of the world beneath. 'I don't know what you see in it, Su.'

'Don't call me that,' she snapped. 'Say what you've come to say and be done with it.'

'I just don't get it.' Ignoring her, he turned, leaning backwards. 'I don't understand why you're going along with this scheme of Levee's. I mean, you're *faking* an act of God. Bit heretical, ain't it? Just like that stuff with Saint's Cradle. It's bullshit, all bullshit.'

'Nobody asked you,' said Ursula. 'What are you so afraid of?'

Seawall laughed, a sound so unusual, so rasping, that she felt the urge to cover her ears. 'Nothing.'

'No, you are. You're afraid things are going to change.' She couldn't help herself. His laugh had loosened something within her. 'You're afraid people will feel like they're special, and worthy, and blessed. And then they might start treating each other decently. And thinking for themselves. And looking after one another. And we can come together and live the way Gaia intended us to, as a community of people, living in harmony with the sweet Earth. We will have no need for guns, no need for sheriffs. In fact, we shall cast them out. Cast them out and supplicate ourselves at our Mother's feet to *beg* forgiveness that we ever let such scum taint Her surface!'

Ursula stopped. She had somehow gotten close to him, closer than she intended, and she could see his eyes – the sardonic amusement, and, deeper still, the utter lack of anything, of any faith, any light. He wiped a fleck of spit from his cheek.

'You're a hypocrite,' he said mildly. 'All this talk of *Mother Earth,* and you don't live anywhere near the ground.'

'God claimed this vessel. It belongs to her.'

'No, Ursula. It belongs to me.'

Then – slowly, gently, as if he were going in for a kiss – Seawall planted two hands on the High Preacher's chest and pushed her over the rail.

AIDAN DID NOT wait around to see the grisly fruits of his labour. It was going to be a busy day. He radioed his sub-deputy and told him that the High Preacher had committed suicide.

'Don't scrape the body off just yet, mind. The more people see, the better.'

A new regime was dawning. The time for discretion was gone.

He took the elevator downstairs to the lab entrance and told the guard there that nobody was to come in or out, and if anyone tried, he had permission to use lethal force. As he was leaving he saw the freak mercenary with the sunglasses staring at him from afar, but being freshly a murderer and in no mood for conversation, he turned and left.

No PANIC ATTACK is ever timely. But some times are worse than others.

It was the Deputy's voice – the way he said, *'Lethal force, y'hear?'* in that slow drawl with a razor blade at the centre – that nearly knocked Kei over. It was a kind of time travel; she was back there again, back in that moment when the bullet had hit and everything fallen apart.

Through some remarkable reflex she managed not to drop the crate, and once it sank in that he had not recognised her she turned around and started walking as fast as she could. She needed somewhere to hide. Could that officer see how hard she was breathing? Sweat seeped from her hands, it was hard to grip. She needed –

– a toilet? Perfect.

The door locked behind her and she dropped down, not minding as the books spilled everywhere, hugging herself as she waited for the merry-go-round in her head to stop. She'd been insane to come back, insane to trap herself again inside this humming, airless monolith, chasing a shadow, chasing a corpse, the corpse of a woman who'd been too good for her even when she was alive. Noelle and the pilot and the pilot's family and the scientists and the soldiers and the rest of them were all dead, she was the sole survivor, and pretty soon she'd be dead too, because there was no way she could walk away from this place twice, no—

It was the colour that caught her eye. A dark, rich green, like the leaves that grew around Nana's runner beans. The book was large, but thinner than the others, so that when she pulled it free from the pile it nearly bent. Brown pencil sketches of half a dozen baby birds crowded in at the base, watched over, with an adoring black eye, by the mother bird. The title was *Make Way for Ducklings*.

She opened it and found the illustration of the duck family marching proudly across a busy street.

Then Kei began to cry.

SUB-OFFICER MAGNUS DEALT in violence. It was his trade, his bread and butter. And so it was the greatest shame of Magnus's short life that he'd never killed anyone before.

Three years he'd worked as a Sheriff's apprentice, but not once had the disaster he'd dreamed of ever come to pass – no bandit raiders riding in from the wastelands to blow up the bank, no bands of escaped convicts taking the innkeeper hostage. He'd roughed up a few horse thieves and pulled his gun on a tax-dodger once, but outside of daily target practice he'd never had the chance to pull his trigger. He thought being stationed in the city would give him a chance at some action, but all he did all day was turn away people with the wrong paperwork. The tedium drove him mad.

Today was different. Magnus's moment had finally come. *Deputy Seawall himself* had given him the go-ahead to shoot aggressors on sight – practically *insisted* on it. Clearly there was something happening, some big event about to go down, and Magnus had a part to play in it. Maybe he'd have a toe-to-toe fight with a rogue officer, or gun down a barrage of crazed heretics who were coming to storm the labs. The labs had to be protected at all costs. For some reason. Magnus didn't know the details, but he was ready to fight to his last breath.

It was disappointing, then, when the next person who appeared was a lone woman. Magnus considered himself a hero and a gentleman and this challenger did not suit his tastes. Sure, she looked a *little* dangerous – her crooked nose suggested one or two clobbers to the face – but not scary at all. In fact she was smiling, and at the raising of his rifle her smile broadened, but there was not a trace of malice in it, and he could see that she was unarmed, and all she had in her hands was a broad green book.

'Hey, now,' she said.

'Back off.' Magnus shuffled his feet around, trying to find the most intimidating stance. 'Nobody goes in or out. Deputy's orders.'

'Out?' She tilted her head. 'So someone's in there?'

'Uh…'

'Who?'

'That's classified,' he said, because he didn't know, 'now back off.' He jabbed the rifle in her chest, but her smile did not flicker.

'What's your name?'

Magnus was getting nervous. Normally when people asked him what his name was it was so they could go and report him to the boss. Did she have that kind of authority?

'Mag—' he started, before realising that it would be prudent to lie. But he couldn't think of another name that started with Mag, except for Maggie, which was a girl's name, and wouldn't do at all. '—nus,' he finished, crumpling a little.

'Magnus, my name is Kei.' She put a hand on her chest. 'Kei Marshal.'

'Nice to meet you,' said Magnus automatically, and then was instantly annoyed with himself.

'I need to deliver this book.' She held it up so he could see. 'It's really important. Can I go in?'

She was asking, but not in the way that Magnus liked people to ask him for things, in a sad and whiny tone that made him feel even better when he said *no*. It was like she was doing him a courtesy by not just walking in.

'I'll be two minutes. That's it.'

'Okay!' Magnus blurted out. 'But I'm gonna time it!'

She patted him on the shoulder. 'You do that.'

Magnus watched her disappear through the automatic door. And then he started counting.

THE LAB WAS silent, save for the scribbling of paper on pen, and the whirring of machinery. She was standing at a countertop, scribbling something down in a book, turned so Kei could look at her in profile. Still perfect. But not the exact same – her face had a gaunt shading to it, the frazzled look of a long night of research multiplied by a dozen. But it was her.

Noelle hadn't heard the door, which Kei didn't find surprising. When she was thinking she had a way of putting the entire universe on hold. Kei loved seeing her like that: the micro-expressions and the way her lips moved to form the words as she wrote them. She let herself enjoy it for another second.

Then she asked, 'What're you working on?'

Noelle turned her head. She dropped the pen and almost fell back, catching herself on the table, bringing her hand up to stifle a scream. Her eyes were huge and shimmering. Kei buried her face into her neck and inhaled and she could hear Noelle saying, 'What? What? What?' with a shock that was slowly morphing into pure joy. She pulled away and Noelle looked up at her and said, again, 'What?'

'It's me.'

'Kei.' Noelle cupped her face with both hands, checking she was real, looking at every inch of her. 'You look so tired.'

'I am. I haven't—' Kei forced herself to take a breath. 'I thought you were dead.'

'I'm not,' Noelle said, laughing.

'Yeah.'

Noelle tucked a strand of hair behind Kei's ear. 'Your hair is so long.'

'Is it?' Kei wrapped her fingers around Noelle's. 'I hadn't noticed.'

Silence fell between them, melting like wax, the silence that Kei had been missing for months and months. It was music to her ears.

* * *

'118, 119, 120!'

Sub-Officer Magnus kicked his way into the lab. For a moment he just stared at the two of them. Blood rushed hot into his cheeks, and he raised his rifle and yelled, 'Stop kissing! Put your hands up!'

The woman in the lab coat burst out laughing, and Kei joined in: 'Okay, Magnus. You got me.' She raised her hands and walked towards him.

'Good. Now—' Magnus wasn't sure what to do next. He was saved the trouble of deciding when Kei shoved the rifle's stock upwards into his face. His skull smacked the back wall and he slid to the ground.

Both of them were still flushed and giddy, but Kei remained aware of the danger. 'The others. Are they here?'

Noelle looked away. 'They stayed with the wreck,' she said. 'But I had to go, I had to find you.' Her eyes welled. 'We lost – we lost some people in the crash. Jules.'

Kei felt a twist in her chest. She took Noelle around the shoulders and asked, 'What happened? When did they get you?'

'You're so melodramatic.' She snorted, wiping her eyes with the heel of her palm. 'They didn't *get* me. We made a deal. He said if I helped him he'd send people out to find you, said it would be faster than searching alone. But things keep getting stranger and stranger… they stopped letting me outside. I was so stupid, Kei. I should have just gone after you myself.'

'It's alright. Come on. We can slip out through the loading yard. I know the way.'

'Oh…' Noelle sniffed, looking up at her. '…now?'

'Yes, now.' Kei saw the look on her face. 'You've gotta be kidding me—'

'Kei. Listen to me. Listen.'

'Do you have any idea what—'

'I'm sorry. There's one more thing I need to do. Then we can go.'

'Noelle, *no.*'

'You don't even know what it is!'

'*I don't care!*' Kei yelled. But it was no use, and she knew that. 'You're exhausting.'

Noelle stood up on her toes and kissed Kei's forehead. 'I love you.'

'I love you too. Let's get this over with.'

'The *New Destiny* was a late-era colony ship. It was designed to create a self-sustaining agricultural community on landing at a destination planet. Of course the ship never made it, and ever since he found the wreckage fifty years ago Levee – the High Sheriff – has been trying to launch that same colonisation programme *here,* on Earth.'

She spoke in a rush, pacing back and forth between the machinery. Kei didn't care, but it was so good to hear Noelle's voice – to hear that bright, pragmatic brilliance – that she tried anyway.

'The results he's achieved are incredible. Unprecedented. If he hadn't torpedoed my ship I'd almost admire him.'

'*Our* ship,' Kei grumbled.

'The issue is, Earth is staggeringly dry, and all the moisture is locked in these vast, sterile oceans. Sooner or later the groundwater is going to run out. They're living on borrowed time. *That* was the issue that Levee brought me in to fix. And I've fixed it, Kei.' Her eyes were burning. 'It took months of reading and scanning and tinkering and frankly it might all fall apart but I've fixed it – with this thing.'

Sweepingly, she gestured to a device that Kei had up until that point mistaken for a pile of garbage. A pair of large cylinders welded together and bound, on closer inspection, by what looked to be repurposed backpack straps, with a bent antenna and a domed solar panel attached at the top.

'This is a long-range precipitation generator. Vintage terraforming gear. I'll not explain it because it's rather complex but essentially, you secure this in a high enough place and it will—'

'Charge particles in the air? Form clouds?'

Noelle gaped. 'How would *you* of all people—'

'There's a city to the west. I think they have a prototype.'

'And – and it works?'

'Like a charm.'

Noelle's hands squeezed at her sides, and it seemed to take her a great deal of restraint to not to jump up and down. 'Superb,' she said fiercely. 'This is superb news.' She walked to the generator, lifting it into her arms with maternal care. 'It's ready to go. I wanted another few hours to fiddle with the programming but – I think we're out of time.'

'So where do you want to set it up?'

'We'll need to go to the top. The very top.'

Kei felt her heart sink. 'Oh.'

'There's a private elevator that'll take us there, but… I'm not supposed to leave the labs unescorted.'

'It's okay.' Kei took out her sunglasses and slid them on. 'I have a plan.'

'Did you do that just for effect?'

'No, it's – they're for the plan.'

Noelle did not look convinced.

'I'm in disguise.'

'Oh.' Noelle frowned. 'As who?'

'I don't know.'

'That doesn't seem a very well-thought-out plan.'

'It's not – look, just come with me, okay?'

They walked away from the labs, Noelle holding the generator, and Kei, by the elbow, holding Noelle. It was such a strange mix of feelings – the joy of being together again, so strong Kei thought her fingernails would glow with it, and also the fear, the sense of how tenuous it all was, how easy to rupture. She was doubly free, doubly vulnerable.

'You're squeezing, love,' Noelle whispered, looking ahead.

'Sorry.' Kei forced her fingers to loosen.

The High Sheriff's private elevator was easily distinguished, signposted in gold, and protected by another armed guard. Kei got back into character by wiping any trace of emotion from her face and lowering her voice an octave. 'Move.'

The guard paled a fraction, but she stood her ground. 'Lifts are off limits,' she answered. 'Order of the Deputy.'

'Yeah, the Deputy ordered me to take her up.'

'But the lifts are off limits.'

Kei bent down, holding her gaze through the dark glass. 'Don't argue now.'

The officer shifted, grimacing. 'Let's see your pass then.'

'My pass?'

'Your access pass. Come on.'

Noelle was a terrible actress, and the panic on her face was clear as day – as was the shock when Kei pulled a battered plastic card from her back pocket. The guard pressed the card against the call button, and it flashed green.

'A-apologies,' she stuttered as Kei shoved past her, yanking Noelle along.

The doors closed.

'You're so *scary*,' said Noelle.

'Shush.' Kei stifled a smile.

'Wherever did you get the card?'

Kei opened her mouth to answer, and then her mind filled with burning pipes, powdered eyes, organ music. 'Long story. I'll tell you later.'

Another silence fell, more pregnant than the last. The lift buzzed as it rose.

'By the way…' Kei trailed away. She did not want to mention her last visit to the top floor, to taint this reality with that one. But she couldn't lie to Noelle, not even by omission. 'I was shot. The last time I came here.'

'Shot?' Noelle repeated the word like she didn't know what it meant.

'Yes. The Deputy did it. Seawall. He told me you'd died, and then he shot me.' *Harriet. Seamstress.* 'He killed a friend of mine, too.'

She thought for a moment that Noelle hadn't heard her. She had a distant look on her face, like intense concentration.

'Noelle?'

'Yes. Sorry.' Noelle emerged from her reverie. 'It's strange. I've never felt such a powerful desire to hurt someone before.'

Kei had to hold back a laugh. '*You* want to *hurt* Seawall?'

'I really do,' she said, quietly mystified. 'If he was here I think I would kick him to death.'

Kei really did laugh then, not at the image, but at her sheer fearlessness. 'It's gonna be different this time.

We've got the lead. And now he's got to deal with you and your violent rage.'

'He will,' Noelle replied, no trace of humour.

The lift doors slid open – not onto the curved porcelain walls that Kei remembered but a dusky hallway, wood flooring and densely patterned wallpaper trimmed in brushed steel. Noelle stepped out confidently; from the throw of her shoulders Kei could tell that she'd been here before. 'We'll have to go through his room,' she said.

'The *High Sheriff's* room?'

'Yes. There's an airlock hatch that leads out to the upper walkway.'

'What if he calls someone in?'

'Trust me, he won't. He wants this to happen. Maybe even more than I do.'

Reluctantly, Kei followed Noelle through a discreet entranceway into the central chamber. The room held silence like a box of velvet. Padded surfaces everywhere, and a cloying smell that clung to them. Once her eyes adjusted to the dimness, they were drawn to the centre, to an antique four-poster bed.

When picturing the High Sheriff, Kei had always imagined someone like Seawall – lean and light, quiet with cunning. Instead she found a bald-headed old man breathing through a tube, propped up and dozing in the cradle of half a dozen pillows. Her instinct was to sneak past, but his eyelids fluttered, opened.

'Well, well.' He spoke slowly, pausing often to take slow, sucking breaths. His tone was genial. 'Doctor. A rare pleasure, that face of yours. Did you get those books I ordered?'

'I did.' There was a softness in the way Noelle looked at him – not pity, but one of pity's cousins. Even Kei found it hard to marry the idea of all the pain she'd been through with the skeletal figure on the bed.

'And who is your friend here? I don't believe I've had the pleasure. Come now, I don't bite.' The High Sheriff stuck a trembling hand out at Kei.

Kei leant down, struck mute by the strangeness of it all.

'This is *Kei*.'

'Oh, my Captain, my Captain.' He looked at her with a glimmer of mischief and had a grip that belied his tiny frame. 'So we find one another at last. Gotta say, I've heard some good things. Lots of good things.' He released the hand. 'I suppose you've come to spirit my good doctor away.'

Kei considered wiping her hand on her jacket, but thought better of it. She nodded.

'The generator is ready,' said Noelle. 'We're going to attach it now. But then – yes. We're leaving.'

'Still going ahead with it, eh? You've got principles.' The effort of talking to them seemed to have exhausted him, and he lay back a little, speaking quieter now, almost to himself. 'My ancestors were principled people. And I've had to live with the consequences of those principles every damn day of my life.'

Noelle caught Kei's eye, nodded her head towards the circular hatch built into the ceiling. Kei nodded back.

'Oh, Captain?' The High Sheriff lifted his head a fraction. 'Come here a moment, now.'

Awkwardly Kei moved around to the old man's bedside and, at his beckoning, lowered her ear to his mouth, so she could feel the warm, fetid breath against her cheek. 'I won't say I'm sorry,' he whispered, 'cuz I'm not. Our God is mighty delicate, Captain. She can't compete with angels from the sky. But still, I hope you'll accept a token of my gratitude.' She felt the weight of the thing as he slipped it into her hands, the familiar plastic grip. He gave her a wink and a pat on the arm. 'I nicked this from Aidan. It's yours, ain't it?'

In the time it took her to formulate a response, the High Sheriff fell asleep.

LEVEE WATCHED THEM disappear through softly slanted eyelids. The Captain was tall, and she helped the Doctor up first, before taking her hand and following her up. *Lucky young devil,* he thought. The hatch door shut automatically with a clang, and then he was alone again.

From the side of his bed he took a remote – the one he used to call in his nurse – and moved a slider. With a steady whirr the blinds on the ceiling pulled back, revealing a skylight, a circle of untainted blue, directly above the bed. The brightness made his head ache, but he didn't care. It would not stay that bright for long.

The door to the antechamber slid open, and from the noiseless steps he knew it was Aidan. 'You're just in time, boy.'

'Enjoying the sun, are you, sir?' Aidan came to the side of his bed. The sight of that face, once so young, now nicked and weathered, made Levee sad in a way that was deeper than he could understand. 'Aidan, when did you get old? I didn't give you permission to do that.'

'Speak for yourself.'

Levee looked back up to the skylight. 'Take a seat. It's gonna start any minute.'

'What's gonna start?'

'For the big show.'

'You don't mean—' A frost took hold of Aidan's voice. 'The Project? Right now?'

'The good Doctor just went up. And Aidan – he was too old to be frightened of anyone, and loved a bit of trouble – you'll never guess who was with her.'

There was a moment, glorious as the first rays of dawn, when Aidan's mask of an expression melted away into pure gormless shock, like some cartoon wolf about to be squished by his own boulder. If Levee had the energy he would have clapped for the karmic joy of it. Instead he chuckled.

'You're a silly lad. Do you think I don't know what you get up to? It's too late, Aidan. There's nothing you can do. Now come on, sit with me. Watch the show. There's a drop of bourbon in the cupboard…'

And here now is the real tragedy. Because Levee had caught Aidan red-handed plenty of times before – caught him trying to set up a weapons market, caught him trying to raise the price of medicine, caught him trying to burn out the musical people who lived in the bowels of the ship. He'd caught him plenty times as a boy, pulling the legs off crickets, burning things. This was a familiar dance. But there had never been any indiscretion that couldn't be settled with an apology and a pinch on the cheek. Levee always forgave. He liked that the boy was practical, and it was good to have someone who assumed the worst in people. It balanced out with Ursula, who always assumed the best.

But Aidan did not take a seat.

'You looking for the bourbon?' he asked. Aidan didn't respond. Levee heard a click. The respirator fell silent.

The effect was instant – a dry drowning. Levee let out a painfully quiet yell and scrambled desperately for his remote. He could see it, right there. On the table. He reached for it, but the remote leapt away from his fingers and scattered on the floor, smoking and bent, with a blackened hole at the centre.

Aidan holstered his revolver. 'Stupid old bastard.' He wrenched the hatch open and climbed up inside.

AT THE OPENING of the second hatch the airlock flooded with a wind so fierce that for a disorienting moment Kei thought they had truly opened themselves out to the vacuum of space. But with the wind came light; and she was still breathing, though the air was so desperately thin and parched it was like missing a lung. They emerged on a narrow gangway connecting to a wire tower, at the peak of which spun a red signal light. Noelle pointed to the tower, and together they started to stagger towards it, cut sideways by the gale.

Most of the land beneath them was hidden in a pearly blue haze, but Kei could make out the dark outline of Underland, the curve of a far-off mountain range. A premature star glowed feebly in the northern sky. She followed behind Noelle, one arm extended gingerly outwards to catch her on the off-chance she fell. They came to the caged ladder that ran up to the flashing beacon. Noelle slung the straps of the generator over her shoulders and turned to say something to Kei, but instead paled, and pointed to something over her shoulder.

A hand gripped the lid of the hatch, soon joined by another, and arms slithering up, until the form of Deputy Seawall lurched wholly from the body of the ship.

Kei kissed Noelle's cheek. 'Go on.'

Noelle's mouth formed a determined line and she

nodded, gripped the ladder, and began to climb. Kei regarded Seawall, who staggered once in the wind before pulling fully up to his feet. He looked at her with an even and detached disgust.

In that moment, just as they laid eyes on one another, something funny happened. Kei felt safe.

It came over her in a wave, a sensation not of sinking or lifting, but of being where she was, of being okay. It was a familiar feeling. Those last few months on the *Ladybug*; the party when they'd crossed the border; that night when Noelle had carried her home through the snow. Fiddles on a distant rooftop. Dancing together. The wholeness of it all.

Seawall's revolver was drawn. He was firing.

He was going to fire?

No, he had fired.

It was too late, it had already happened.

Kei looked down. She thought she'd see a bullet wound. But no, there was no blood, and her gun was drawn – *her gun*, the heat pistol, at home in her hand – drawn and smoking, faintly. Seawall was unhurt, and his revolver was intact.

What had happened to the bullets?

Then Kei realised, her mind catching up to what her body had done.

They had eaten one another in mid-air.

Seawall fired. It happened again. A hot flash of light, no bullet. Just like a magic trick.

'*Are you fuckin' kidding me?*' Seawall screamed. Kei wondered how many rounds he had left. She wondered how far Noelle was up the tower. But none of these questions frightened her. It was clear to her now that everything would be okay.

'Turn back,' she said.

'Listen to me.' Seawall's cropped hair whipped his face, and he spoke with tightly wound panic, like he was talking her off the edge of a bridge. 'You can't do this. It's not fair. It's not fucking—'

'I'm not arguing with you. Go back.'

Seawall fired, and again the bullet vanished, and he howled in frustration and sprinted at her headlong down the walkway. Kei grabbed the rails at either side, leant back, and slammed the edge of her heel into the soft place beneath Seawall's jaw. He fell and dropped his revolver, which slid down the side of the curved hull and into the ether.

Kei raised her gun. 'Turn back.'

'You and your bitch of a—'

The pistol flashed, and a glowing hole appeared in the ground between the Deputy's legs. He scrambled back. Another flash, this one grazing the sole of his boot. And she chased him, shot after shot, scrabbling on his hands and feet until he finally fell back into the open hatch and slammed the lid shut behind him.

Kei holstered her gun. The wind had died to a whisper, and she could swear the sky around her was thickening somehow. It hid away the mountains, the city, even the blinking light, moving inwards. Moving towards the tower. Then she understood.

She was standing in a cloud.

LEVEE'S ROOM STANK of elderly flesh, but it had plenty of oxygen, and Aidan breathed with relish. He needed to think. It had been a mistake to talk, to try to use reason. But the Captain had made a greater mistake by letting him go. He'd set up a barricade here. Block their way out. Send wave after wave of bullets and bodies until they gave in from either blood loss or despair.

So rapt was he with visions of retribution that he failed to notice the presence behind him, failed to realise that he was not alone until he felt a hand on his shoulder and then, lower down, the slow push of something sharp right through the centre of his back. A noise like a gasp came out of him, and he collapsed, pulling his assailant with him to the ground.

Tongue struggling for purchase on the air, he was desperate to speak, to say something. It brought to mind his mother's last moments – paperish lips, crusted in bile, whispering: '*This was meant to be. This is how it was meant to be.*'

He wanted to say: *It's not fair.*

That was all he'd ever wanted to say. To everyone, every happy child he'd ever met, every soul who walked carefree upon the Earth; to the Earth herself, so capricious with her punishments. *It's not fair.*

Aidan Seawall spluttered and bled.

And Levee Brown dreamed…

He dreamed himself as a young man, first beholding the glory of the fallen leviathan. How perfectly it was shaped, like a hole cut surgically from the sky. How he'd wept dry tears at the sight of it. Many miles he had crawled from the God-fearing, rat-eating, bandit-ravaged encampment where he had been raised, in search of something better. And here it was. As soon as he laid eyes on the ship called the *New Destiny* he knew that it had called him there, called him to spring a bouquet of wildflowers from its hollow carcass like in the tales the preachers told. He resolved to build a world of lost wonders; to send his own name down through the generations as the venerated founder, lawkeeper and saint to the forgotten people of Earth.

It had taken him three months just to clear the corpses out. Most of the passengers had been in stasis during the botched launch, and the crash had ruptured their life support system, starving them while they slept. They rested now in a mass grave somewhere beneath the foundations of Underland. Reclaimed by Gaia, or so Ursula would have said.

Now it was his turn to melt into the Earth, to fertilise the skin of his so-called God. But he'd done the one thing he'd always wished to do as a starving boy, gazing each night at the world they'd denied him. He'd reached up and brushed his fingers against the cold indifferent stars.

That was what he dreamed of as he clung to Aidan's twitching body. By the time the women from space returned, the High Sheriff and his Deputy were both stone dead.

THE AIR TASTED different. It was the first thing Kei noticed when they stepped from the ship; not just a drop in temperature, but a new flavour, a richness on the tip of her tongue. The sky was greying and already people were stepping outside, looking up and pointing, fear and excitement swirling in the air. They walked hand in hand through the crowd, saying little – the bodies in the bedroom had knocked away much of the triumph – but still with a little conspiratorial humour between them.

Kei had some money, but not enough to afford anything

that ran on fuel. At a farm half a mile to the west of Underland they managed to barter for a stout draught horse, saddled with a thin pad and, with a fair amount of persuasion, ready to go. Kei took great pleasure in the look on Noelle's face as she stepped up into the stirrup and swung herself smoothly over the side.

'I cannot believe this,' Noelle said, as Kei cantered proudly up and down the track. 'You've gone native, Captain.'

'Yee haw,' she said matter-of-factly. 'You coming?'

Gallantly, she extended a hand down, and Noelle took it, yelling in protest as Kei hauled her up and over.

'Gently! Gently! *Shit!*'

Kei leant over, guiding Noelle's hands to take the reins. 'Hey, now. It's not so bad, see?'

'Lunacy,' Noelle muttered. 'Utter lunacy.'

'We can find somewhere to sell him when we get further out. But I want to get as far away from that city as I can.'

'Agreed.'

Kei nudged with her heels, and the horse set out at a steady walk. There was a definite chill in the air now, enough to tingle the fingertips, and the gathering clouds had become an unbroken white blanket, low in the sky. 'You were right, by the way,' she said.

'How so?' Noelle's eyes pricked upwards.

'You told me I'd love it here. I think I do.'

'Really? Not a *madhouse* after all?'

Kei laughed. 'Oh, it's a madhouse, alright.' She rested her chin on the crown of Noelle's head. 'So when do we get our first rainstorm?'

'Actually...' Noelle cleared her throat. 'It will settle into intermittent rain eventually. But Levee wanted something special to start with. So I programmed in a unique weather event for the first time the generator is activated – this will only happen *once*, mind you, it's neither practical nor sustainable—'

'Uh-huh.' Kei stifled a yawn. The tip of her nose was reddening.

'—but, well, I loved the idea, if I'm honest, I just couldn't resist. He wanted to give people something to celebrate. A reward for all their faith.'

'Mmm. Great guy.'

Noelle glanced up. 'I didn't like him much. But – that idea, I did like. About faith.'

'I found my faith when I met you.'

Silence, for a moment. Noelle felt Kei's fingers slipping, so she wound them around her own as she held the saddle straps. She could feel Kei's chest against her back, her slow, even breaths.

'You know the most amazing thing I found out these last few months?' Noelle said. 'I was always taught that Earth was ruined irrevocably. Too much garbage, too much waste in the air. But just in the time I've been here I've detected a steady cooling in the atmosphere. Too slight to notice without instruments – but if it goes on – who knows? Maybe the damage wasn't permanent after all.'

As she spoke, the first few delicate flakes drifted down, alighting on the horse's mane, melting into their hands. The dirt plains around them began to vanish under a thin coat of snow.

Kei said nothing. She'd long since fallen asleep.

ACKNOWLEDGEMENTS

THIS BOOK EXISTS thanks to the efforts of the following excellent people: special agent Zoë Plant, god-tier editor Kwaku Osei-Afrifa, the delightful Jim Killen, learned teachers Kirsten Smith, Raffaella Barker and K.R. Moorhead, my lovely parents Tom and Andrea Curtis, and of course my sister Esme, who I admire more than anyone else in the world. Thank you, thank you, thank you.

ABOUT THE AUTHOR

GRACE CURTIS IS a freelance writer & ugly jumper enthusiast from Newcastle-Upon-Tyne. When she's not dreaming up pulpy sci-fi stories, Grace usually writes about video games, with work appearing in publications including Eurogamer and Edge Magazine.

FIND US ONLINE!

www.rebellionpublishing.com

/solarisbooks   /solarisbks   /solarisbooks

SIGN UP TO OUR NEWSLETTER!

rebellionpublishing.com/newsletter

YOUR REVIEWS MATTER!

Enjoy this book? Got something to say?

Leave a review on Amazon, GoodReads or with your
favourite bookseller and let the world know!